Praise for the authors in *Hot Pursuit*

Karen Rose

"Rose is certain to get a large following."
—*Romantic Times*

"Rose . . . stokes the tension to a fever pitch."
—*Publishers Weekly*

"Absolutely astounding. . . . Rose kept me glued to the pages."
—*Rendezvous*

Annie Solomon

"A nail-biter through and through . . . absolutely riveting."
—*Iris Johansen*

"Sizzle and suspense. . . . Solomon earns her place as a powerful new voice in romantic suspense."
—*Romantic Times*

"Will captivate the reader until the final page."
—*The Best Reviews*

Carla Cassidy

"Ms. Cassidy has created larger-than-life characters and kept this reader on the edge of her seat. Energetic, heart-warming, and terrifying all at the same time."
—*Rendezvous*

"Entertaining . . . delightful. . . . Fans will appreciate this action-packed romantic suspense."
—*Midwest Book Review*

"Exciting . . . romantic . . . a tense, chilling thriller."
—*The Best Reviews*

HOT PURSUIT

Karen Rose
Annie Solomon
Carla Cassidy

A SIGNET ECLIPSE BOOK

SIGNET ECLIPSE
Published by New American Library, a division of
Penguin Group (USA) Inc., 375 Hudson Street,
New York, New York 10014, USA
Penguin Group (Canada), 90 Eglinton Avenue East, Suite 700, Toronto,
Ontario M4P 2Y3, Canada (a division of Pearson Penguin Canada Inc.)
Penguin Books Ltd., 80 Strand, London WC2R 0RL, England
Penguin Ireland, 25 St. Stephen's Green, Dublin 2,
Ireland (a division of Penguin Books Ltd.)
Penguin Group (Australia), 250 Camberwell Road, Camberwell, Victoria 3124,
Australia (a division of Pearson Australia Group Pty. Ltd.)
Penguin Books India Pvt. Ltd., 11 Community Centre, Panchsheel Park,
New Delhi - 110 017, India
Penguin Group (NZ), cnr Airborne and Rosedale Roads, Albany,
Auckland 1310, New Zealand (a division of Pearson New Zealand Ltd.)
Penguin Books (South Africa) (Pty.) Ltd., 24 Sturdee Avenue,
Rosebank, Johannesburg 2196, South Africa

Penguin Books Ltd., Registered Offices:
80 Strand, London WC2R 0RL, England

First published by Signet Eclipse, an imprint of New American Library,
a division of Penguin Group (USA) Inc.

First Printing, December 2005
10 9 8 7 6 5 4 3 2 1

Contents

DIRTY SECRETS

Karen Rose

To my own dear guy-friend from high school who had the courage to write me a love letter I never saw. I hope your life has been as wonderful as mine.

To my husband, Martin, whom I might never have met had I read that high school love letter all those years ago. Looking back, I'd change nothing. You are my everything.

Prologue

St. Petersburg, Florida, Friday, February 19, 1 A.M.

He stood in the darkness, waiting. Nauseous. Trembling, for God's sake.

It had been far, far worse than he'd ever imagined. But then, he never imagined he'd ever take another man's life in cold blood. Never imagined he'd sit there and watch as another man gasped and clawed and begged for mercy.

But he had.

He had.

He lifted his head when he heard the crunch of gravel . . . coming closer, louder. A shadow appeared beneath the trees where he waited. Large, looming. Menacing by the light of day. But by night. He fought the shudder and squared his shoulders for what needed to be done. Andrews was coming.

"Is it done?" Andrews asked.

As if he'd dare show his face were it not. He nodded once. "It's done."

"You're sure he's dead?"

"I checked his pulse," he returned bitterly. "He's dead."

"And it looked like an accident?"

He swallowed hard, remembering how the young man had gasped and clawed, his face going a bluish-purple before the gurgling finally stopped. "Yeah. I made it look like he'd accidentally ingested one of the chemicals he'd been researching. It was the middle of the night and he was drinking coffee in the lab. They'll find the chemical in his

5

coffee cup. They'll rule it accidental contamination. No one will suspect."

"Excellent. And the book?"

He reached in his briefcase and pulled out a hardbound notebook encased in a plastic ziplock bag. "This is what he was working on. Leave it in the bag unless you're wearing gloves."

Andrews's eyes narrowed doubtfully and a spurt of fury bubbled up to mix with his nausea. He shoved the book into Andrews's meaty hands. "Take it, dammit," he snarled. "This is what you damn well wanted." *This is what I killed for.* Another wave of nausea rolled and he swallowed it back.

"You replaced it with another book?"

"I did." He was still huffing, his heart still racing. "No one will suspect."

Andrews slipped the book into his own briefcase. "Until someone else gets too close."

His throat closed at the unspoken command. "*No.* No way in hell will I do this again. *No.*"

Andrews just smiled, his teeth flashing white in the darkness. "Of course you will. I'd only borrowed you before. I own you now."

Chapter 1

In numb silence Christopher Walker watched the police photographer flashing pictures of Darrell Roberts's body sprawled on the pristine white tile of the research lab. Darrell's face was bloated, discolored. His open eyes unseeing. His mouth twisted and open as if his last moments had been a struggle for breath.

Christopher knew he'd never get the sight out of his mind.

"This can't be happening," he murmured, wishing it was a dream. That he could wake up and find it never happened. That Darrell Roberts was still alive and healthy.

But it was no dream. Darrell was dead.

He felt a hand on his arm and turned to find the University police officer who'd been the first to respond to his frantic call for help. "Professor, there's a detective from St. Pete PD here to talk to you."

Christopher's eyes flicked to the detective who was giving him a measuring stare, then back at the University cop. But he could still feel the detective watching him. It made him feel uneasy, his shoulders tight, constricted, and he frowned at the University cop, confused. "I thought you guys had jurisdiction here."

The University cop traded a guarded glance with the St. Pete detective. "We contract St. Pete PD to investigate all unexplained deaths related to campus activity, Professor. We're a small force with limited experience in such things." He lifted a brow and a shoulder. "Lawsuits."

7

Christopher stared down at Darrell's body. Lawsuits. His student, his friend was dead and the University was worrying about lawsuits. He gritted his teeth and met the detective's steady gaze. The man was in his forties, his dark hair graying at the temples. He wore a jacket and tightly knotted tie. His eyes were narrowed and piercing. Suspicious. Christopher fought the urge to wipe his sweaty palms on his slacks. Ridiculous. *I haven't done anything. He's trying to unnerve me.*

"I'm Detective Harris," the man said, and firmly guided Christopher through the door of the lab into the adjoining lounge. "Sit down, Professor."

Christopher sat, his eyes drawn to the lab door. To Darrell. Lying dead on the floor. His skin cold. His limbs stiff. Someone had propped the door open with a stack of textbooks and Christopher could hear the conversation inside the other room. Someone was asking if the photographer was finished and could they take him now.

Take him. To the morgue. They'd zip his body in a bag and take him to the morgue. Because he was dead. *Darrell was dead.*

"I have to call his mother," Christopher murmured. How could he tell Darrell's mother? That her son was never coming home, that he'd died so unnecessarily. He couldn't even imagine her pain, couldn't imagine how he'd feel if someone told him his own precious child, his Megan was never coming home again. He started to stand up and the detective pushed him back down.

"Professor, I know this is a bad time, but I need to ask you some questions."

"Right." He turned from the door, giving the detective his full attention. "I'm sorry. I'm having trouble connecting my thoughts."

"That's normal. Can you tell me about the victim?"

Victim. Christopher's stomach did a nasty roll and he swallowed hard. "His name is . . . was Darrell Roberts. He's a grad student in my department." *Was.* Damn it all.

"You're a chemistry professor?"

"Yes. Darrell was about six months from earning his doctorate."

"Who found him?"

Christopher swallowed again, the image of Darrell's face filling his mind. "I did."

Harris pulled a little notebook from his pocket. "What time was that?"

"A little before seven. The card reader could give you the exact time."

Harris looked up sharply. "The card reader?"

Christopher touched the photo ID hanging around his neck. "Nobody gets in or out of the lab without one of these. It's a restricted area."

"Why?"

"We're doing federally funded research and many of our chemicals are toxic."

"Like cyanide?"

Christopher flinched. He'd smelled the telltale odor of bitter almonds when he'd bent over Darrell's body. "Yes. We have cyanide here. I smelled it, Detective. I told the officers and the medical examiners as soon as they arrived on the scene so they could protect themselves. Even small exposures to cyanide can be harmful."

"And we appreciate the heads-up, Professor Walker," Harris said mildly. "Was Darrell normally alone in the lab in the middle of the night?"

"No. I like my grad students to work in pairs if they're going to be here after hours. Tanya Meyer was supposed to be here with him last night. I called her after I called 911. She told me she was feeling sick last night and Darrell sent her home. She said she left at nine. He was very alive then."

Harris noted Tanya's name. "Okay. Did Darrell seem depressed recently?"

Christopher's brain suddenly woke up. He lurched to his feet, furious. "Whoa. Wait just a minute here. This was an accident. A horrible accident. Darrell wouldn't commit suicide, Detective. I've known this boy since he was eighteen years old. He would never commit suicide."

Harris nodded. "I'm sure you're right, but I get paid to ask the questions, Professor. So Darrell didn't seem depressed?"

"No. He was a little tired maybe. He's been working hard on our project and working part-time waiting tables.

He had other classes, too. I know he's pulled a few all-nighters recently, but that's pretty par for the course. It's a university. That's what students do." Chris could hear the desperation in his own voice and forced himself to calm down. To sit down. "He was getting married this June. He was . . . happy." He whispered the last word, his throat suddenly thick.

"I'll need the name of his fiancée."

"Laurie Gaynor. You'll find her at Edgewater Elementary School. She's an education major doing her student teaching. She's going to be . . . devastated."

The detective's voice softened a little bit. "So you were close to Darrell?"

Fatigue hit Christopher like a brick and he slumped in the chair. "I've known him for seven years, ever since he was a freshman. His dad died when he was a sophomore. I've been . . . kind of a substitute. Combination big brother, uncle. Mentor. There is no way Darrell Roberts would take his own life. His mom and his younger brothers depended on him." Chris thought of the poverty in which Darrell's family lived, wondered what the Roberts family would do now. "He kept his little brothers in school, out of drugs. As soon as he finished his degree he planned to buy them a house in a nice neighborhood, with good schools."

"So what do you think happened, Professor?" Harris asked, gently now.

Christopher closed his eyes. "There's a coffee cup on the counter next to where I found him. We have a strict rule— no food or drinks in the lab. The risk of accidental ingestion is just too high. I don't even allow water bottles. Darrell knew this and I've never known him to disobey the rule. But he must have been tired. Got a cup of coffee to keep himself awake. Dammit." Anger surged, both for the loss and for its needlessness. "He knew better," he whispered harshly, and fought back the tears that stung his eyes.

"You smelled the cyanide. Why didn't Darrell?"

Christopher shrugged. "Not everyone can smell it. About a tenth of the population can't. It's genetic, like being able to curl your tongue. Darrell was one of those people."

"One last question, Professor. What are you working on in there?"

Behind him Christopher heard the squeaking of wheels. They were pushing the gurney into the lab. They'd zip Darrell into a body bag and take him away. Bracing himself, he kept his eyes on Harris's face, away from the door. "We're working with the USDA on improved methods for soil testing."

Harris frowned. "Soil testing?"

"For contaminants. Dioxins." Christopher rubbed his forehead. "Cyanides, too."

"So Darrell would have been handling the cyanide as part of his work?"

"Yeah. There's a bottle of potassium cyanide next to his cup. He was making controls, samples with known contamination levels to use for testing."

"Do you have any records of his work, Professor? Anything that I can use in my report to support this being an accident?"

"Each grad student keeps a notebook. I'll get Darrell's for you." Wearily he rose, just as the gurney came rolling out of the lab, the body bag strapped down. And dammit, he couldn't tear his eyes away. Couldn't stop the tears that slid down his face.

"Professor?" Harris gently prodded. "The book?"

Christopher jerked his eyes away. "I'll get it for you." He made himself walk into the lab, past the now empty tile. He glanced at Darrell's notebook, open on the table, the familiar handwriting like a knife in his heart. *Dammit, why weren't you more careful?*

"Chris? Chris, what's going on here? *Chris!*"

"You can't come in here, sir. This is a crime scene. *Sir.*"

Christopher looked up to find Jerry Grayson struggling with the University cop. Jerry was a physics professor and his closest friend. They'd been undergraduates together, fellow geeks who'd just loved academia too much to leave, so they'd come here to teach. Jerry had been with him through most of the critical times in his life, high and low. Best man at his wedding, godfather to his daughter. Jerry had been Christopher's main support during his divorce. And now this. Now this.

"Chris?" Jerry's pale face made his beard seem blacker. "I saw the ambulance out front. They were putting a body bag in it. I thought . . ." He swallowed hard, struggling for control. His voice cracked. "I thought it was you, that something had happened to you. What happened?"

Christopher picked up Darrell's notebook, conscious of Detective Harris watching them both. Not really caring anymore. "Darrell's dead," he said dully.

"Chris." Jerry had stopped struggling and the cop loosened his hold. "God, I'm sorry. How did it happen? What can I do?"

Christopher met Jerry's eyes, saw his friend's unswerving support. "I have to tell his mother."

"I'll go with you."

"Thanks."

Cincinnati, Ohio, Friday, February 19, 10:06 P.M.

Emma Townsend stood on the airport escalator, her palm vibrating as she gripped the heavy black rubber handrail. After a week of lecturing and a six-hour flight from Seattle she should be asleep on her feet, but the throbbing in her head and the dread clawing at her stomach assured her that she was very much awake indeed.

There were about ten million places on earth that she'd rather be at this moment, but here she was in the Cincinnati airport, steadily rising toward the arrival area where loved ones waited. A sea of faces anxiously peered over the railing from the balcony above, some waving, nearly all smiling. And as if magnetized, her eyes were drawn to the place where Will had always waited with a beaming smile of welcome and a single red rose. A middle-aged man stood in Will's place, holding a bouquet of pink carnations. Waving at someone else. A shard of pain pierced her chest.

This is why I hate this airport, she thought. *This is why I've avoided coming back for so long.* It hurt too much. Resolutely she averted her eyes and concentrated on keeping her footing at the end of the escalator, on looking for the driver that should be holding a sign bearing her name. She spotted the black-clad woman quickly, her sign neatly lettered. DR. EMMA TOWNSEND.

That would be me, Emma thought and approached the driver with what she hoped was a friendly smile. It wasn't the driver's fault that there were ten million places on the planet she'd rather be. "I'm Dr. Townsend," she said and shook the driver's hand. "I'll have to get my luggage from the baggage claim, then I'll be ready to go."

The woman gave a brisk nod. "I'm Linda Raines. I was hired by your assistant to drive you to Lexington tonight. Did you have a good flight from Seattle?"

Emma nodded even though the flight had been truly horrendous. Bumpy and nauseating. She tried to tell herself it was the turbulent flight that had caused the butterflies in her stomach, but deep down she knew better. It was the prospect of facing this airport, this city, and everything it represented. She'd be gone soon enough though. She was just passing through Cincinnati on her way to Lexington where she'd spend the next week lecturing to auditoriums packed with strangers. She'd planned to fly into Lexington, but Kate had called with a last-minute itinerary change. Emma's flight into Lexington had been cancelled. The only other flight was into Cincinnati.

Kate booked all of Emma's lectures and travel, managed the details of Emma's personal and private business. But Kate was far more than an assistant. She was Emma's best friend. She'd been Will's friend as well. Kate knew exactly what flying into this airport would mean for Emma and had apologized profusely, but there had been no way around it. Emma had a book signing in Lexington at two tomorrow afternoon. She had to make it in from the West Coast tonight or she'd miss her commitment.

Raines cleared her throat. "We should be in Lexington by twelve thirty or so if we don't have to wait too long for your luggage. Point out your bags when they come 'round and I'll get them to the limo."

Emma stood far enough back from the luggage carousel to be able to see her large suitcase that held two weeks' worth of suits while standing apart from the throng of people. She'd gotten quite good at that, standing apart from a crowd even as she stood among them. Someone cleared her throat behind Emma and she turned to find a shy-looking woman in her midsixties standing behind her with red cheeks and a book in her hand. A familiar face stared up from the book's back jacket cover, Emma's own. She forced a smile and the woman smiled back.

"Dr. Townsend, I'm sorry to bother you," the woman

said softly, her voice barely audible over the roar of ten
luggage carousels and the conversations of fifty times that
many people. "I just wanted you to know how much I
enjoyed your book. I brought it with me to read on the
plane." She faltered, dropping her eyes. "Your book has
helped me a great deal. I lost my son recently and, well . . ."
The woman let the thought trail with a self-conscious grimace. "I suppose you hear this all the time."

Emma did, in every city she toured, every standing-room-
only hall in which she'd lectured over the past year. *Bite-
Sized* had struck an instant chord with the public, hitting
and staying on the bestseller lists for more than six weeks.
Bite-Sized discussed the ways to cut grief and loss into man-
ageable pieces, suggested practical ways to get through each
day after the loss of someone dear. The book was the product of eight years of conducting therapy groups for the
bereaved. It had been Emma's life's work.

Now . . . it was her life.

"You're not alone," Emma said quietly. "Have you
found a support group?"

The woman bobbed her head. "Yes, yes, I have. And it
does help. My son . . . he was all I had left." She swallowed
hard and Emma found herself doing the same. Found herself watching from the corner of her eye the middle-aged
man with the pink carnations who'd been standing in Will's
place. Now he stood next to the luggage carousel with his
arm around the shoulders of a plump middle-aged woman
who held the pink carnations carelessly in one hand. They
were talking animatedly with big smiles and an occasional
hug. The pressure in Emma's chest increased and she
dragged her eyes back to the woman holding the book.

The woman hesitated, then blurted, "I read you lost your
husband recently. I'm so sorry."

Emma's smile was now brittle, her heart thundering. It
wasn't recently. It had been a year. A year without him. A
year alone. It was not the first time a reader had expressed
condolences, but to hear it *here* . . . The air suddenly
seemed thick, impossible to breathe. *I need to get out of
here.* She wanted to bolt, to run far away from this damn
airport and all the memories it dredged up. She wanted to
tell the woman with the book to mind her own damn busi-

ness. Instead, she drew a quiet breath and made herself say, "Thank you."

"At least you know how to get through the pain."

You'd think so, Emma thought. "Yes," she lied. She'd gotten good at that over the last year, too. Lying, not getting through the pain.

The woman hesitated again, then held her book out. "Would you mind signing it?"

At least this was something concrete she could do, Emma thought, reaching for a pen. "Not at all. What's your name, ma'am?"

"Alice."

"To Alice," Emma said aloud while writing. "Bite off what you can chew, one day at a time." The hypocrisy of the message had ceased to sting after several hundred signings. Now it just left a dull ache in the pit of her stomach. She signed her name and handed the book back to Alice. "Take care and stick with the support group. They'll help you get through. Now, if you'll excuse me, I just flew in from Seattle and I'm very tired. And I think I see my luggage coming round the bend there."

Alice hugged her book to her chest and gave a little wave. "Thank you."

Emma was relieved to find that her luggage truly was coming round the bend. She snagged the large bag from the conveyor and jumped when it was taken from her hand.

Linda Raines. Her driver. Emma had nearly forgotten about her.

"I'll take that, Dr. Townsend. Follow me. The limo's waiting outside."

Emma followed and was ushered into the backseat of a black limo with tinted glass. She could vaguely see that another woman sat in the front passenger seat, her profile hidden by the neat black cap she wore. "My partner," Linda explained. "At night we don't drive alone. She's been driving all day, so she's probably asleep."

Emma slid onto the spacious seat with a sigh. "I'm sure I will be, too, as soon as we start rolling." She had her eyes closed before Linda shut the door and barely felt the trunk slam as her bag was stowed. Then they were off. Away from the dreaded airport, away from the city where she and Will had lived for the entire twelve years of their marriage. Away from the home they'd built together, laughed in, loved in together. The home in which she hadn't set foot in nearly six months.

She always had a good reason to bypass Cincinnati. A last minute lecture, a meeting with fellow psychologists in whatever city she was in, a meeting with her publisher in New York. She flew through JFK often enough that she'd finally leased a small furnished apartment in New York, just to have a place to stay, to store her suits. It was there she went whenever she hadn't been able to make weekend plans. It was there Kate forwarded her mail, sometimes bringing it in person so they could visit. Go shopping. Walk the streets of Manhattan. It was there Emma hid.

You should go home, said the nagging voice inside her head. *I will when I have a schedule break.* But she knew she was booked all the way through June. *So I'll go home in July. I'll call Kate tomorrow and ask her to set it up. Tonight, I'm going to Lexington where I'll sign books and lecture until next week when I go to Baton Rouge. Then St. Louis, then Houston.* And so on.

She opened her eyes, looked at the highway signs stretched across the interstate. Then sat up straight as the limo passed the Lexington exit, going north instead. Her heart started pumping hard. They were headed away from Lexington. The wrong way. *I never checked Raines's ID,* she thought. *I should have checked her ID.*

She tapped on the glass separating the front and back seats. "Excuse me," she said loudly. "You missed the exit. Hello." She tapped the glass again. "You missed the Lexington exit."

Linda Raines lowered the window. "You're not going to Lexington, Dr. Townsend."

Emma's heart stopped. She licked her lips, made herself breathe. Slipped her hand into her coat pocket and flipped open her cell phone, prepared to dial 911 by touch. "Then where am I going?"

Raines's partner twisted in her seat, yanking off her hat. Emma could only blink, her heart settling back into a somewhat normal rhythm as irritation flared high. "Kate." Her assistant. Her best friend. "What the hell is going on? Where are we going?"

Kate's brows lifted. "You're going home, Emma. You've run long enough."

"But . . ." Emma stuttered. "What about Lexington? The signings, the lectures?"

"I rescheduled Lexington. Baton Rouge, St. Louis and Houston, too. You're taking a break, Emma. And you're going to deal with that house and everything in it."

Chapter 2

Someone had set an empty chair on one end of the semicircle. Sitting on the edge of his desk, Christopher swallowed hard as he stared at the empty chair, then made himself meet the grieving eyes of his graduate students. Tanya was crying, quietly. Nate looked like he was trying hard not to. Ian just looked mad.

Christopher knew how they all felt. For three days he'd been bouncing between rage and grief. He hadn't slept more than an hour at a time, seeing Darrell's lifeless eyes every time he closed his own. For three days he'd been hounded by the press, begging for a comment, but even that wasn't as bad as the reaction of his own bosses.

He'd been summoned by the University administration, for God's sake. They'd called him into the dean's office Friday afternoon, every face tight with concern. For themselves. "Don't say anything that would make us liable," the University's lawyer had warned, and it had taken every ounce of strength he possessed to keep his fury contained, to promise his "cooperation on the subject." They didn't care that one of his students had died, only that the University wasn't held responsible.

But his students didn't need his rage right now. They needed him to be calm and strong so they could begin to heal and go on.

"I don't know how to start," Christopher said. This was the first time they'd all been together since Darrell's death, three days before. "I still remember Darrell when he was

18

a freshman. Seven years ago." One corner of his mouth
lifted in a sad half smile. "He was this scrawny, skinny kid
carrying this backpack that looked heavier than he was. He
told me that his mother had worked two jobs scrubbing
floors to help him buy the books in his backpack and that
someday he'd pay her back." Christopher's eyes stung as
he remembered that first day, the fire in Darrell's dark
eyes, the boy's determination to succeed. "I asked him
what he wanted to do with his life." The memory lightened
and a real smile curved his lips. "He said he wanted my
job."

This earned him a tremulous smile from Tanya and a sad
chuckle from Nate. Ian was unmoved, still angry. "I
watched him grow from that scrawny, skinny kid to the
man you knew. I was so proud of him." Christopher sighed,
hating what would come next. "But Darrell was careless
Thursday night, which was so unlike him. We have to talk
about this, even though I know it'll be hard."

"He wasn't bloody careless," Ian bit out, his brogue
thickening more than usual. "Darrell was more careful than
the lot of us put together."

Ian and Darrell had been close friends. Accepting Darrell's death would be hard under any circumstances, but
knowing his death had been avoidable had to be particu-
larly hard for Ian to bear. Christopher leaned forward,
squeezed Ian's arm. "Normally, I'd agree with you. But I
saw the coffee cup with my own eyes, Ian."

Ian jerked his arm away. "There has to be another explanation, that's all."

"Ian." Nate shook his head. "Let it go, man."

"Darrell was tired, Ian," Tanya murmured wearily.
"He'd been pulling all-nighters that whole week before. I
guess he just needed the caffeine to stay awake."

"He would have drunk it in the lounge, *not* the fuckin'
lab." Ian lurched to his feet, paced to the window where
he stared out at the courtyard, his arms crossed hard over
his chest. He turned, his eyes flashing. "I will *not* believe
he was careless."

Christopher slowly pushed away from the edge of his
desk and met Ian's turbulent eyes with deliberate care.
"And I will not believe Darrell Roberts took his own life,"
he said quietly. "I had to tell his mother he was dead, Ian."

He swallowed hard, remembering the anguished shock in Yvonne Roberts's eyes, the pitiful choking sound of her sobs when the awful truth sank in. He'd held her, let her cry. Cried with her. Then sat by her side as she told Darrell's four younger brothers the devastating news. The big brother they idolized had made a mistake that cost him his life. He was never coming home. "It was one of the hardest things I ever had to do." He had Ian's attention now. The younger man's eyes narrowed as he listened. "I can't even imagine telling his mother he did this to himself. He wouldn't. You know he wouldn't."

"That detective asked me if Darrell had been depressed." Tanya's voice was rough from a weekend of tears. "I was so mad, I told him what he could do with his question."

"Pissing off the cops isn't going to solve anything," Nate said rationally, if unsteadily. Nate's calm was surprising, Christopher thought. Nate had a history of being a hothead, of leading with his gut. Darrell had always been the voice of reason among the grad students. Perhaps Nate recognized that and was trying to fill the void.

"I wasn't pissed off, actually."

Everyone immediately turned to the door to Christopher's office where Detective Harris stood, his eyes sharp and assessing. A chill crept down Christopher's back as he met Harris's cold gaze. "Detective Harris. What can we do for you?"

"I need to talk to you."

Christopher raised a brow. His heart was beating hard and somehow he just knew he wouldn't like what was coming. "Just me, Detective, or all of us?"

Harris's eyes fell on the empty chair. "All of you, I think." He came into Christopher's office and perched on the corner of the desk. "I got some interesting information from *my* lab this morning," he said, his eyes scanning every face. "The ME says the concentration of cyanide in Mr. Roberts's stomach was four times higher than the concentration of cyanide in his coffee cup. Now, I'm no chemist, but that just doesn't seem right to me. Professor Walker, what do you think?"

Stunned, Christopher could only stare at him. "What?"

"My ME tells me the numbers should have been

switched. That the concentration in the cup should have been higher. That the poison in the coffee should have been diluted in his stomach."

Nate shook his head. Hard. "No way. That has to be a mistake. It has to be."

"My ME thought so, too. So he reran the test. Twice more. Had a colleague do the same. The numbers were consistent with every test."

Tanya was pale. "Your equipment . . . maybe it needs to be calibrated."

Harris regarded her with a level stare. "It's a police crime lab, Miss Meyer," he said dryly and Christopher got the impression that while Tanya hadn't pissed him off before, she'd done so now. "Our equipment is every bit as sophisticated as yours."

Christopher pulled the heels of his hands down his face, his stomach churning once more at what the detective had left unsaid. "Wait. You're saying it wasn't an accident? That Darrell did this to himself? That's as impossible to believe today as it was on Friday. Darrell Roberts would never have taken his own life."

Harris just looked at him. "I agree, Professor."

For a moment, Christopher just looked back. Then cognition hit and he could feel the color draining from his face. "Oh, my God. You're saying somebody else did this? That somebody murdered him? That's . . ." He dropped into the chair behind his desk. Searched the faces of his students. All three looked as sick as he felt.

Harris's face didn't change, not a muscle moved. "We found Darrell's fingerprints on the cup, but no trace of his DNA on the cup."

"Maybe he wiped it off." Tanya's whisper was thin.

Harris's smile was sardonic. "There was no trace of DNA in the coffee left behind, either. We didn't find any trace of a straw near his body, either, so don't even try. What do you conclude from this, Professor?"

Christopher met Harris's gaze unwaveringly. Made himself remain calm at the implied accusation. It's a police technique, he thought. *But I have nothing to hide.* "I'd have to say the cyanide was introduced from two different sources, Detective. But while this seems to rule out accidental ingestion, it doesn't definitively prove foul play."

"Spoken like a lawyer," Harris observed. "Not a chemist."

"I watch TV," Christopher replied evenly, then clenched his jaw. "Look, Harris, I still can't believe Darrell would kill himself, but if somebody killed him, that person would have to have access to this lab. And that's us. So if that's the direction you're going, just spit it out."

Harris didn't blink. "All right. So where were you between ten p.m. Thursday night and one a.m. Friday morning, Professor?"

Nate covered his face with his hands. "This isn't happening," he whispered.

Christopher let out a controlled breath. Commanded his heart to slow down. "I was home with my daughter, Megan. She went to bed at ten thirty. I called my mother at eleven thirty. I imagine you can check my phone records to confirm this."

"Kind of late to be calling your mother, isn't it?"

"She lives in California. It was only eight thirty there."

Harris nodded, took out his notebook and jotted it all down. "All right. Any way to prove where you were between midnight and one?"

"No. I'm divorced, so I have no wife to verify my alibi." And Mona wouldn't have if she had been there, Christopher thought grimly. "I did do some research on the University's online library between twelve and one. The server records should verify it."

Harris turned to Tanya. "And you, Miss Meyer?"

Tanya was white-faced and trembling. "I was home sick. My aunt can tell you."

"Your aunt was awake all night?"

"She came in once, when I was throwing up in the bathroom. I don't know exactly what time it was, but it was before one a.m."

"All right. Mr. Bass?"

Nate jolted. "I was with my girlfriend. All night," he said meaningfully. "You can ask her yourself. Look, man, I don't even own a car and the buses don't run that late."

"Relax, Mr. Bass. I'm just asking questions." He turned to Ian. "Mr. Delenn. I understand you're here on a student visa from the UK. Where exactly are you from?"

Ian clenched his fists at his sides. "I'm from Glasgow, but what does my student visa have to do with anything?"

Harris shrugged. "So where were you that night, Mr. Delenn?"

Ian pursed his lips. "Home. Alone. No girlfriend, no daughter, no bloody mother to call long distance, so nobody to confirm my alibi." The last words were muttered from behind clenched teeth.

Harris nodded benignly, as if not even noticing Ian's anger. "Thank you all. Professor, who else has one of those key cards that you all wear around your neck?"

Christopher shook his head. "Only us. And my boss, Dr. Stossel. He's the department chair. But he's out of the country at a symposium."

"Who can I contact for a record of key card use for that door?"

"Try the IT department," Christopher answered wearily. "They're the guys who come when it breaks down and we can't get in."

Harris stood up. "Thank you. Please stay available in case I have other questions."

"In other words," Ian gritted, "don't leave town."

Christopher shot him a quelling look. "Be quiet, Ian. You're not helping. Detective, when can we get back to work in the lab?" The door was still crisscrossed with yellow crime scene tape.

"When we're done investigating."

Christopher held up his hand to stop Ian from making what would likely have been another antagonistic comment. "Detective. We have a contract with the US Department of Agriculture. I understand that you need to keep your scene protected, but we need to give our sponsor notice if we're going to be late with our deadline."

Harris frowned. "Should be by the end of the week." He headed for the door.

"Thank you. And Detective?" Christopher waited until Harris turned around. "When will you release Darrell's body? I promised his mother I would handle the burial arrangements." Something flickered in Harris's eyes. Controlled compassion.

"The ME signed the paperwork this morning. The body should be released before noon. I'll show myself out."

Christopher sighed. "Looks like we're taking a break, gang. Catch up on your other classes. Get some sleep. Go down to the beach and catch some sun. But don't talk to the press. Please. This is bad enough without us contributing more to it."

Tanya and Nate filed out. Ian remained and Christopher waited patiently for the young man to have his say. "Professor, something's been bothering me. I, for one, am not surprised that the detective thinks Darrell was murdered. I knew he'd be too careful to have an accident like that and the idea of him committin' suicide is just damn ludicrous. I was thinking . . . Do you remember last month when we had that break-in?"

A sharp pain arced up Christopher's neck as his muscles tensed. "Yeah, I do." Three of their gas chromatograph machines had been destroyed, and with it countless soil samples that had been painstakingly prepared. "We haven't regenerated that data."

"Professor, those samples were Darrell's. That they may be connected is not somethin' we can ignore."

The pain in his neck spiked sharper. "Hell. I'll let Harris know."

Cincinnati, Monday, February 22, 10:30 A.M.

"Hot chocolate break?"

Emma looked up from a box of Will's old college books to see a tray rising from the hole in the attic floor, Kate's hands keeping it steady. Crawling across the attic floor, Emma took the tray and set it on the floor. "You're too tall to fit up here."

"Spoken like a short person." Kate climbed the rest of the way up and sat cross-legged and hunched, looking around with interest. "Your attic looks bigger than mine."

"Because mine's not as full of junk as yours," Emma said and took a mug of steaming cocoa from the tray. "This is good."

"Thank you." Kate regarded her over the rim of her mug. "Are you all right?"

"I've survived the trauma of being kidnapped," Emma replied dryly.

"I wouldn't have done it if I hadn't been desperate. You wouldn't come home when I asked. And you were never in danger for a minute." She grinned. "But wasn't Linda wonderful? You never suspected a thing."

"No, I didn't. And if you ever do anything like that again, I'm calling the cops."

"I hope I won't have to," Kate said pointedly, then sobered. "So how are you, Em?"

Emma looked away. "I'm all right. The past few days have been hard, going through his things." She looked back at Kate's concerned face and forced her lips into a rueful smile. "I wouldn't have believed clothes could hold a man's scent for more than a year." But they could. Emma hadn't known just how badly a heart could break until she'd pulled one of Will's sweaters from a drawer and . . . smelled him.

She'd held back the tears until that moment, but smelling his woodsy cologne was somehow worse than everything else. The dam had broken then and Will's sweater became a crying rag. Kate had raced to her side and held her through the torrent and when the weeping had passed, Kate pressed a hot cloth to her face and popped aspirin down her throat to take the edge off the resulting headache. But the headache was long gone now, in its place a . . . peace, a relief she'd long seen in the clients she'd counseled over the years as they too had come to grips with their loss, with having to refind their place in the world without that special person.

Kate gripped her hand and squeezed hard. "But you needed to do it, Emma. I couldn't stand watching you hide any longer. This is your home. You need to live here, not in hotels or in New York. You needed to grieve."

"I've been thinking about that," Emma said thoughtfully, fixing her gaze out the attic window where snowflakes were silently falling. "I know you think I hadn't grieved Will because I wouldn't come home." She shrugged. "I didn't think I had either. But I did, in my own way. Every time I went to bed alone in a strange hotel, I missed him. Every time his favorite show came on TV or I heard one of his favorite songs on the radio, I missed him. But every day it got a little easier. Eventually, I stopped reaching for him in the night. I stopped listening for him to call my name in a crowd. Friday night was the first time I'd slept in our bed since he died. And . . ." She drew a breath. "I missed him. But it wasn't as hard as I thought it would be."

Kate's eyes were shiny. "I'm sorry, Em."

"So am I." She sighed and crawled back to the box of

books she'd been cataloging. "I found the newspaper clippings, by the way. Clever, hiding them in with the bag of peanut M&M's you brought with you."

Kate bit her lip. "I was half-hoping you would find them and half-hoping you wouldn't. I didn't know if you'd kept up with the case."

Emma stared down in the box of books, controlling a sudden rush of grief and helpless rage. "I checked the *Post* online every day from wherever I was. And the detective called when the trial started." The trial of the nineteen-year-old that had walked into a convenience store with a loaded gun and changed her life forever. "I was ready to come back if they needed me to testify, but the store video gave the police all the evidence they needed. The police were really wonderful. They faxed a letter to me when I was in LA last year. It was from the mother of the little boy Will pushed out of the way." Will had saved the child, putting himself in the path of the robber's bullet instead. Emma's voice softened, trembled. "The mother was . . . very grateful."

"She testified," Kate said quietly. "The mother, that is. She was a very convincing eyewitness. She had the jury in tears when she told how Will saved her little boy."

Emma blinked at Kate. "You went to the trial?"

"Every damn day. I figured it was the least I could do for you."

Emma's eyes stung. "Oh, Kate."

"I cheered when they sentenced the bastard to life without parole," Kate said forcefully. "He'll never touch anyone else."

"Which is justice, but small consolation." Emma pulled Will's books from the box, needing to change the subject before she started crying again. "I wonder how much the used bookstore would pay for these?"

Kate's eyes narrowed, but she went along with the subject change. "Not much. You might do better to donate them to the library or to the Salvation Army along with his clothes." She scooted to another pile of boxes. "What's all this?"

Emma cocked her head. "No idea. Open it and see."

Kate ripped the tape off the box flaps and laughed out

loud. "Lookee here. It's your old high school yearbooks. This one's from 1989."

Emma groaned. "My junior year."

"What was your maiden name?"

"Kate, please . . . Oh, hell. You'll pester me until I tell you. It was Wilson."

Kate flipped pages and let out another laugh. "Look at you. Your glasses were bigger than your whole face. Here, look."

"I don't want to." Emma shuddered. "I remember keenly. I was a nerd."

"You were not. You were cute. What's this?" Kate waved a folded sheet of paper.

Emma glanced up from yet another box of Will's books. "I have no idea. Read it."

"Oh my," Kate murmured. "Oh my, oh my. Emma, you never told me."

"Told you what?"

"That you'd had a torrid romance in high school."

Emma's eyes widened. "Because I didn't. Will was the first man I ever dated and I didn't meet him till college. What is that?"

"It fell out of the yearbook." Kate waggled her brows. "It starts with 'Emma, my love' and ends with 'All my love, Christopher.' "

Emma carefully put down the book she'd pulled from the box. "Excuse me? Did you say *Christopher*?"

"I certainly did. 'Emma, mi querida.' " Kate looked up, her eyes twinkling. "That means 'my love.' "

"I took six years of Spanish in junior high and high school, so I know what 'mi querida' means," Emma said impatiently. "What else does it say?"

" 'I've sat next to you for two years and only now have the courage to tell you what's in my heart. We danced last night and for the first time my dreams became real.' "

Emma closed her eyes, remembering both Christopher Walker and that one dance. "It was our junior prom and we'd gone together. As friends."

Kate hummed. "Uh-huh."

"It's true. That's what I thought at first anyway. But that night he asked me to dance and . . . I wondered." Emma bit her lower lip. "He was my best guy-friend. We were lab partners in chemistry and we took Spanish together, too. Our seats were always assigned next to each other, since both our names started with W. He broke up with his girlfriend the week before the prom and I'd never had a boyfriend, so we decided to go together."

Kate tapped his yearbook photo. "He's cute with all that curly brown hair. Nice eyes, too. Kind of skinny, though."

"He was six feet tall and all arms and legs," Emma said fondly, then paused and frowned. "Well, is there more, or does he stop there?"

Kate blinked. "You mean you've really never seen this letter? Holy Moses. Okay. Here's the rest. 'When I held you in my arms I let myself hope that you might feel the same way. I know we haven't always seen eye to eye, but if you let yourself, you might find we have more in common than you realize.'" Kate lowered the letter, brows raised. "You argued with him?"

"About everything. World politics, movies, football . . . Sometimes I'd stand on a chair to argue with him nose to nose. I never knew . . . never dreamed he felt that way."

"I'd say that's a given." Kate shook the notebook paper dramatically. "But there's more. 'I think we could have something special. I love your mind and your heart. But above all else I treasure your friendship. I haven't said anything before now because I've been terrified I'd lose you. If friends is all you want us to be, then that will have to be enough. If you say nothing, I'll know you just want to stay friends. But if you want more, I'll be waiting. All my love, Christopher.'" Kate let out a breath. "Oh my, oh my."

Emma clasped her hand to her heart, felt it beating hard. "Oh, Kate, I never said a word. I must have hurt him so badly. How could I have missed this letter?"

"It fell out of two pages that were stuck together. Emma, you look like I hit you."

"I should be hit. Kate, I broke his heart."

"I'm sure he's recovered by now," Kate said wryly. "It's been seventeen years."

Emma shook her head, her thoughts spinning. "You don't understand, Kate. I sat next to him in Spanish class the next year. I never said a word and after a few weeks, he dropped the class. Said he wanted to take band. Play the trombone of all things. He must have been so mad at me."

"Emma, this was another lifetime ago. You can't change this."

Emma frowned, picked up Will's old college book. "*This* was another lifetime ago, Kate. *This* is what I can't change. I can't bring Will back. But I can change how Christopher feels. How he remembers me and himself. I can't go on letting him think he was rejected all those years ago, or worse, that I was too cruel to acknowledge his feelings. Hell, I thought I felt a spark when we danced that one time, but I was so inexperienced, I didn't know how to pursue it. And when he dropped Spanish, I thought it was because I'd danced too close that night. I compulsed about it for weeks."

"You? Compulsing about something? Say it isn't so."

"This is serious, Kate. I have to do something about this."

Kate looked worried. "Like what? Find him?"

"Maybe." Emma sat up straighter. "Maybe I will."

Kate also sat up straighter and bumped her head on the attic roof. "Bad idea, Em," she said, rubbing her head. "Really, really bad idea. Maybe he's married. You don't want to barge in on his marriage. Old flames make current wives very mad. Trust me."

"Then I'll hire a private detective to find out. If he's married, I'll leave it alone. If he's not, I'll have the detective ask him to call me. If he does, great. If not . . . well, the decision will be in his hands this time."

"Em, this is your grief talking. Don't do this."

"Maybe it is my grief. All I know is that I feel something besides lonely for the first time in a year. As luck would have it, what I feel is shame. I broke a boy's heart and I never even knew. Look, Kate, what harm could it possibly do to have a private detective poke around? God knows I can afford it. Between Will's life insurance and royalties on *Bite-Sized,* I have more money than I'll ever need."

Kate sighed. "If he's married, you walk away. Promise me, Em."

Emma raised three fingers. "Promise. Scout's Honor."

St. Pete, Monday, February 22, 2:40 P.M.

Detective Wes Harris hung up the phone with a thoughtful frown.

"Well?" His captain perched on the edge of Harris's desk. "Walker must have had something pretty important to tell you. He's left five messages since nine a.m."

"He said that they'd had a break-in last month. Some samples were destroyed that belonged to the Roberts kid. Apparently the female grad student, Tanya Meyer, had her ID stolen. That's how the vandals got in the lab."

"Coincidence?" Captain Thomas asked.

Harris shrugged. "Maybe. Unlikely."

"Walker? What about him?"

"He's got a solid alibi. Besides, my gut says he didn't do it. I was there when he told the mother. He cried right along with her and if it wasn't genuine, the Professor deserves an Oscar. His grad students I'm not so sure about. On one hand, they'd know how not to goof the cyanide concentrations of the stomach and cup. But then again, they might have purposely made the mistake thinking it would shield them from suspicion. I'll watch them."

"Any video cameras around?"

Harris sighed. "Yep, but somebody had turned them off. I'm looking into that, too. I've got the lab checking out the kid's notebook. It all looked like Greek to me, but they'll be able to read it. All of their alibis check out, although Nate Bass's girlfriend sounded a little too rehearsed. I did get the printout of the key card reader. Nobody besides Darrell Roberts came in or out of the lab between the time Tanya Meyer left and Walker showed up. Whoever came in, Roberts opened the door and let him in."

Captain Thomas stood up. "Find out who else is a player here. Check out the kid's family, his friends outside of school. Let's get a few suspects on the board, Wes."

Chapter 3

"Daddy." Megan's voice lifted over the quiet strains of Bach. The sober music suited his mood. "The phone's for you."

Christopher opened one eye and looked at his daughter standing in the doorway of his study, still wearing the black dress she'd worn to Darrell's funeral. She was a good girl, he thought, pride mixing with the sadness that hadn't given him a moment's peace in a week. She'd stood by him today, her hand in his, even though at thirteen she'd started pulling away from such public displays of affection.

"Can you take a message, honey?"

Her brown curls bounced as she shook her head. "It's that private detective again. He's called four times since yesterday afternoon. Maybe you should just talk to him so he'll go away."

Christopher pushed out of his easy chair with a sigh of extreme irritation. "Him again? I'll take it in here." He switched off the stereo and picked up the phone at his desk, turning the ringer back on. He'd turned it off to have some peace and quiet, but it didn't look like he was going to find either. "This is Christopher Walker," he said briskly.

"Dr. Walker, my name is Richard Snowden."

"And you're a private investigator," Christopher responded impatiently, pulling his tie off. "You've called me five times, harassed my daughter, my staff, and my boss's secretary." They'd told him so today, at Darrell's funeral.

"I didn't harass your boss's secretary or your staff, Dr.

31

Walker," Snowden said mildly. "I merely asked them if your biography listed your hometown and high school."

Suspicion prickled at the back of Christopher's neck. "Can you please state your business, sir? Because this is really not a good time."

"I'm sorry, Dr. Walker. I understand condolences are in order. I'm sorry for the loss of your student."

"Thank you," Christopher said tightly. This guy knew about Darrell. The press had been everywhere—outside his office, his gym, even outside the church during the funeral, looking for information about the investigation, which so far hadn't turned up any leads on Darrell's death. For two days Christopher had been looking over his shoulder, expecting Detective Harris to jump out from behind a palm tree and arrest him, and his nerves were fried. "Look, if you're a reporter, you can go—"

"I'm not a reporter, Dr. Walker. I'll make this brief. I've been retained by one of your former high school classmates to locate you."

Christopher almost laughed. "High school?" After the dark events of the day, even the notion of looking up old classmates seemed annoyingly ludicrous. "You're kidding."

"No, sir, I'm very serious. Dr. Townsend has been quite anxious to speak to you."

Christopher frowned. "You must have the wrong Walker, Mr. Snowden, because I don't remember anybody named Townsend in my graduating class."

"She was Wilson then. Emma Wilson."

It was as if he'd been nailed in the gut by a sledgehammer. Christopher felt his breath leave his chest in a painful huff and he lowered himself into the chair behind his desk, his knees like jelly. "Emma Wilson?" Emma Wilson who'd owned every teenaged dream and fantasy? Emma Wilson who'd laughed and argued and brightened every day of his high school existence until one day he'd gotten the nerve to immortalize his feelings in one very ill-advised letter?

Emma Wilson who'd told him she didn't feel about him as he'd felt about her? Without words of course. She'd ignored his letter, acted like it had never happened. *Like you told her to,* he thought. But still . . . It had been the most traumatic event of his life. Until Mona, that was.

Compared to Mona, Emma had been a mere amateur in the pain department. "Did you say Emma Wilson?"

"I did."

"What does she want?" His heart was beating harder now.

"She wants to talk to you. Face to face if that's possible."

The thought of seeing Emma again made his mouth actually water. *It's pathetic,* he thought. *Worse than Pavlov's damn dogs.* But it was the reaction he'd had every time Emma Wilson had entered a room, all five-feet-two curvy inches of her. He'd drooled enough over Emma through high school to fill a damn swimming pool.

"Where is she now?"

"Dr. Townsend lives in Cincinnati, but she said she'd be more than willing to meet you in St. Pete. She doesn't want to inconvenience you, just talk to you."

Dr. Townsend? He wondered what kind of doctor she was, medical or Ph.D. Either way he was proud of her. *Good girl, Em.* "Why didn't she call me herself?"

"She didn't want to put you on the spot. She thought if you didn't want to see her you'd find it easier to say so to me than to her. And she didn't want to cause any trouble if you were married."

Christopher swallowed. Hard. "I'm not."

"I know. She wouldn't let me contact you until I'd made sure of that. What should I tell Dr. Townsend? Would you be willing to meet with her?"

Yes. Yes. Yes. Christopher drew a breath, made himself slow down. "I'm not sure yet. Is she married?"

"She's a widow."

Hello. A jolt of pleasure rushed through him, followed quickly by shame. Her husband was dead. That was no reason for celebration. "Why does she want to talk to me? Now, after all this time?" *It doesn't matter, idiot. Just say yes.*

"That she wouldn't say. Well? What should I tell her?"

"Where and when was she thinking?"

"She was thinking you could choose a restaurant. Name a time and place and she'll fly down to meet you."

"Just like that? She's going to hop on a plane just like that?"

"Dr. Walker, do you want to meet with Dr. Townsend or not?"

Christopher sighed. *Of course I do.* "Tell her to meet me at Crabby Bill's on St. Pete Beach. It's a fairly well-known restaurant, so she shouldn't have any trouble finding it."

"Crabby Bill's. And what day and time, Dr. Walker?"

"Saturday night? Seven?"

"I'll tell her. She'll meet you there."

It was . . . surreal, Christopher thought as he hung up the phone. And the timing . . . On one hand it couldn't have been better. On the other, it couldn't have been worse.

"Daddy?" He turned to find Megan wearing a frown. "Is everything okay?"

"Everything's fine, honey. That didn't have anything to do with Darrell or the trouble at school." He was unwilling to tell his daughter about Emma Wilson's visit. He'd purposely stayed alone since his divorce. It had been so hard on Megan, he hadn't wanted to add to the disruption in her life with a parade of girlfriends. So his love life had remained unfulfilled for three years. As had his sex life.

But Emma was coming. He gritted his teeth against a sudden surge of need. *Don't be a fool.* They'd have dinner. They'd talk. And she'd go home to Cincinnati, her curiosity appeased. And he would remain a single dad, which was his most important priority anyway. He put his arm around Megan's shoulders and sniffed. "What smells so good? Did you cook dinner?"

"If I did, it wouldn't smell so good. Uncle Jerry brought a bucket of KFC. Come on, Dad, sit down and eat."

As Megan's godfather, Jerry had been "Uncle" since she'd learned how to talk. What a huge help he'd been in planning the funeral. Darrell had been one of Jerry's physics students, so he'd known him, although not as well as Christopher had. That Jerry brought food was a typically thoughtful gesture. "That was nice of him. Let's go before he eats it all." He found Jerry standing at the kitchen window, staring at the channel that flowed past the end of Christopher's back yard on its way to Tampa Bay. "Jerry?"

Jerry turned, a drumstick in one hand. The sadness in his eyes disappeared as he forced a smile for their benefit. "I got twenty pieces. You can eat it tomorrow, too."

Christopher moved the bucket to the table while Megan pulled down plates and glasses. "Sit, Jerry. You look as tired as I feel."

Jerry sat with a sigh. "How is Darrell's mother?"

"About like you'd think. Some people from her church brought casseroles and cakes, so the boys won't go hungry, but without Darrell's salary . . . I don't know what they're going to do."

Then in a moment that he knew he'd always remember, his daughter bit at her lower lip, then shrugged. "I have a little of my own in savings, Daddy, almost fourteen hundred dollars. Give it to Mrs. Roberts."

Christopher sat still, pursing his lips against the sudden rise of emotion, prouder than he'd ever been. "You were saving that money for a car, Megan."

"I won't be able to drive for three years anyway. That gives me time to save more."

Jerry cleared his throat, his eyes moist. "And who says America's teenagers are selfish? Chris, I've got some rainy day cash set aside. You can have that, too."

"Maybe we can have a fundraiser," Megan said, excitement lifting her voice for the first time in days. "All the students can help. Tanya and Ian and Nate. And we can call the students that graduated last year and the year before. I know they'll want to help."

"I've got a friend at the University TV station," Jerry said. "He can help you get the word out."

Megan beamed. "That's great. We can do a car wash and a raffle."

Christopher sat back and listened to her plan, but the car washes and raffles began to run together and his mind began to wander. To Saturday night. Emma was coming.

St. Pete, Thursday, February 25, 2:00 A.M.

"You fucked up."

He closed his eyes, his stomach liquid and queasy. "I know." They'd kill him now. Maybe it would be for the best. He'd never be able to live with what he'd done.

"You said they'd think it was an accident."

"I thought they would."

"Don't lie to me."

He stiffened when a rope was pulled tight around his throat. Then loosened, left to lie on his shoulders, taunting him. "If you're going to kill me, then do it, for God's sake."

The rope tightened, leaving just enough space for him to take a labored breath. "I'll kill you when and if I'm ready. Now I want information. There's a private detective asking questions about Walker. Why?"

"I don't know." The rope tightened and he gave in to reflex and tried to pull it away from his throat, tried to free even a millimeter for breath to flow. "I swear it!" The rope loosened and he drew a gasping breath. "Dammit."

"Find out why. For now, all roads lead to you. If you're caught, you take the fall. And if you even consider revealing an iota of the nature of our relationship . . ." The rope jerked tight, then loosened once again. "These ropes come in all sizes."

Fear iced his heart. "What's that supposed to mean?"

"I think you'll keep your mouth shut, because you're smart. If you don't, you'll watch the people you care about die one by one. This isn't a game. We're serious. We will not be caught, no matter what. Do you understand?"

He nodded, trembling so hard he could barely stand. The rope was yanked from his throat, leaving a strip of red, raw skin. He dropped to his hands and knees and heard the gravel crunch as the footsteps moved away. Then like the cowardly dog he was, he threw up.

Chapter 4

Emma shivered. It had been a beautiful day, the warmth welcome after the snow in Cincinnati. But the air cooled quickly as she watched the sun set from the wide balcony outside Crabby Bill's bar. She pulled on the jacket that went with the dress she'd agonized over for hours. Was it too dressy? She didn't want to look too dressy. She didn't want him to get the idea that she'd come to take him up on his seventeen-year-old offer. Was it too casual? She didn't want that either, didn't want him to think that this apology was something she just did because she had nothing better to do.

Emma drew a breath and huffed it out on a laugh. She was compulsing, as usual. He'd probably come in khaki pants and a polo shirt like everybody else here. They'd have a relaxed dinner, she'd humble herself in apology, then she'd go home to Cincinnati, her conscience appeased. He'd return to the life he'd built here. He was divorced with a daughter. That's all she knew. That's all she'd allowed the PI to tell her.

"Emma?" said a voice she'd recognize if she lived to be a hundred.

It was him. Slowly turning, she caught her first glimpse of him and was glad she'd worn the dress, because he stood behind her in a dark suit with a garishly bright orange tie with green palm trees. She braced her back against the balcony railing and herself for whatever reaction she'd see in his face, praying it wouldn't be hostility or disdain. She lifted

37

her gaze higher until she'd locked on those blue eyes she remembered so well. When he was young, they'd flash with anger, crinkle with humor, widen with surprise when he learned something new. Now, tiny crow's feet marked the corners, but the color was still that same vibrant blue. They stared at one another, then the crow's feet became crinkles as the corners of his mouth tipped up in welcome.

"You look the same," he said and she rolled her eyes.

"I do not." She studied him as fully as she dared without giving him the wrong idea. "Neither do you. Your curls are all gone."

He brushed his large hand over his dark close-cut hair self-consciously. "Curls work better on kids." He came a few steps closer and took a lock of her hair between his thumb and forefinger. "You're a lot blonder," he said teasingly, his mouth still bent in that little smile, and the air seemed suddenly thicker.

She made herself chuckle. "Without chemicals, life itself would be impossible," she said, quoting their old chemistry teacher, then drew in a surprised breath when he grinned. As a young boy he'd been cute, lanky. Awkward. As a grown man he was no longer lanky, but filled out and muscular. Very attractive. But when he grinned . . . Her heart resumed, at a less than steady beat. Dear Lord, that smile was potent. Or perhaps it was the waves and the palm trees and the lanterns bobbing in the warm gulf breeze. *Or perhaps it's just the pathetic wishing of a lonely woman.* Maybe Kate was right and she never should have come. Recovering, she tapped her temples. "You've acquired some new colors yourself."

He lifted a broad shoulder. "Gray hair is distinguished on men."

"Which is so blatantly unfair."

His chuckle was deep and rich. It was his turn to inspect and he did so with a careful precision that sent her pulse scrambling anew. "Your glasses are gone."

"Contacts," she said with a grimace. "Still blind as a bat without them."

He tilted his head to one side. "And you're taller."

"Heels, I'm afraid."

He was quiet a moment, then his shoulders settled as if he'd been holding them rigid. "It's good to see you again, Emma."

"It's . . ." She cleared her throat. "It's good to see you, too."

"I thought we could meet here because it's easy to find, but you're dressed for something nicer, I think."

She smiled up at him. "So are you. But is the food good?"

"Best seafood platter on the beach."

"And is Bill really crabby?"

He grinned again and her heart thumped. "Nah. Last time I was here it was some couple's fiftieth anniversary and he treated the whole place to free beer."

"Now that's a glowing endorsement," Emma laughed. "We're here, Christopher. Let's just stay here. I didn't come for the food or the ambiance, anyway."

He sobered at that. "Why did you come, Emma? And why the detective?"

Emma sobered as well. "Let's go grab a seat and get a drink. I may need one."

And with that she started down the stairs from the bar to the restaurant, leaving him to stare. At the swing of the blonder hair that fit her so well. At the rear of the black dress she wore, which fit even better. He used to love watching Emma taking her turn at the blackboard in high school, the way her round rear sashayed as she conjugated Spanish verbs. She'd only improved with age. He caught up with her and neither said a word as the waitress found them seats and took their drink order.

She wasn't looking at him now, her eyes fixed on the menu. He took the opportunity to study her the way he'd really wanted to. If anything, she was curvier than she'd been in high school. Regardless, the impact on his body had been exactly the same. One look at those big brown eyes and big round breasts and he'd been rock hard. Her face was the same, no matter what she'd said. Not a single wrinkle marred the skin he'd so often dreamed of caressing. He still did.

The waitress came back with two ice cold mugs of beer. "You ready to order?"

Emma looked up at her with a smile. "I hear you have the best seafood platter on the beach."

"We do."

"That's what I'll have then."

Christopher handed the waitress his menu. "Make that

two." When the waitress was gone, he grabbed his courage and reached across the table and squeezed Emma's hand. "Now, we're sitting down and you have your drink. Talk to me, Emma."

She drew a very deep breath and huffed it upward, sending her bangs flying. "I got married in college," she said, looking away.

He felt an instant and searing jealousy for the lucky man. "I know."

"His name was Will Townsend. He was a good man. One of the best I've ever known." She swallowed hard and pursed her lips, still looking away. "A little over a year ago I was in New York on business and I got a phone call. Will had been shot in a convenience store robbery about five miles from where we lived in Cincinnati. He . . . he died on the operating table. Before I was able to get home."

He still held her hand and squeezed again. Gently. "I'm so sorry, Emma."

"Thank you. Anyway, I was terribly foolish and cowardly and avoided my house. My job required I travel, but I traveled a lot more than I needed to. I just couldn't go home and face his things. But to make a long story short, last weekend I did. I was in the attic packing his books to give to charity when my friend found my old yearbook." From her purse she pulled out a single piece of folded paper and his heart started galloping in his chest. "This fell out." She looked up at him, finally meeting his eyes, hers full of honest anguish. "I never saw it, Christopher. I never knew. I'm so sorry."

He took the paper. Carefully unfolded it. Reread the words he'd agonized over so many years ago, a thousand thoughts struggling for center stage in his mind. *She'd never read it.* She was telling the bitter truth, of that there was no question. She hadn't rejected him, blown him off like he was nothing.

She'd never read it. But what might have been if she had?

She cleared her throat and he looked up, met her eyes once more. "When I saw the letter, I knew I had to make things right. My best friend was with me at the time and made me promise to make sure you weren't married or engaged or anything, because an old friend, even a platonic one, could wreak havoc on an existing relationship. That's why I hired the detective. I wanted to make sure you knew the truth in a way that didn't jeopardize the life you'd built for yourself."

Without her. The life he'd built without her. Because she'd never read his letter.

He moistened his dry lips. Screwed up the courage to pose the question that screamed to be answered. "And if you'd seen it, Emma? What would you have done?"

She blinked once. Twice. "I don't know how things would have turned out, Christopher. We can never know, after all. But I know I cared about you. And I wondered . . ." She dropped her eyes to the tablecloth, her cheeks heating in a blush. "I don't know what I would have said." She lifted her gaze bravely, pinning him. "But I would have said something. I thought when you dropped our class . . ." She shrugged, shyly now, and looked away. "I thought you didn't want to be around me anymore."

His mind had wiped completely blank and he wasn't sure he'd ever breathe again. "Emma." It was the only word that his brain would provide. The only one that mattered. She'd wanted him too. *She wanted me.*

Maybe . . . just maybe she still did. Or would again. Either way, this was a chance people didn't get every day. To go back and correct a cruel twist of fate. He'd let her slip through his fingers once. But smart men didn't make the same mistake twice and Christopher Walker was a very smart man.

"Emma." He reached across the table and took both her hands in his. They were cold, her hands, and trembling. She was here. *She came to me.* What courage it must have taken to come, to say she was sorry for something she'd never even known she'd done. To admit that she really had cared, that was even braver. "Please look at me." He waited until she did so, dragging her eyes upward until they met his probing gaze. "I left that class because I couldn't stand sitting next to you every day knowing I'd never have you. I know I said in my letter that friendship would be enough, but I found out that wasn't true. If I'd known, if I'd had any inkling you felt the same way . . ." He let the thought trail, squeezing her hands, hard.

And watched her eyes widen. Change. Sorrow and apology became awareness. And heat. Her cheeks grew rosier still as her lips parted, just a hair. And it took everything he had to stay in his chair, not to leap across the table and crush her in his arms and kiss those lips the way he'd dreamed countless times.

"Two seafood platters," the waitress announced and two large plates were unceremoniously deposited in front of them.

Their hands jerked apart with a jolt, a shiver racing down Emma's spine. Dear Lord, it had taken every ounce of discipline she possessed not to leap across the table and kiss him. She hadn't experienced any kind of desire in more than a year. *But I still can,* she thought. After a year of lonely solitude, she felt like a woman again. And how could she not, sitting across the table from a gorgeous man with broad shoulders and eyes so blue she could drown in them. That's how she'd felt, like she was drowning. There'd been a moment of panic, but it quickly became thrill as she let herself wonder what it would be like to be held by those strong arms. From the look on his face, he'd been wondering the same thing.

Their food had arrived at a fortuitous moment. They were flying on memories of adolescent desire and the high of healing a painful misunderstanding. Time to step back. To be an adult. "Tell me about yourself, Christopher."

His tanned cheeks stained with a dark flush as he visibly got control of himself and lifted a dark brow. "Your PI didn't tell you?"

"Only that you're not married and you have a daughter. That's all I wanted to know."

"I'm divorced," he said, then smiled warmly. "My daughter's name is Megan. She's thirteen and the best thing that ever happened to me." And she listened as he talked about Megan, his obvious love for his daughter warming Emma's heart. *He's a good father,* she thought. *I knew he would be.* He talked about his teaching and the University and his grad students, a shadow crossing his face as he told her about the student who had recently died. Who the police thought might have been murdered. He hadn't accepted it yet, that his friend could have been killed, and she understood that, too.

"I'm sorry, Christopher," she said simply. "I know how hard it is to lose someone you care about."

"I guess you do," he murmured. "I'm the one who

should be sorry. I didn't mean to depress you with my problems." He resettled himself in his chair, pushing aside his empty plate. "Tell me about Emma. Your PI said you were Dr. Townsend."

"I got my PhD in psychology," she said and he blinked in surprise.

"Really? I always thought you'd major in chemistry like I did. We used to have such good times in that class and you always had the best grades."

"Second to yours," she replied, smiling at the memory. "I did major in chemistry. I'd planned to be a doctor but I did some volunteering at the local hospital and found I was more interested in the people's emotions than in their anatomy and physiology."

"So you switched majors?"

"No. I was almost done with the chemistry degree. It didn't make sense to abandon it, so I just added psychology as a second major. After I got my doctorate I started a private practice focused on grief counseling. Now I travel, lecturing."

"Grief counseling," he said thoughtfully. "We've heard a lot about that in the last week. The University's counselors have met with all of us. They left me with a list of support groups and this book they said was the latest rage in coping with grief."

"Did it help?"

He grimaced, thinking of the session with the University shrinks. He didn't put much stock in therapists, but he wouldn't say that to Emma. He did, however, put even less stock in books. "I'm not much on those self-help books. How to diet. How to quit smoking. How to find your inner child, for God's sake. I'll miss Darrell like hell, but I can't see how any book can help me any more than just the good old-fashioned passage of time. And work. I keep busy. It helps more than any book."

Emma tilted her head. "Do you remember the title of the book?"

"Baby something. No, that's not it. Bite . . . *Bite-Sized*. Why, have you heard of it?"

Her lips twitched. "Kind of. I wrote it."

Christopher's jaw dropped and he felt his cheeks go hot. "Oh, hell." But she was chuckling good-naturedly so he did the same. "Open mouth, extract foot."

She shook her head, sending her blond hair swinging across her jawline. "Self-help books aren't for everyone, Christopher. Some people they do help. Others manage via different avenues. You sound like you have a wonderful natural support network, with your daughter and all your students. Go with that. Do what makes you happy."

He stilled, realizing she meant her words one way, but taking them another. At this moment he couldn't think of anything that would make him happier than exploring this second chance she'd given them both. "I will." He pushed back from the table. "Now, how do you feel about a walk on the beach to work off all that fried shrimp?"

"I'm wearing high heels," she said, her expression doubtful.

He stood up, looked down into her eyes. "Take them off." He'd meant it to be a teasing command, but his voice emerged raw and husky.

She swallowed hard and again his body responded to the sight of her. To the very thought of her. "I'm . . ." She faltered, her eyes wide. She was nervous, he realized, and the knowledge should have been sobering, but instead it thrilled. "I've got stockings."

"Take them off, too."

She hesitated for a full minute, then stood up. "All right. Let's take a walk."

Saturday, February 27, 8:30 P.M.

Walker had met a woman. He'd watched him emerge from his house on the canal earlier this evening, all dressed up in a suit and looking ready to go to church. He'd expected him to meet a man. The PI that had been asking about Walker had been male. But instead Walker had met a woman he didn't recognize at a restaurant. He'd taken a table for one, ordered dinner, and watched them, at the wrong angle to clearly see her face and too far away to hear what they were saying. Whatever it was, it was serious. A paper was exchanged, which Walker folded and slipped in his coat pocket. There had been some light conversation, but mostly heavily serious dialogue. Then they'd abruptly left without waiting for the check, Walker leaving cash on the table.

He got up and followed them, only to be stopped by an even voice by the front door.

"Did you forget something, sir? Perhaps your check?"

He gut tightened as he turned, Walker and the woman disappearing from his view. *Dammit. Dammit to hell.* "I'm sorry. I thought I saw someone I knew and I got so carried away I forgot to pay the bill." He pulled out a few bills, pressed them in the waiter's hand and burst into the parking lot. But they were gone and he panicked.

He found Walker's car still in the parking lot and sighed in relief. He waited for a few minutes, but when they didn't come back to the car he assumed they'd gone down to the beach. He scanned the sand but in the dark, all the strolling couples looked the same. He wasn't sure which way they'd walked and he didn't want to pick the wrong direction. This woman could just be a date, he thought. But Walker didn't date. Everybody knew that. And she'd given him a paper, days after a private detective was poking around. It was too much coincidence to be safe. He touched his throat, still raw from the rope. He needed to file a report by tomorrow. He needed the woman's name before then. He certainly didn't want to be late. Or wrong.

He'd stay here and wait for Walker to come back to his car.

Saturday, February 27, 9:30 P.M.

"This will work," Emma said, pointing at a smooth stretch of sand just beyond a four-foot-high dune. "That dune will block some of that cool wind." She sat down, tucking her bare feet under her skirt, and looked up at him. "Well, are you going to sit or not?"

Christopher frowned down at her. "Your dress will be ruined."

They'd walked an hour down the beach, reminiscing, chatting easily about everything under the sun. Or moon, as it were. It was amazing how quickly they'd returned to the camaraderie they'd shared in their high school days. But beneath the conversation ran a current of tension, an awareness that sensitized her skin, making her anticipate the casual brush of his hand against hers as they walked. Making her wonder if he'd hold her hand again, as he'd done in the restaurant. He didn't and finally Emma took the initiative, reaching up to grab his hand and pull him down beside her.

"Stop worrying about my dress, Christopher, and relax." She fixed her eyes on the water as he settled on the sand, stretching his long legs out in front of him. "It's a beautiful evening and I want to enjoy watching the water a little longer."

His shoulder brushed her upper arm, sending a shiver through her body, and he frowned again. "Are you cold? We should go back before you catch pneumonia."

Emma laughed. "Christopher, it was twenty-five and snowing when I left Cincinnati this morning. This is like a tropical paradise in comparison." But he was already shrugging out of his suit coat and wrapping it around her. Another shiver shook her as his hands lingered on her shoulders a few beats of her heart longer than necessary.

Her deep breath drew in his scent from his coat, warm and citrusy. Different from Will's. She felt a small pang of guilt at the thought, but rationally knew Will wouldn't want that. He'd have been the first to want her to go on with her life. He'd have been furious with the way she'd locked herself away for a year. Well, she wasn't locked away any longer. Be it Christopher or someone else in the future, her life had to go on.

Her sigh was nearly lost on the breeze. "I never dreamed I'd end up like this, Christopher."

"Which part, Em? Your husband dying, you becoming rich and famous, or ending up here with me after all these years?"

She studied his profile, the hard line of his jaw. "All of the above, I guess."

He looked down and her breath caught in her throat at the expression in his vivid blue eyes. So intense. Compelling. "Would you have changed it if you could?"

She said nothing for a moment, just looked into his eyes. Then shook her head, soberly. "No. I might have missed the pain, but I would have missed the dance." The song to which they'd danced rumbled through her mind even as she said the words. Garth Brooks's "The Dance," haunting and so very appropriate to her life. Then and now.

His eyes flashed. "You remembered."

One corner of her mouth lifted. "How could I ever forget? It was my first dance, Christopher. My first prom. My first date. I was such a nerd then. I thought you'd asked me out of a combination of pity, friendship and pragmatism."

His jaw tightened. "For a very smart girl, that was very dumb."

"Probably," she said lightly and turned back to the water, unable to endure another second of his intense stare. *You're just vulnerable,* she told herself, *and needy. Back off, Em.* He crooked his finger under her chin and pulled until she looked up. And once again she caught her breath. His eyes . . . smoldered. There was no other word for it.

"Emma, I felt a hell of a lot of things for you then, but pity was never among them."

She stared up at him, every word in her mind . . . gone. Vaporized like mist in sunlight. Then even that thought was gone as he slowly threaded his fingers through her hair, cupping the side of her head, lifting her face as he lowered his.

And he kissed her.

And oh, it was good. His lips were warm and hard and soft all at the same time. Her heart thundered until all she could hear was the blood rushing in her head, all she could feel was the yearning of her own body, the tightening of her nipples, the sweet tug of desire pooling between her clenched thighs. His coat fell to the sand as she lifted her hands to his face, her palms bracketing his jaws, her thumbs rasping gently against the stubble on his cheeks.

And he groaned.

Setting her tingling body on fire. She opened her mouth, seeking, allowing him entry. His tongue found hers and her hands found their way around his neck. A few seconds later he was pushing her to her back, any residual worries about sand on her dress completely forgotten. His mouth was ravenous, eating at hers like a starving man. Like he'd never get enough.

And his hand . . .

God, his hand was on her breast. And it felt so good. His thumb pressed against her nipple, flicking it through the fabric of her dress, and she whimpered.

He lifted his head, breathing like he'd run a marathon. His eyes burned. "I wanted you then, Emma," he gritted.

"Every damn day. God help me, I want you now." His lips
dropped to her throat. Moved lower to her breast. Then
his mouth closed over her breast and she moaned. Clasped
his head in her shaking hands and held him close while he
ravaged, sucking until she thought she'd come, right there
on the beach.

She tried to speak, but no words would come. She, a
woman who made her living speaking, could not form a
single syllable. *Emma, stop this. Get a hold of yourself.*

She didn't want to. She didn't want to get a hold of
herself more than she'd ever not wanted to do anything in
her life. But because she didn't, she forced herself to speak.
"Christopher, wait. Please." She tugged at his head.
"Stop."

He went stiff, then still. Lifted his head and met her eyes.
"I don't want to apologize," he said, his voice hoarse and
rough, sending another shiver of electric desire through her
body. She was cold without him pressed against her. She
wanted to be warm again. She wanted him.

"I don't want you to apologize. I just think I'm not quite
ready for this."

He swallowed hard. "Your body thinks otherwise."

"My body hasn't had sex in a year," she shot back, then
closed her eyes on a soft groan. "I didn't mean to say that
out loud." He didn't move and she finally opened her eyes
to see him staring down at her, not one whit of his intensity abated.

"Mine hasn't had any in three," he said quietly. "But
that has nothing to do with this. I've always wanted you,
Emma. Always. And now, you walk back into my life and
I have to believe it's for a reason. I've waited for you for
more than seventeen years. I can wait a little longer. But
be advised, Emma. I will have you." She shuddered violently, again speechless under his gaze, under the mesmeriz-
ing timbre of his voice. "I will have you and your body will
know you're mine." Her hips lifted of their own volition
and he smiled, a tiny little smile of male triumph that did
nothing to cool her down. "Your body already knows it. I
can wait for your heart to catch up."

She was afraid her heart wasn't too far behind. Still she
cleared her throat. "You . . . you could be right. You probably are right."

He lifted a brow.

"Okay, Christopher, you're right," she said with no small irritation. "But for now . . . I want to slow it down. When and if we do . . ."

"Make love," he purred and her insides felt like they were turning inside out.

"When and if—"

"When, Emma. Not if."

She sighed. "Christopher." Then he grinned and made her laugh before she sobered again. "*If* we make love I want it to be for the right reason," she said softly. "Because it's the right time, not because we're two people trying to recapture the past."

"Is that what you think?"

She sighed. "I don't know. But regardless, Christopher, to risk sounding trite, I'm not that kind of girl."

He sat up at that and pulled her so she sat next to him. "I know you're not. You never were. That's one of the things I loved about you then, Emma." He shoved his fingers through his short hair. "I should really apologize. But I still don't want to."

"Then don't. I feel . . . incredibly flattered."

"You should," he said grumpily. "I've waited for you more than half my life."

"You didn't wait," she pointed out. "You got married, too."

A frown shadowed his eyes. "Not well."

"I'm sorry, Christopher. I wish your marriage could have been like mine."

He lifted a shoulder in a half shrug. "It takes two to tango. I made mistakes, too. I worked a lot early on. We were college kids up in Michigan and I was working two part-time jobs and going to school at the same time. Then when Megan was born I had just started grad school, still working two part-time jobs."

"Then after?"

He grimaced. "I worked for a chemical company for a few years, but I hated it. Mona was moving up the ladder in her company and they offered her a promotion. She could choose one of three cities and our best friend from college had already moved down here so we picked St. Pete. My friend was a physics professor at the University and loved it, and I missed academia. I got a position as an assistant professor. I could finally slow down and be a father to Megan. That was seven years ago."

"And your wife?"

He stared out at the water, his jaw tightening. "Mona got busier and busier with her career. Started traveling around the world and she'd be gone for weeks at a time."

"Weeks? That must have been hard on your daughter. And you."

His laugh was harsh. "You could say that. Megan would cry at night, missing her. When Mona would come home, she'd be more and more distant. One day, she said her company wanted her to take a job in South America and she'd accepted it."

"Without discussing it with you?" Emma asked, startled. "Will never would—" She broke it off abruptly. "I'm sorry. That was thoughtless of me."

"What, that your husband never would have made a major life decision without discussing it with you? Don't be sorry. I think that's how normal couples do things. I'm not sure Mona and I ever were normal. Anyway, I didn't want to uproot Megan, or myself, if I'm honest. We fought about it and she said I was a selfish bastard and I could go with her or she'd leave us. The next time I saw Mona she was sitting on the other side of the table in the divorce attorney's office."

"And Megan?"

"She was devastated. Mostly because Mona never even contested my sole custody petition."

"Poor little girl," Emma murmured. "She must have felt so rejected."

"She *was* rejected," Christopher said bitterly. "I'd already accepted that things were coming to that, but Megan was just a little girl. It broke my heart to see her holding out hope that her mother would actually want her. Mona sees her whenever she comes back to the States on a business trip, but only when it's convenient. Megan hasn't seen her mother in almost a year."

"I'm sorry."

"Me, too." He let out a sigh. "But I don't want to talk about Mona any more. I want to talk about you. There are still so many things I want to know."

"Okay. What do you want to know?"

He was quiet for few moments. "Why did you wait a whole year before dealing with your husband's things?"

Emma huffed a surprised laugh. "You cut right to the chase, don't you? Gosh." She blew out a breath, sending her bangs dancing. "I was afraid."

"Of what?"

Emma fixed her gaze on the gentle waves, remembering exactly what. "A few years before Will died, I was on an airplane, coming home from some conference. Sitting next to me was this old woman, crying. I asked her what was wrong and she told me that she was on her way home to Wisconsin. That her husband of forty-seven years had died the year before and her sister had come to help her with the funeral. After the funeral, her sister invited her to her condo in Florida for a few days, to rest. On the flight to her sister's, the woman broke her hip and was forced to stay with her sister until she could move on her own, almost a year later.

"I'll never forget how she cried. She said her husband's shoes would still be in their foyer and his coat on the kitchen chair. She said going home after a year was like he'd died all over again. She had me crying so hard with her that the flight attendant thought she was my grandmother."

Christopher was touched. Emma had always had such a tender heart. He'd always loved that about her. "You remembered that when your husband died."

"Yeah. I was in New York when Will was killed. My book had just come out and hit the bestseller lists and I'd done a short interview on one of the TV morning shows. I was on top of the world and when I got home, Will and I were going out to celebrate. Instead, I got home just in time to sign the organ donor releases. My friend Kate took me home and I thought about that old woman as I was walking up to my front door. I couldn't go in. Couldn't stand to see his shoes in the foyer. I slept at Kate's that night. Eventually I did go inside the house, but it was so hard." She shrugged uncomfortably. "The next week, I got an invitation to lecture about the book, so I went away again. The next time I came home it was harder to go in and I stayed an even shorter time. Suddenly a year had passed and I realized what a coward I'd been."

Christopher hated to hear her beat herself up. "Maybe you knew too much, Emma. Listening to all those grieving people in your practice all those years, maybe you knew how hard the road to acceptance was going to be. Sometimes knowing how long the road is makes it harder to take the first step."

"Or the first bite," Emma murmured. "That's very wise, Christopher." She looked up at him, admiration in her eyes, and his heart stumbled. "Thank you."

His chest was tight, pressured. His groin even more so. He wanted her with every fiber of his being and if he didn't move now, he'd never be able to give her the space and time she'd asked for. Abruptly he stood up. "We should be going now." He pulled her to her feet, ignoring her surprised squeak. Gathered his coat and her shoes and started back toward the restaurant and his car.

"Christopher!" He stopped and looked back. She stood there, hands on her hips. Her very curvy hips. His mouth watered as it always had. "What's wrong with you?"

He hesitated, then in three long strides was standing in front of her. His coat and her shoes were back on the sand and his arms were around her and his mouth was crushing hers. And she was kissing him back, frantically, as if she'd never get enough. Her arms lifted around his neck, her breasts pressed into his chest and he knew this was the dream he'd had every miserable night of his adolescent life. And longer.

She was on her toes, leaning up into him. Then her round, curvy ass was filling his hands and he lifted her off her feet, needing to feel her against him. Needing her to feel how much he wanted her. Her wild little whimpers of pleasure drove him insane and he ground himself into her softness, rubbing her up and down his rock hard, aching length. Torturing them both. He could have her here. *Right here. Right now.*

But they were on a public beach. His sanity returned with a slam and with it a healthy dose of guilt. He'd promised to give her time. He released her, sliding her body down until her toes made purchase with the sand. Then let her go, turning to the water, his lungs working like a bellows. She should be angry with him. Maybe even slap his face. Instead, she rested her forehead against his upper arm and sighed.

"I think you're right," she said. "We should be going now."

* * *

They walked back to the restaurant in half the time it had taken them to walk the beach. Earlier they'd been strolling and chatting. Now they were power walking and silent. His car stood nearly alone in Crabby Bill's parking lot.

"Where's your car?" he asked.

"I took a cab," she said. "I'll take one now. You can go home. Megan will be waiting for you."

"Megan's at her friend's pajama party and I'm not going to let you take a cab. I'll drive you to the hotel." When she hesitated he rolled his eyes. "I'm not going to attack you in the car. Get in, Emma." He pulled out of the parking lot and looked over at her. She was looking out the window, her lower lip pulled between her teeth. "Where are you staying?"

"The Don CeSar," she murmured.

No other words were exchanged until he pulled in front of the St. Pete landmark hotel where uniformed doormen waited to assist the guests. "Not yet," Christopher barked when one of them tried to open her door. He gentled his voice. "Emma. I'm sorry. I shouldn't have kissed you like that when I promised to give you time."

Her smile was rueful. "I wanted it as much as you did, Christopher. Which is why I can't ask you to come up."

He ignored the spear of disappointment. "I understand. Can I see you tomorrow?"

Her smile faltered. "My flight leaves at seven thirty in the morning."

His heart stopped. "You're leaving? You can't."

"I didn't plan to stay, Christopher. I'd planned to come, say my piece, and leave."

He gritted his teeth. "Emma, I just got you back after seventeen fucking years. You're not leaving me again."

She sighed. "Tonight was so much more than I ever expected. *You're* so much more than I expected." She took his hand and squeezed it. "I need to cool down. So do you. Let me go home and sort this out in my mind. I'll come back. I promise." She leaned over and kissed him quickly on the lips. "Thank you, Christopher Walker. For making me feel alive again." Then she was gone before he could say good-bye.

Chapter 5

Emma stood on the airport escalator, her palm vibrating as she gripped the heavy black rubber handrail. What a difference a week made. No longer did she dread the airport, the city. The house.

She still felt a sharp pang of loss when she glanced up to the place where Will had always waited with a single red rose. But it wasn't *as* sharp, and the realization was a comfort in and of itself. The next time she came through it would be a little less sharp still. Until one day she'd be able to look up with a smile and think, *that's where Will used to wait for me.* Christopher had been right. She'd known the road to acceptance all along, she'd just been overwhelmed by the sheer magnitude of the trip.

She glanced down at the handful of wildflowers she'd gripped all the way from Florida with a wistful smile. He'd been waiting for her in the lobby of her hotel this morning at six a.m., the wildflowers in his hand, and her heart had jumped for joy even as her mind screamed caution. He couldn't let her go without saying good-bye, he'd said, so sweetly. Plus, she hadn't given him her address and phone number. So he'd come back, early, and waited for her to come down.

Then driven her to the airport where he'd said his good-bye, a lusty kiss with his tongue in her mouth and his hand in her hair. Then he'd pressed a heavy manila envelope into her hand that wasn't grasping the remaining life out of the wildflowers he'd picked in his own garden. "Read it when you're alone," he whispered, then kissed her again, leaving her knees weak and her heart racing.

She hadn't read it yet. She would when she got home. Anxious to get there, she sailed past the poor souls that had checked luggage, her overnight bag over her shoulder, to where Kate waited outside with her car.

"Well, how did it go?" she asked when Emma hopped in.

Emma slanted her a wary look. "Fine."

Kate's lips twitched. "Nice flowers."

Emma chuckled. "Drive me home and I'll tell you all about it."

St. Pete, Sunday, February 28, 9:15 A.M.

The lights were on in the lab and the yellow police tape no longer blocked the door. Pulling on a pair of protective goggles, Christopher ran his key card through the slot and pushed the door open, finding all three of his students hard at work putting the lab back to rights. "I guess Harris called you guys, too." He'd found the detective's message on his home answering machine when he'd returned from taking Emma to the airport.

Ian looked up from the gas chromatograph he was recalibrating, his eyes narrowed behind his goggles. "He did. He also said we're still not to consider leavin' town."

"He said we should stay available to answer any questions," Nate corrected mildly.

"It's the same thing," Ian insisted. "Especially since that damned detective has been doggin' our every damn move. He's going to get me deported."

"He can't do that," Nate sighed, as if Ian's concern had been voiced once too often.

"Well, I'm just glad to be getting back to work," Tanya said quietly. "I've been going nuts with all that time to think."

They all went still for a moment, all eyes drifting to the table where Darrell had worked. Christopher sighed. "It's never going to be the same." Then he straightened. "But we do have a deadline. Sutton at the USDA is waiting for our next report. When can we have it done?"

The three students looked at one another. "It'll take us at least a week to do the samples that Darrell was working on," Tanya said. "On top of our own work."

"And another week to redo the samples that got destroyed in the break-in last month," Ian added. "Perhaps another three to four weeks, Professor. Will they give us that much time?"

"I hope so. I know they were hoping to start testing the new methods in their own labs by spring."

"Suppose you all tell me about these new methods."

They turned as one. Detective Harris stood in the door, holding Darrell's key card in his hand. Under one arm he carried the notebook Darrell had been using the night he was killed. Nate just sighed. Ian scowled. Tanya looked rattled.

Christopher frowned. "Harris. If you're going to come in here you have to wear goggles." He gave him a pair. "I thought you'd cleared us to get back to work."

Harris put the goggles on without argument. "I did. I was hoping you'd all rush back here, because I wanted to talk to you all together. I need to know more about the work you're doing here."

Christopher shrugged, puzzled. "It's no government secret, Detective. We're working on some new ways to test for soil contaminants. Soil gets tested as part of environmental maintenance around factories and in construction sites before building permits can be issued. Private labs all over the country do this testing, but if they're certified labs, they use standardized methods blessed by the USDA."

"These are the same methods you're working on," Harris said.

"Improved methods," Christopher clarified. "Ways to do the testing faster, but with equal or better accuracy. Part of proving our new methods are just as accurate as the old methods is by testing samples side by side with old and new methods. We've gathered soil samples from all over the state, sandy, peat, rocky—all different soil compositions. Now it's just a matter of testing and recording data and cranking out the comparisons, old to new. It's not rocket science. Really."

Harris nodded. "And you record all your data where?"

Ian tapped his hardbound notebook. "First in these, then into the computer. That's how we do all the statistical comparisons. With the computer."

"Can you show me your notebooks?"

More puzzled, each of them did so, watching as Harris leafed through each page. "And when you're done with one notebook," he asked, "what do you do with it?"

"They're official records," Christopher said. "They can be used in court or for patents, that kind of thing, so we want to ensure we keep the data safe. When one notebook is finished, it's sent to the University library to be copied. We used to microfiche in the old days, but now they put the copies on a CD. Then the library returns the notebooks and a CD to us so we can reference them as needed."

"Why are you asking all these questions about our notebooks?" Ian asked.

Harris pointed at the bookshelf that sagged with old notebooks. "Can I see the book Darrell Roberts was working in before this one?" he asked, ignoring Ian's question.

Annoyed, Ian pulled out Darrell's last finished notebook. "This is it."

"Put it on the table," Harris directed, then put Darrell's unfinished notebook beside it. He flipped through the older book, then opened the newer one.

Tanya made a distressed sound. "That's not Darrell's notebook."

Harris raised a brow. "I know. But why did you say so?"

Tanya bit her lip. "Darrell was halfway through his book. That one only has a few pages. And the handwriting's sloppy. Darrell was never sloppy."

Harris looked at Christopher. "Our lab checked this book out. It's Roberts's handwriting, but it's shaky. And all the pages were written at the same time, even though they're dated days apart."

Christopher slowly examined both books. "And there are gaps in the dates themselves from book to book," he said heavily. He hadn't really believed Darrell had been murdered until this moment. "Whoever killed him, took his latest notebook with him, because it wasn't here when I found him. Why? These are just soil samples." His throat thickened as the enormity of the situation struck him hard. "It's just dirt."

"Somebody didn't want him testing their dirt, Professor," Ian said quietly.

"This isn't possible," Nate protested weakly. "It's . . . too fantastic."

Christopher could not tear his eyes away from the fake notebook. It was Darrell's handwriting, but Tanya was quite right. It was sloppy and that was something Darrell had never been. "Whatever was in that book is gone."

"No, it's not," Tanya whispered and all eyes were suddenly on her pale face.

"What do you mean, Miss Meyer?" Harris asked sharply.

She licked her lips nervously. "After Darrell lost all his samples in the break-in last month, he got hypercompulsive about losing his data. He started scanning his notebook pages every night before he went home." She looked over to the computer in the corner. "The files are on the hard drive."

Christopher shook his head. "I don't understand, Tanya. If he was so worried, why didn't he say anything?"

Tanya sighed. "He thought it was too fantastic himself and he didn't want you to think he was losing it. He said he knew he had to be wrong." Her lips trembled and she pursed them hard. "He said it was just dirt."

There was silence until Harris cleared his throat. "I'll need access to the files that he scanned from his missing book," Harris said and Christopher nodded, numbly.

"Right away."

"I appreciate it." Harris backed out the door, taking off his goggles. "And if you're planning to work after hours, make sure you're not alone." He gave each of them a hard look before walking away.

Christopher waited until he heard the outer door slam. "Make sure you burn a copy of those files for me as well," he said tersely. "I'll be in my office."

Cincinnati, Sunday, February 28, 1:00 P.M.

Emma put down the last page from Christopher's envelope and carefully smoothed the worn page with a trembling hand. The envelope had been filled with letters. The yearbook letter and dozens of others. Some were love letters, but most were ordinary "here's what happened to me today" kind of letters. All ended "All my love, Christopher." All were letters he'd never sent, dating from their freshman year of high school until his sophomore year of college when they stopped. Abruptly.

That would have been the year he met and married Mona.

Dear Lord, she thought. All those years. *He was in love with me all that time.*

But on top of the stack had been a letter he'd penned last night after dropping her off at the hotel. She read it again, her cheeks on fire. It was by turns sweet . . . and hot. Filled with longing, both emotional and most definitely physical, Christopher Walker had taken the term "chemistry" to a whole new level. She'd come home to cool down, but that didn't look like it was going to happen any time soon.

She gathered the papers into a neat stack and carried them to her bedroom, loathe to leave the letters out where just anyone could see them. Specifically, where Kate's prying eyes might spy them. Even though Kate knew the basic events of the weekend, the words in these letters were Christopher's mind and heart and needed to be protected. On an impulse she slid them in the middle of a stack of printed pages that was the beginning of her next manuscript, the follow-up to *Bite-Sized* that her publisher had been asking for. That she'd had trouble writing.

Every time she sat down to write she'd felt like a cheat, a fraud. She'd been sure she'd be found out, exposed, the psychologist telling everyone how to deal with their grief when she'd been running from her own. Now she sat down in front of her computer, new ideas filling her mind. And she began to write the story of the old woman she'd met on the plane all those years ago. The woman who was afraid to go home because her husband's shoes were in the foyer. The paragraphs flowed and the old woman's story became her own. A story she was now unafraid to write.

So deep was she into her work that she didn't notice the sunlight growing dim or the shadows growing longer as the sun went down. She didn't hear the creak of her kitchen door opening, nor the footsteps on the stairs. A split second of warning was all she had before a big gloved hand covered her mouth and yanked her to her feet.

She struggled, her feet blindly kicking behind her. *No.* She bit the hand that covered her mouth and drew a breath to scream when with a grunt the hand let go. But her scream was cut off, a rag shoved in her throat, so deep she gagged.

He'll rape me, she thought, her lungs unable to get enough air. *God, please. No. I just started over. Please . . .* She was pushed to her bed, the man's knee shoved into her kidney as he held her down. Tears stung her eyes. Pain and fear warred as her mind tried to stay calm. He yanked at her hands, tying them behind her back. Then he tied her feet and wrapped another rag around her eyes.

The pressure lifted from her back and she gritted her teeth, preparing herself . . .

The bed creaked as he got to his feet.

But he didn't touch her. Emma fought to breathe evenly through her nose as she listened. He was unzipping her overnight bag, dumping it on the floor. Ripping drawers from her bureau. She heard more sounds from over by her desk, the scrape of plastic, the dull clang of metal. A muttered curse.

Then he left her room. She heard him downstairs, moving all the boxes she and Kate had packed. She heard tape ripping from cardboard, again and again.

I have to get help, she thought. He could come back when he finished doing . . . whatever it was he was doing. There was a phone on her nightstand. *I can do this,* she thought. *I've answered that phone in the dark a hundred times.* She inched toward the top corner of her bed, like a caterpillar, swung her legs over the side of the bed and struggled to sit up, as soundlessly as possible. The nightstand was against her knee. She leaned over, knocked the receiver off the phone with her chin. Nearly fainted with relief when she heard the dial tone. Nearly fainted from terror when she realized that he might hear it, too. He was still downstairs. In the kitchen now. She could hear the occasional clatter of dishes or silverware as he continued his search.

For what? Right now, that didn't matter. What only mattered was calling for help. She bent her face close to the buttons and carefully she ran the tip of her nose over each one, grateful Will had insisted on a no-nonsense office-style phone. She pictured the position of the numbers nine and one.

911. She pushed the buttons with her nose, cursing the shrill tones that seemed to echo off the walls. She could clearly hear the calm voice of the operator asking her to state the nature of her emergency. Her grunts were muffled, but the operator understood. Help was on the way.

Downstairs, his movements went quiet, then she heard a

click as he picked up the extension in the kitchen. She winced at the crack when he threw the phone to the marble counter-top in her kitchen. Held her breath as the back door creaked open.

And closed. She let the breath out, let the tears come. He was gone.

St. Pete, Sunday, February 28, 7:00 P.M.

"Daddy! I'm home!" Megan's voice jerked Christopher's attention from the book in which he'd spent the better part of the afternoon, totally engrossed. Megan had spent the night at a friend's pajama party. She'd been concerned about going to a party so soon after Darrell's funeral, but he'd urged her to go. To have fun. Life went on after all. She poked her head through the door of his study. "What are you reading?"

Christopher flashed the book her direction. "It's a book the campus counselor suggested we read. It's about how to deal with the death of someone close to you."

He'd picked it up in his office after Harris left. Brought it home, needing the connection to Emma after coming to grips with the stark truth that Darrell had been murdered after all. He'd thought he'd skim it. But one page had turned into fifty, then a hundred. She wrote like she talked, wry and funny and so damn sincere. It was almost like she was talking, just to him. He could see why her book had been such a success.

Megan flopped into the chair next to his desk. "It must be good. You never even heard me come in."

He turned the book, looked at Emma's face smiling up at him from the back cover. If he'd looked at the book the day the counselor had given it to him he could have found her himself. But she'd found him just two days later. It was fate, plain and simple.

"It's very good," he said quietly. "Better than I thought it could ever be." He considered telling his daughter about Emma then, but she started bubbling about the time she'd had with her friends at the party, the movie they'd seen, the pizza they'd made from scratch. She'd been so sweet since Darrell's death, trying to cheer him up.

"From scratch?" he said, smiling. "You never make any-thing from scratch for us."

"At a party it's fun. Every night . . ." She grimaced. "Too much trouble." Then she bit her lip. "But I could if you wanted me to."

"Delivery from the place on the corner is fine with me, Punkin," he said, lapsing into the pet name he'd had for her when she was small. "In fact, let's do that tonight."

She grinned her relief. "How about I order us a pizza with everything?" Without waiting for his reply, she bounced to her feet and bounded from the room.

"Bye," he said to the place where she'd been standing moments before. *Oh, to be a teenager again,* he thought. But he couldn't think about being a teenager without thinking of Emma. About how perfect she'd felt in his arms. Her wild cries of pleasure when he'd fondled and suckled her breasts, and that had been with her dress in the way. He could only imagine what she'd be like when he finally got her naked. In his bed. Panting and begging. Her legs wrapped around his hips. His name on her lips.

He'd imagined it all night long. He was imagining it right now. Damn, he was hard as a rock from all the imagining. It was all he'd been able to do not to buy himself a plane ticket to Cincinnati. To give her the time and space she'd asked for.

She hadn't called him yet. He wondered if she'd read his letters. Especially the one he'd written last night. There would be no doubt in her mind what he wanted from her once she'd read that last letter. He leaned back in his chair with a sigh. He missed her already. Missed the way she smiled, the way her brown eyes could hold so many different emotions. The way he felt . . . complete and at peace.

He needed her right now, as his thoughts seesawed to Darrell and the detective's visit that afternoon. His friend had been murdered. Over dirt.

It was still too impossible to be true. But it was. They'd gone over his old notebooks, looking for something suspicious. But all they found was a list of more than fifty samples Darrell had been preparing to run. The fifty samples came from at least two dozen different places. They'd seen no pattern. No smoking gun, as it were. The only thing they could do was re-create Darrell's tests, to find out what it was that someone didn't want him to learn.

The phone rang and out of habit he let Megan pick it up. It was always one of her friends anyway. Until he saw the

513 area code on the caller ID. Cincinnati. *Emma.* "Hello?" he and Megan both said together. "I've got it, Megan. You can hang up." He waited until he heard the click before uttering a smooth, "Are you ready to come back?"

"Chr-Christopher?" Her voice was shaking and instantly he was sober. And afraid.

"Emma? What's wrong?" He listened as she stuttered the details, his blood running cold. His fist clenched around the phone. "Are you hurt?"

"No." He heard her shudder. "Not like you think. He didn't touch me. Not like that."

Staggering relief stole his breath. "Then he just robbed you."

"No," she murmured. "No, he didn't do that either."

"Then what did he do, Emma?"

"He . . . he was looking for something."

Christopher's cold blood turned to ice. "*What?*"

"He was looking for something." He heard her swallow. "He ripped my hard drive out of my computer. He went through all my papers, all the boxes I'd packed of Will's things. He threw Will's things all over the house." She choked back a sob. "Now I have to pack them away all over again."

The bastard had gone through her papers. Emma's papers. Darrell's notebooks. It seemed too fantastic, but so had the idea of Darrell being murdered. He closed his eyes and took a hard hold on his churning gut. "Emma, honey, where are you now?"

"With my friend K-Kate. She came and got me after the police came and untied me." She was shivering, her teeth chattering. In shock.

The thought of her tied and gagged . . . and afraid . . . It made him want to find the bastard who'd terrorized her and rip him from limb to limb. "I'm coming."

"Christopher, no. I just needed to hear your voice. I really am fine."

"No, you're not. Emma, I just lost a graduate student because he was working on something somebody didn't want him to know. Now you're attacked in your own home." He gritted his teeth, feeling so helpless. "Don't you think that's coincidental?"

"Oh, God. Christopher, I never . . ." Her breath was labored. "But you're right. It is too coincidental to be ignored."

"Put your friend on the phone. Please." Trapping the phone between his shoulder and ear, he put both hands on his keyboard and pulled up a travel Web site. By the time her friend Kate said hello, he'd booked one flight up and two flights back.

"This is Kate. Christopher?"

"Yes. Tell me the truth. Is she all right?"

"She's shaken up and bruised, but other than that she's not hurt. The guy tore up her house. He was looking for something, the cops were sure of it. Why would somebody think Emma had anything of yours in her possession?" Kate's voice was slightly accusing but mostly terrified, and Christopher couldn't blame her a bit for either.

"I gave her an envelope this morning at the airport. If someone was watching me . . . Dammit. Listen, I've got a ticket on the seven a.m. flight tomorrow morning. I've got two seats on the eleven a.m. flight back here. I'm going to bring her here, where I can keep her safe. Can you make sure she has a packed bag?"

"I will. I'll bring her to meet you at the airport. Thank you, Christopher. I'll see you tomorrow."

Christopher hung up the phone and sat still. He was trembling. Shaking. She'd been in danger. His woman had been in danger and he'd been too far away to help. His hands were barely steady enough to dial, but he punched in Harris's number with single-minded intent. "It's Christopher Walker from the University." Haltingly, Christopher told Harris what had happened. "I could be making a major deal out of something unrelated, but I'm not willing to take a chance with her life."

Harris was quiet for a moment. "I don't think you're overreacting, Professor."

"I'm going to Cincinnati tomorrow to get her and bring her back here. I just thought you should know I'm leaving town, but I won't be gone more than a day."

"For what it's worth, I never thought you had a hand in Roberts's murder. Is your lady friend all right?"

"Yes, thanks to her own ingenuity."

"She sounds like a plucky lady. Who knew you two were going to meet last night?"

"Only the detective she'd hired and I don't think he would have done this."

"No, that doesn't make sense. Nobody else?"

"I didn't even tell my daughter. But . . ." He rubbed his forehead wearily. "But the private detective did talk to a number of people about me. He called my daughter and my grad students and my boss's secretary. And during the funeral on Wednesday, all of them told me he'd called them. Anyone could have heard."

"I think you've got someone watching you, Professor. You need to be careful. Who will watch your daughter while you're away tomorrow?"

Christopher's heart just stopped. Simply . . . stopped. "Oh, my God. Megan. I . . ." He got hold of himself. "She'll be in school tomorrow. I can have my friend drop her off and pick her up from school." Jerry would help. No question.

Papers rustled in the background. "She's at St. Pete Middle, right?"

"Yes. She's in the eighth grade."

"We have a resource officer there at the school. She'll be safe there. I'll tell him to keep an eye on her."

"Thank you."

"No problem. Call me if you find anything more in those notebooks."

It all came down to what Darrell had been working on. Somebody thought he knew something, that he'd passed information to Emma. "I will."

"You will what, Daddy?"

Christopher turned to find Megan staring at him from the study door. His hand bobbled the receiver as he hung it up. "How long have you been standing there?"

Megan was frowning. "Long enough to know you're going away tomorrow and bringing somebody back. What's going on here, Daddy? And who is she?"

"She's an old friend, Megan. It was why that private detective was calling me. He was trying to pass on a message from her. I met her for dinner last night. She went home and someone broke into her house. She's shaken and scared."

Megan's face went carefully blank. "Why can't she be shaken and scared in her own house? Why does she need to come here?"

Christopher flinched at the utter lack of compassion in his daughter's tone. "Megan."

Megan turned on her heel. "Never mind. It doesn't matter. I'll call Debbie and ask if I can spend the night with her. That way you won't have to worry about me at all tomorrow. For now, I have homework to do."

Christopher scrambled to his feet. "Megan, wait. We need to talk."

"No, we don't. Call me when the pizza gets here."

He flinched again at the sound of her bedroom door slamming and slumped into his chair. "Hell." She'd been so sweet this last week. He swore he'd never understand the mercurial mood changes of adolescent girls.

His daughter wasn't a baby anymore. *But she's still* my *baby.* His gut clenched at Harris's warning. Someone had been watching him. That same someone might be watching Megan as well, and while the police meant well, they wouldn't be able to watch her constantly.

Christopher picked up the phone and dialed Jerry. "Hey, buddy, I need your help."

He could hear a television being turned down in the background. "Name it."

He told Jerry about Emma, about Darrell, about Harris's concerns for Megan. "I'm going to Cincinnati tomorrow. Can you make sure Megan gets to school and then to her friend's house after school?"

"My God, Chris." Jerry's voice shook a little. "This is insane."

"I know. I can't believe any of this is happening, but it is. Can you watch Megan?"

"You know I will. Do you need me to come over?"

"No. She's going to her friend's house tonight. Just make sure she gets in the school building tomorrow morning. She'll be safe there. They have resource officers patrolling the halls." He'd hated the thought that his daughter's school needed officers, but at this moment he was damn glad they were there. "I'll call you when I get back."

St. Pete, Sunday, February 28, 8:30 P.M.

The phone rang. He closed his eyes, the ceramic tile cold against his cheek. The pain still too intense to move. The ringing ceased, only to start all over again. Groaning, he grabbed the edge of the kitchen counter and pulled himself to his knees. He picked up the phone, a spear of white hot pain shooting up his arm and down his back. "Yeah."

"You were wrong," Andrews said. "He didn't give the Townsend woman anything."

He'd figured that out himself. Having one of Andrews's Neanderthals attack him in his own kitchen was a major clue. He had at least three broken ribs and cuts and bruises all over his chest, back, and abdomen, none of which would show when he put on his shirt tomorrow. Which, he supposed, had been the point. "I'm sorry."

"Lie to me again and you'll be dead."

He hurt too much to be afraid or to argue, but he hadn't lied. He'd followed Walker to the airport that morning, watched him slip a thick envelope into the hands of the same woman he'd had dinner with the night before. She'd zipped the envelope securely into her overnight bag and he couldn't get it without her raising a public fuss. So he'd managed to get in line behind her while she waited to go through airport security. She was so intent on sniffing her flowers that she didn't even notice that he was looking over her shoulder at the ID she held with her boarding pass. Her driver's license said she was Emma Townsend of Cincinnati, Ohio. Then he'd mumbled something about forgetting something to the person behind him, got out of line and called Andrews.

He let Andrews know Walker had passed information to this woman, that she was romantically involved with him, clearly evident from their good-bye kiss. Andrews had cursed him for not getting the envelope, muttering that he'd have someone else get it. *They moved more quickly than I expected.* "Is she?" he asked. "Dead, that is?"

"No. Our guy was supposed to make it look like a robbery, but he got interrupted when the woman managed to call the police. Now they'll be doubly suspicious. You'd better find out what Walker knows."

The phone clicked in his ear just as someone started knocking at his front door, and he bit back a groan. He pulled on a shirt and fumbled with the buttons, wincing at the pain. "I'm coming." He opened his door and blinked. "Tanya."

Tanya's eyes were red and puffy. She'd been crying. But now her eyes were dry. And narrowed. She pushed her way in and slammed the door. "We have to talk."

Chapter 6

"The view looks different from up here," Emma murmured, looking down over the balcony at Monday morning commuters streaming up the airport escalators. She had always been the one coming up the escalator. Never a traveler, Will had always waited above.

Kate put her arm around her shoulders and squeezed. "He should be here soon."

"This is just so unreal." Emma rested her head against Kate's shoulder. "I know I've said that a million times already."

"Doesn't make it any less true. Emma, when you get down there with him . . . I just don't want you to get hurt rushing into anything. Y'know?"

Emma sighed. "I know. But he wouldn't hurt me, Kate."

"Not on purpose. Just be careful, Emma. Every which way."

Emma's stomach tightened as a familiar form became visible below, his dark head and broad shoulders above the crowd. "That's him."

From behind her Kate hummed her appreciation. "Oh, Emma. Very nice."

Emma wasn't listening, every nerve in her body vibrating, waiting for him. He was halfway up the escalator when he caught her eye and her blood surged. *He's here. He came for me.* Then he walked off the escalator and she was in his arms, held so tightly she had a hard time drawing breath. He lifted her against him and her arms were around his neck, holding on for dear life. They stayed that way for a long moment, and she could feel his heart racing in his chest. Its beat matched her own.

Shuddering, he let her go, carefully setting her on her feet. "I'm sorry I held you so hard. I forgot you're bruised," he said, his eyes critically assessing her face, darkening with fury when he saw the bruise on her cheek. "He hit you."

Self-consciously she touched her fingertips to her cheek. "When I tried to get away."

"Dammit, Emma," he hissed. "I'm sorry."

"It's all right."

It wasn't all right, he thought. He'd make sure no one hurt her again. He lifted his eyes from her face to the tall thin woman who stood behind her. "You're Kate."

"Yes." Kate unabashedly searched his eyes, then nodded. "You'll keep her safe?"

"You can count on it."

"Your flight doesn't leave for another hour and a half," Kate said. "Let's go grab a cup of coffee. I'd like to get to know you a little better."

Christopher slipped his arm around Emma's waist. "Coffee sounds like heaven right now." They'd started in the direction of a coffee shop when his cell phone rang. "Walker." At the sound of Ian's voice, he stopped short, earning quelling stares from the passengers that were forced to go around them. Ian's words didn't seem to make any sense. "What do you mean Tanya's gone?"

"Tanya's gone," Ian repeated. "She didn't show up for our eight o'clock class this morning and her aunt says she didn't come home last night. Her aunt was frantic."

Christopher clenched his jaw. "Call Harris."

"I did. He says he'll send a squad car 'round to check out her aunt's house."

"Call me the minute you hear something," he gritted, hung up and dialed Jerry's cell. "Did Megan get to school all right?" he asked and Emma looked up at him, her eyes grown wide. He squeezed her shoulder lightly, reassuring her.

"I walked her in myself, Chris," Jerry said. He laughed shakily. "She probably won't speak to me for a month, she was so embarrassed."

"She'll survive a little embarrassment," Christopher said

grimly. "I fly back in a little more than an hour, so I'll be home in time to pick her up from school. Thanks, buddy."

"Anytime. Call me if you get delayed. I've got one of my grad students ready to cover my afternoon classes in case I need to pick Megan up."

"Thanks, Jerry." He slipped his phone in his pocket and started moving again. Kate was leading the way toward the coffee shop on the upper level. "Megan is fine."

Emma's sandy brows were puckered. "But Tanya isn't?"

Christopher swallowed hard, not even wanting to contemplate the possibilities. "Tanya's another one of my grad students. She's missing."

"And she's not one to just take off for a weekend getaway and not come back."

"No." Christopher clenched his jaw. "She's a first-year grad student, six months out of the undergrad program, but she's always seemed so much older. More mature. She'd never just up and leave, especially knowing how much we'd worry."

Emma laid her head on his shoulder. "You shouldn't have come up here to get me," she said softly. "I could have flown down on my own."

He looked down at her, at the bruise on her cheek left by some thug looking for something someone had already killed for. At least once. "I know you could have. But I needed to see you with my own eyes. To know you're safe."

Her eyes were sober. "I'm fine, Christopher. Let's make sure the other people in your life stay that way."

St. Pete, Monday, March 1, 2:30 P.M.

"It's not much, but it's home," Christopher said, setting her small suitcase on a ceramic tiled entryway. But Emma wasn't looking at the house. With a delighted smile she walked to the back wall, which was all glass, and looked out onto a narrow channel that flowed at the back of his property. A small two-person fishing boat bobbed in the current, tied up to a weathered dock on which rested a fat pelican. The sky was blue, the air warm, without a hint of the winter she'd left behind.

"You're right on the bay," she exclaimed. "How lovely."

He stood behind her, his hands on her shoulders, and an involuntary shiver raced down her back. For the first time since Saturday night on the beach, they were truly alone. His thumbs brushed lightly, rhythmically across the curve of her neck. "It's technically on the channel," he said, his voice husky, and she gave in to the need to lean back into him. "Even a shack on the beach is well out of my price range."

"It's still water," she murmured. "I always found the water to be soothing." His arms settled around her waist, his hands loosely linked on her stomach. Rocking her gently. Soothing her in a different way. Then his lips brushed the sensitive curve of her neck and she drew in a startled breath as her nerves scrambled.

"Should I stop?" he whispered and she shook her head.

"No," she whispered back. "It's just still so unexpected. How you make me feel."

His lips trailed a warm path up the side of her face, pressing a kiss against her temple. "How do I make you feel?"

Another shiver shook her. "Alive." She swallowed hard, tilted her head to one side to give him better access. "Like a woman should feel."

"Hmm." His hum of appreciation tickled her skin and he turned her in his arms, his hands cupping her face, his lips taking hers in a hot, sensual kiss that left her senses reeling. "I can't take any credit for that, Emma. You're all a woman should be. I've been wanting to really kiss you since I left you at the airport yesterday morning." His hands rested lightly at the small of her back, undemanding.

She lifted on her toes, her arms around his neck. "So what's stopping you?"

His eyes heated. "I was afraid you were too sore."

"Just my ribs, and only a little." She nibbled at the corner of his mouth, desperately wanting to feel the force of his passion again, as she had on the beach when he'd pressed the hardness of his erection against the softness between her legs. It had been so tempting. Tantalizing. "Kiss me, Christopher." She pulled herself an inch higher on her toes and felt his body shudder. Felt that tempting ridge once again, but pocketed against her stomach, still not low enough to feel relief. With a growl he cupped her behind and lifted her, bracing her against the wall of glass, and he thrust, drawing a whimper from her throat. His hands slid lower, lifting her thighs so that she gripped his hips, enabling her to grind hard against him, to feel him pulsing against her even through the double denim barrier of their jeans. And he kissed her like he'd kissed her on the beach, open-mouthed and totally sexual, nothing hidden, nothing withheld.

She kissed him back, greedily, ignoring the twinges in her bruised ribs. Threaded her fingers through his short-cropped hair and moved his head this way and that, getting the most she could out of that kiss. Then froze when his fingers on her thighs brushed inward and upward. Butterfly caresses against the part of her that throbbed for him. How could a touch so light rock her body like that?

It had been a long time. *Too long,* she told herself. *Long enough that your body will get ahead of your brain if you're not careful.* She remembered the last letter he'd written, the desires he'd spelled out in graphic detail. And she wanted to fulfill each and every one of them. Right this very moment. *But she shouldn't.* She forced her head to lift and her eyes to open. Found him breathing hard, his eyes nearly black. His fingertips continued to brush against the juncture of her thighs, so softly. She opened her mouth to speak, to tell him to stop, but no words came out. She hung there, steeped in the sensations with which he gifted her, her body trembling, her heart racing.

Then his fingers withdrew and he shifted her away from his pulsing erection, slid her thighs down his legs and gently pressed her hips downward until her feet were steady on the floor once more.

"I didn't mean to do that." His voice cracked, raspy and harsh. "I only meant to kiss you, but I can't seem to stop myself where you're concerned." He attempted a smile, but it came out more like a grimace. "I guess I have too much want for you built up."

Emma licked her lips, tasting him still. "It's a two-way street, Christopher. But I'm not ready to go to bed with you. Not yet."

He was quiet for a minute, then raised a brow. "Did you read my last letter?"'

Heat flooded her cheeks and he chuckled. "You should

have put a warning on the envelope," she said with mock severity. "Rated R or something."

He was grinning now. "I did tell you to open it when you were alone." His hands had returned to the small of her back where they simply rested. "I read your book."

She tucked her tongue in her cheek. "Did you find your inner child?"

His lips twitched. "No. But I could hear you on every page. It's good stuff."

"From a man who finds self-help books no help, I take that as a compliment." She sobered, flattening her palms and running them up his arms to his shoulders. "I'm sorry, Christopher. I'm sorry that Darrell's gone. The pain of losing someone to an act of purposeful violence is different from any other kind of grief."

Christopher's throat worked. "And Tanya's still missing. I still can't believe this is happening." He'd called the detective working the case as soon as he'd set foot off the plane in Florida. The grad student was nowhere to be found. He cleared his throat. "I have to go pick up Megan from school. Let me show you where you'll be sleeping. You can just relax while I'm gone."

He withdrew from her arms, his manner suddenly brisk. But Emma didn't take offense. It was his way of coping with a situation that had rocked his world. She followed him to the back of the house where he put her suitcase in a modest little room with a double bed. He surveyed the room with a critical eye. "Like I said, not much." He trailed his finger through a thin layer of dust on the nightstand. "Sorry. We're not much into housekeeping, Megan and I."

"Christopher, after hotel rooms that all look the same, this is perfect." She brought his face down to her level for a soft peck on the lips. "Go get your daughter. I'll be fine." She walked him to the door, gripped by a longing as real as the doorknob she clutched as he drove away. A picture had inserted itself into her imagination, her waving him good-bye every morning from this very door. He'd go to work at the University and she could stay here and write. With the blue sky and the balmy breeze and the swooping birds . . . Who could ask for a better place to just . . . be?

She shook her head at her own wishing as she closed and locked the door. It was normal to want a home again

after living alone. But she'd seen too many clients rush into
relationships after the death of their partners, because the
loneliness was so severe. Sometimes these new relationships
worked, but more often they crumbled. Emma had broken
Christopher's heart once before. She wouldn't do that to
him again. If they were meant to be, it would work out. In
its own time. She wouldn't rush it.

But she could make him and his daughter dinner, she
thought, and headed for the kitchen. It had been more than
a year since she'd cooked an entire meal, but . . .

"Like falling off a bike," she muttered.

Her grandmother's Alfredo sauce was simmering on the
stove when the front door slammed and a panicked voice
called out.

"Chris! Megan!"

Frowning, Emma peeked around the kitchen doorway to
see a man roughly her own age pocketing a key. He was
burly with a neatly trimmed beard and a pipe clamped between his teeth that made her think of Hemingway. This
would be Jerry, she thought. Christopher had told her
about his friend, the physics professor, shown her a picture
of the two of them together with Megan. It had been a
Christmas photo and they'd all been smiling. Jerry wasn't
smiling now, his mouth bent into a frown.

Emma emerged from the kitchen, unsettled at the sight
of a strange man. She told herself it was simply a residual
reaction to the man who'd broken into her home and tied
her up the day before. She was shaky after an assault.
Go figure.

"He's not here," she said, a wooden spoon in one hand.
She wasn't sure why she'd kept it in her hand. It would
suck as a weapon anyway. "But he should be back soon."

The man narrowed his eyes at her. "You're either Emma
or Chris has finally broken down and hired a housekeeper."

"The first one. I'd be pretty lousy at the second.
You're Jerry."

His eyes popped wide. "How did you know?"

"Christopher showed me a picture. He's gone to pick
up Megan."

The frown smoothed from the man's face. "Thank God.
I hadn't heard from him this afternoon, so I went by the

school just in case he hadn't gotten back in time to get Megan, but she wasn't standing out in front like I'd told her to. I almost had a heart attack." Jerry dropped onto the soft sofa, his eyes closed, his cheeks gray above his dark beard. "I tried to call him on his cell, but I kept getting voice mail."

"He was probably talking to that detective, or his students," Emma supplied and walked over to him, appraising him with a critical eye. "Are you all right?" He did look like a man on the verge of a heart attack. "Can I get you some water?"

He opened one eye. "As long as it has scotch mixed with it. Light on the water."

Emma poured him a drink from the bottle she'd found in the kitchen. She watched him down the drink in one gulp and hold out the glass for seconds. Perhaps Jerry had more in common with the alcoholic Ernest Hemingway than a pipe and a beard.

But before she could tell him the bar was closed, the front door opened and a young girl came in. Christopher followed and took an appreciative whiff. "You brought dinner, Jerry. You didn't have to do that."

Jerry shook his head and aimed his thumb at Emma. "No. She's cooking something." He struggled to his feet, his eyes on Megan even though his words were for Christopher. "You didn't call. I was worried sick."

Christopher's face fell. "I'm sorry, Jerry. Detective Harris called when I got off the plane and I got sidetracked." He turned his attention to the young girl who had dropped her backpack to the floor next to the door. She'd been standing there, regarding Emma through narrowed, hostile eyes, but standing behind her, Christopher hadn't seen that. "Megan, I want you to meet Dr. Emma Townsend. Emma and I went to high school together. Emma, this is my daughter Megan."

Emma took a step forward, her hand outstretched despite the girl's obvious hesitance. "It's nice to meet you, Megan."

Megan took a step back, her dark eyes blazing. "It's not nice to meet you," she said and Christopher gasped.

"Megan! What's wrong with you?"

Megan lifted her brows, her expression one of furious disdain. "What's wrong with me? What's wrong with you, Dad? Bringing her *here*, to our *house*."

Christopher looked utterly shocked. "Megan, you've never even met Emma."

"I didn't have to," Megan said bitterly. "I know plenty about her. She's the reason for your divorce."

And with that startling statement Megan stormed to her room and the whole house shook with the force of her slamming door.

Stunned, Christopher could only stare for a long moment. Then grimly he followed, carefully closing the door his daughter had slammed. Emma drew a breath, her heart beating like a war drum. Chanced a glance at Jerry, who was staring at Megan's closed door. Then he turned angry, narrowed eyes on her and Emma opened her mouth in her own defense.

"The last time I saw Christopher was at our high school graduation," she said quietly. "Then I saw him Saturday night. I never knew his wife. I never even knew where he was living."

Jerry eyed the front door as if considering escape, then shook his head. "I'll wait for the official statement," he said dryly and refilled his own glass. "Never a dull moment in this house, I will say that." He gestured with his pipe at the wooden spoon still clutched in her hand. "Your sauce is burning."

Emma rolled her eyes. "Hell."

Christopher leaned back against Megan's door, completely at a loss for words. His daughter sat on her bed, arms crossed tightly over her chest, her face to the wall, her back to him. He racked his brain, trying to think of one time, any one time he'd mentioned Emma. He couldn't think of a single time.

"Megan. Talk to me, honey." He stepped forward, put a hand on her shoulder. She jerked it away. "Megan, please."

"Please what, Dad?" Her voice was cold. Terribly adult.

Christopher shook his head helplessly. "I don't understand." Again he put his hand on her shoulder. Again she pulled away. "Megan . . . I never even talked to Dr. Townsend after high school. She had nothing to do with your mother and me."

Megan's laugh was bitter. "She had everything to do with the two of you."

He pushed a stuffed bear off her desk chair and sank into it. "Megan, I was never unfaithful to your mother. Not once. Not ever."

Megan kept her gaze fixed steadfastly on the wall. "Mom found a stack of letters, Dad." She twisted to pin him with a glare. "Love letters that went way beyond high school."

Christopher blinked. Mona had seen the letters he'd written to Emma. They'd been largely innocent. The musings of a young college boy, miles from home. Truly alone for the first time in his life. Almost like a diary, they'd been. But he'd stopped writing them. The day he'd decided to propose to Mona he put the stack of letters away, determined to never write another. And he hadn't. Not until Saturday night. *I should have torn them up,* he thought, damning his own sentimentality.

He cleared his throat. "Your mother must have been hurt," he said quietly.

Megan chuckled harshly. "You think?"

"I never wrote any letters after I asked your mother to marry me, Megan. That's the truth."

"No, you just said *her* name in your sleep."

Christopher's mouth dropped open. "What? Your mother told you that?"

His daughter sucked in her cheeks, willing herself not to cry. "Once, when she was visiting. Right after your divorce. I went to stay with her in her hotel and I woke up in the night, crying. She was awake. I asked her why she left us. Why she left you. She . . ." Megan looked away, her lips trembling. "She'd been drinking. She told me."

Christopher swallowed hard. He'd suspected Mona drank too much, but to do so when their daughter was with her . . . "She drank when you visited her?"

Megan's fingers nervously plucked at the bedspread. "Yeah. The last time, it was bad. I almost wasn't able to wake her up the next day. When she finally did wake up, she was embarrassed. I think that's why she hasn't come back."

So much for unsupervised visitation, Christopher thought

grimly. He'd make sure that didn't happen again. But that wasn't the biggest problem at the moment. His daughter's resentment of Emma threatened whatever future they could possibly have. "I wish your mother had told me. I could have told her the truth. I may have loved Emma in high school, but your mother was the woman I married. Your mother was the woman I wanted to build a life with. Your mother was the one who chose to walk away, Megan. Not me."

Megan narrowed her eyes, dark like Mona's. "We could have gone with her."

"To South America? Would you have wanted to uproot yourself, to move to a foreign country, learn a new language? She wouldn't have stayed home with us any more there than she did here, honey. We would have been alone there, too."

Her eyes flashed. "Are you sleeping with *her*? With *Emma*?"

Christopher flinched at the venom in her tone. "Megan."

"Well, are you?"

He met her eyes. "No. But if I decide to, that's my business, sweetheart."

Her nervous hands stilled on the bedspread. "And what I say doesn't matter."

Christopher leaned his head back and studied her ceiling for several seconds before once again meeting her eyes. "Of course it does. But, Megan, I've done nothing wrong here. I never once cheated on your mother, no matter what she thought. If she'd trusted me enough to talk to me about this, perhaps it never would have gone this far. But it did and she's gone. I have to go on with my life, too, honey. Emma is a wonderful person. I have confidence that once you give her a chance, you'll see it, too."

Megan turned away. "Don't hold your breath," she muttered.

With a sigh, Christopher stood up. "I'll call you when it's dinnertime."

"Don't bother. I'd rather starve than eat anything *she* made."

Shaking his head, Christopher took his leave, closing her door behind him. He found Emma in the kitchen boiling pasta and Jerry leaning against the doorjamb, silently watching her with a frown. "I'm sorry, Emma," he said and she looked up, troubled, but said nothing. Jerry, on the other hand, didn't seem to have any such hesitation.

"What did she mean?" he asked.

Christopher glanced at Jerry and sighed. "I apparently talk in my sleep. That, paired with some old letters Mona found . . ." He shrugged. "She drew her own conclusions. They were wrong. Unfortunately she told Megan one night when she was drunk." He rubbed his brow. "Mona, not Megan."

"I figured that," Jerry said dryly.

"I never cheated on Mona, Jerry. Not once. She can't say the same though."

Emma's eyes widened, but still she said nothing, just watched while silently stirring the boiling pasta. Jerry cleared his throat.

"How did you know that?"

"She told me, one night when she'd been drinking too much." Christopher poured himself a drink, studied it, then dumped the contents of his glass down the sink in disgust. "Never told me who the guy was. She told me to hurt me. That was a few months before she left. I never understood why she was so angry with me. I still don't understand why she never just asked me."

"Maybe she was afraid of what she'd hear," Jerry said, sadly, Emma thought. "I've got work to do. I'll see you tomorrow, Chris. Emma, a pleasure to meet you."

The front door closed and it was quiet. She could feel Christopher watching her move around his kitchen. "Say something, Emma."

Emma sighed. "I don't know what to say. I've made an enemy of your child, completely unintentionally. I don't want to make it worse. I'll go to a hotel."

He shook his head. "No, you won't. I brought you here to keep you safe. I can't do that if you're in a hotel. Megan will just have to understand."

Emma opened cabinets until she found plates and pulled three from the stack. "Megan is a thirteen-year-old girl. They don't 'understand.' Even if her mother didn't blame me, Megan would have trouble accepting her father with any woman. The Don CeSar has great security. I'll be safe there."

"You're not going anywhere," Christopher insisted with

a frown. "I've done nothing wrong, Emma. You've done nothing wrong. Mona, on the other hand, did quite a bit wrong and she's off in South America living her own life. You're here because there's a real threat. Even Detective Harris thought so. When this is settled, we'll talk about you going to a hotel. But not until then and certainly not tonight."

Emma could see from the set of his jaw that argument was futile at the moment. "So what did the detective say when you talked to him on the way back from Megan's school?" she asked instead, setting the table, pushing aside the terrible feeling that Christopher's daughter could nix whatever new-found relationship they had before it ever really started. Instead Emma wrapped herself in the warmth of setting a table for more than one. Let herself wish. Just a little.

"He asked how far we'd gotten on processing the samples Darrell had been gathering. I told him that with Tanya gone the work would take longer." He clenched his jaw. "I don't want to think about where she is."

"What did the detective say about her?"

"That she's still missing. He's assuming foul play. I guess I know it too, but I don't want to admit it yet." He steeled his shoulders. "He's asked us to step up the pace on testing the samples Darrell was working on when he was killed. I'll go in myself after dinner to do some of her work." He frowned. "I guess you and Megan will have to come with me. I won't leave either of you here alone, especially after dark."

And won't Megan be happy about that? Emma thought wryly, but left it alone. "I can help you with the testing," she said, "as long as it's nothing too complicated. I majored in chemistry, too. I can be a lab assistant if you want." She skimmed a spoon over the simmering sauce and lifted it to his lips, catching his gaze. And her breath.

He touched his tongue to the spoon, his eyes heating. "I'd appreciate the help. You make a good sauce, Emma."

"You're just saying that because it's not Hamburger Helper," she teased, her cheeks warm from his light praise. "You must have two dozen boxes of Hamburger and Tuna Helper in your pantry."

"Neither Megan nor I cook very often," he admitted. "More often than not Jerry brings a bucket of chicken."

"I'd scold you for eating all that fat, but it doesn't seem to have hurt you that much." Her eyes dropped the length of him, all the way to his toes and back up again.

He threaded his fingers through her hair and tilted her face up for a soft kiss. "You didn't age too badly yourself." Quickly he disengaged himself and lifted the pot from the stove. "Let's eat. I'm starving." He glanced at the table where she'd set three places. "Megan said she'd rather starve than eat with us."

"Then we'll make her a plate and she can eat later. Don't push her, Christopher. Give her time to get used to the idea."

Gently he grasped her chin, tilting her face up again. "The idea of what?"

Emma licked her lower lip, then bit it. "Of us. Of me being part of your life."

"Are you getting used to the idea, Emma?"

"Yes. I think I am."

His blue eyes flashed with a look of triumph he either couldn't or didn't bother to hide. "Then Megan will come around. She's a smart girl, loving and generous. She'll eventually see that this makes me happy. That it will make her happy, too."

But Emma remembered the blatant hatred in the girl's eyes and could only pray Christopher was right. Because if his daughter didn't approve . . . Emma had counseled enough "spliced" families to know the pressure angry stepchildren could put on new relationships. Even the best case wasn't good at all.

Chapter 7

Ian inspected Emma's results. "You're a quick study, Dr. Townsend."

Emma lifted one corner of her mouth at the sour admiration in his tone. He'd been vocally opposed to her "help" when Christopher had first brought her to the lab. She'd disturb their samples, she'd do more harm than good. It wasn't until Ian moaned that they'd have to babysit her to make sure she didn't poison herself or blow them all up that Christopher snapped at him to "Be quiet and show her how to run the damned tests." Now, after running several samples with no harm to the lab, its occupants or her own person, it seemed she'd earned a little respect.

"Thank you, Ian. I got nothing out of the ordinary from the samples I tested, though. None of them tested positive for anything."

"Mine either," Nate said grimly from the lab table next to Emma's. "What we have is a shitload of plain dirt. I've been here for seventeen hours and I know nothing more than when I walked in this morning." He threw his pen to the table in disgust. "Dammit."

Her shoulders sagging, Emma looked at the rows of little glass bottles filled with dirt lined up along the lab table, watched them blur. They could be here another seventeen hours and still have more samples to test. Blinking hard, she made her eyes focus on her watch. They'd been hard at work for hours, mostly in silence, Megan Walker asleep on a sofa in the next room. Sleep was beginning to sound pretty good to Emma, too.

"Gentlemen, I'm starting to run on fumes. I didn't sleep most of last night." She glanced across the glaring white of the lab to where Christopher was frowning at a computer screen filled with numbers and graphs.

"He's trying to find anything to tie these samples together," Ian murmured.

But Christopher had found nothing, Emma knew. Not so far. She sat down on the stool at the lab table. "How would anyone know what Darrell was working on? Someone had to have known. He'd be alive otherwise."

Ian rubbed the back of his neck wearily. "I don't know. Detective Harris has asked us that same question, a dozen different ways. Nate and I have wracked our brains trying to think of how anyone would have known, but we come up blank."

Nate scowled. "Nobody knew except us."

"Well, the guy at the USDA office knows," Emma said thoughtfully.

Ian lifted a brow. "Yes, Sutton knows, but none of our reports have listed anything but code numbers for the samples. There was nothing that would seem suspicious."

"To you, perhaps. It meant something to somebody, Ian."

"Tanya knew," Nate said flatly. "Did you see how she went pale when Harris opened Darrell's notebook yesterday morning? She knew something. And now she's gone, too. Doesn't take a rocket scientist to connect the damn dots."

"Christopher said that nothing you were working on was secret. There would have been no reason for her *not* to talk about it. Perhaps she said something innocently."

"To who?" Ian wanted to know. "We're working with dirt here. It's not exciting. Not a bit of intrigue. It's not like the newspapers or anybody else is standing in line to get a peek at our data. The only people who care are at the USDA's office. Bloody hell."

"This new test of yours," Emma said, ignoring his impatience. "It replaces somebody else's test, right?"

Nate nodded. "Yeah. But if you're thinking that the somebody who owns the right to the old test is pissed off about being superseded, you're wrong. The tests aren't like your book," he said, his own impatience combining with a condescension that annoyed her. "It's not like every time somebody uses it to test soil you get a royalty. The test is published in USDA literature. In this business there are no secret tests that could make somebody rich. They just don't exist. So there's no motive there.''

"What about the samples themselves?'' she asked. "You said it was soil samples that were destroyed last month. Where were the samples taken from?''

Ian's tone was downright cross. "We've already looked at that as well, Dr. Townsend. I know you're trying to help, but you're not. Whatever you could think of to ask, we've asked.'' He stopped short of asking her to leave, but his intent was clear.

Emma glanced across the room. Christopher had stopped typing and was watching the conversation with narrowed eyes. He opened his mouth as if to rebuke his students, but Emma shook her head. "Gentlemen. I'm not just 'trying to help' here. I am involved, whether you like it or not. Somebody thought I knew something yesterday. He broke into my house, tied me up, and tore my house apart. I don't know that I wouldn't have ended up like Darrell if I hadn't managed to call the police.'' She let the statement hang, saw their eyes drop. "My house is a crime scene, and I won't feel safe going back there until this thing is cleared up. So if I annoy you by asking questions, that's just too damn bad. Now it's late. I assume you're as tired as I am. Why don't we all get some sleep and come back tomorrow and try this again?''

Nate bit the inside of his jaw. "I'm sorry, Dr. Townsend. You're right. We're tired, but that doesn't excuse us being rude.''

Ian jerked a nod. "Ditto. *Ow*.'' He winced when Nate elbowed him, hard. "I'm sorry, all right?'' He rubbed his side. "Dammit, Nate.''

Emma inclined her head. "All right. Tomorrow, then, gentlemen.'' She waited until they were gone, then turned to Christopher. "Sorry. Your grad students pissed me off.''

One corner of Christopher's mouth lifted. "Do your worst. Nate tends to have a temper and Ian whines. Darrell yelled at them at least once a day. They were due.'' He came to stand behind her, his hands gently massaging her stiff shoulders. "My students get a stipend for their work here. How will I pay you?''

"It's been a long time since I've had a massage. Feels good." She dropped her head to give him access to her neck, lifting her eyes to the long row of samples yet to be tested. "Were all these bottles here the night Darrell was killed?"

His hands stilled. "Yes, why?"

"Why didn't whoever killed him destroy them? They destroyed them before, when they broke in, why not destroy the samples when they killed him?"

Christopher's hands slid from her shoulders. "They wanted it to look like an accident. If they messed up the lab, it wouldn't. Darrell gathered all these samples."

"How do you know where he took them from?"

"Each one is labeled with a code. Darrell kept a list of the codes along with map coordinates. Some of these came from around town. Some came from other parts of the state. I gave the map coordinates to Harris yesterday morning." Christopher frowned, looking at the codes of the untested samples, then at the codes on the empty bottles tested throughout the day. "There's a block of numbers missing."

"What do you mean, missing?"

"The codes go along with geographies. All the numbers starting with one came from here in Pinellas County. All the numbers starting with two came from the county next to us and so on. There are no codes starting with seven. Not one."

Emma sat up straighter, suddenly awake. "Maybe they were taken."

He turned, his brow furrowed. "No. I checked the samples myself against the list Darrell had been working on, after Harris left yesterday morning. I hadn't really believed Darrell had been murdered before that. It was too crazy an idea to be true. I don't think Darrell had finished gathering all the samples."

"So somebody stopped him before he could get to geography number seven?"

Christopher was back at the computer, frantically tapping keys, pulling up the scanned copy of Darrell's last notebook, the one that was missing. The one the murderer had taken with him. "Here are the areas where Darrell was collecting samples. Number seven was an area about a hundred miles north of here."

"Then I guess we're making a trip up there tomorrow," Emma murmured, looking over his shoulder. "Should we take Megan with us?"

"No. She'll be safe in school with the resource officer." He shut off the computer. "Let me wake Megan up so we can get her home and into bed."

Tuesday, March 2, 2:30 A.M.

"Did she ever wake up?" Emma asked when Christopher walked into the kitchen. She was making herself a cup of herbal tea, a ritual she'd developed during her year on the road. She was exhausted, but too wired to sleep.

Christopher pulled a bottle of water from the refrigerator. "Nope. Kid can sleep anywhere, anytime, even on her feet. When Mona was on the road I'd sometimes take Megan into the lab if I needed to check on an experiment that had to run all night. She'd always curl up and sleep on the sofa. Getting her to sleep has never been the problem. Now, getting her to wake up in time for school, that's always fun." He eyed the tea now steeping in a sturdy cup. "Does that help you sleep?"

"Doesn't seem to hurt. Want me to make you some?"

His eyes flashed and her skin begin to heat. His gaze was hot, palpable as a touch. When he'd gotten that look before, he'd kissed her, and she wanted him to, right now. There was something both soothing and dangerous about a kiss in a quiet kitchen. Forbidden, even. But he abruptly dropped his eyes to the bottle he held in his hand.

"Emma, do me a favor and take your tea and go to bed."

Disappointment speared. "Christopher—"

"Please," he interrupted. "I'm tired and worried." He blew out a breath. "And I want you so much I can't think straight, but you said you weren't ready to go to bed with me and I respect that. I just don't think I have enough willpower to do the right thing tonight."

She backed away, unspeakably aroused, the steaming cup of tea hot between her palms, an almost equal heat between her legs. Wondering what the right thing really was. "Good night, Christopher. I'll see you in the morning."

She sat down on the spare bedroom bed, conscious that his bedroom was directly next to hers. The house was Lshaped, their bedroom windows facing both the channel and each other. The light in his room came on and she could see the shadow of his body pacing back and forth. Like a large panther stuck in a small cage. She could feel his worry, his anger. One student dead, another missing. His daughter angry and hurt even though he'd done nothing. *And then there's me,* Emma thought. A face from his past, the one he'd wanted first, with the ardency of young love. He was a good boy. *Now he's a good man.* And Emma knew she wanted him, too.

She heard his muttered oath through the wall and the light in his room switched off. Senses, thoughts, emotions reeling, Emma climbed beneath the covers. A hundred times she told herself to stay where she was, but still she wished. And finally she slept.

Tuesday, March 2, 10:00 P.M.

The trip north to Darrell's area seven was made without incident and with very little conversation. Christopher informed Harris of his plans; then he and Emma drove up the coast, collected samples from the locations Darrell had marked in his notes, then climbed back into Christopher's old car for a quiet ride back, arriving in St. Pete just in time to pick a taciturn Megan up from school. Through the day Christopher was impressed with Emma's ability to respect his need for silence. Many women would have needed to fill the gaps with idle chitchat, but Emma had spoken when necessary, assisted him at every stop, often anticipating his needs before he could voice them.

Back at his house, Emma made dinner as she had the evening before, and as *she* had the evening before, Megan declared she'd rather starve than eat with them. But unlike the evening before, Christopher stood firm. Megan would eat with them, or not at all, so the girl sat at the table angrily eating a grilled pork chop. But Christopher noticed the bone was gnawed clean and not a morsel of vegetables remained on Megan's plate. However Megan felt, she appreciated Emma's culinary skills. That was at least a start.

After dinner the three of them were back at the lab. It was quiet when they arrived, Christopher having called ahead to tell Ian and Nate to go home and get some rest.

"I don't see why I have to come with you again," Megan muttered, throwing herself down on the sofa in the lounge, her algebra book under one arm.

"Because I said so," Christopher returned sharply, then drew a deep breath. "Megan, I know this has been difficult for you, but please put yourself in my place. Darrell is dead and Tanya is missing. Emma was attacked. I need you to be safe."

His daughter's face paled as she fully comprehended the implication. "I could have gone to Uncle Jerry's."

"I should have asked him to come and stay with you, but I didn't think of it. Megan, please. Just do your homework." He sent her a look of paternal entreaty. "Please."

Her teeth gritted, Megan gave a curt nod. "Fine."

Emma was already in the lab, goggles and gloves in place. "Let's get started."

Christopher took the glass bottles filled with dirt samples from the box in which he'd been carrying them. "What if none of these are unusual?"

"We'll cross that bridge when we get there," she replied evenly.

Three hours later she put her pen down. "I've botched this or I found something."

He was at her side in a flash, frowning at the numbers she'd neatly printed in the notebook. "That sample came from where, Emma?"

She consulted her list, then looked up, her eyes deeply troubled. "It was the construction area we visited before lunch. They'd already put up two high rise condos and had a third building mostly done. The sign said it would be a medical center."

Christopher closed his eyes, not wanting to accept the numbers on the page. "Built on land with dioxin levels a hundred times higher than the safe limit. My God. That land is worthless. No one should have built anything there."

"Somebody knew," Emma murmured. "And didn't want you all to find out."

"I need to call Harris," Christopher said.

Harris was a hard man, Emma thought. He reminded her of the detective that had worked Will's murder. She wondered how these men and women dealt with death and the grieving of helpless families day after day. Some turned off their emotions, she supposed. It was purely self-preservation to do so. Now he stood before them, his expression unreadable as he looked at their findings, penned in Emma's own hand.

"This testing should have been done as part of issuing a building permit," Christopher said. "We should look into the company that did the testing. Somebody there should know about this. It could be one tester who was paid to keep the results a secret. It could be the testing company is crooked. Either way, there's no way any test could miss dioxin levels this high."

"What would cause this kind of contamination, Professor?" Harris asked.

Christopher shrugged wearily. "Dioxin is a by-product of a lot of industries. Was, anyway. Most industries have found ways not to produce it, or heavily control the way they dispose of their factory waste. This contamination could have been there for thirty, forty years. Darrell's area seven hit a population boom recently. The land was probably not being used before, but when somebody wanted to build on it, this showed up. I can give you our samples and draw you a map showing where we took these from."

"I'll take the map now, but I think I'll request our lab send someone out for the samples," Harris said. "I don't even like looking at that stuff in the little bottles."

"Think about your kids playing in it," Christopher said, his jaw clenched as he sketched the map. "Sonsofbitches, keeping this secret. Entire towns have been evacuated with dioxin levels this high." He folded the paper with vicious creases. "Well, at least this made your trip out here worthwhile for once."

Harris pocketed the map with a sigh. "Professor, I was actually going to come by here tonight anyway."

Christopher flinched, his face going gray. "Tanya?"

"We found her body," Harris said heavily. "I'm sorry."

Emma slipped her hands over Christopher's shoulders as he sagged onto a stool in front of her. He cleared his throat harshly. "Where did you find her?"

"In the park just outside the University."

"How?"

Harris clearly hesitated. "She was strangled."

Christopher shuddered under her hands. "Have you told her family?"

"Yes. I just came from her aunt's house where her parents were staying. They'd flown in from Iowa yesterday afternoon."

"I should go see them," Christopher murmured, his voice breaking.

Emma lowered her brow to his shoulder. "I'll go with you, if you want."

He jerked a nod, for a moment unable to speak. Then he whispered, "Emma, she was only twenty-two years old. Just a kid. How could this happen?"

Emma jumped when Harris gripped Christopher's arm. The detective's eyes flickered with compassion. "Professor, do you know if she was seeing someone?"

"No, I don't. She could have been, I guess, but she never mentioned anyone."

"Did she go out a lot, with other friends, maybe?"

Christopher's laugh was mirthless. "She was a grad student. She didn't have any money for entertain . . ." The thought trailed off and he sucked in a breath, straightening his spine. "Wait. About two weeks ago, she was heating up a meal in the microwave in the lounge. It wasn't her usual Chef Boyardee and I remember asking her about it. She said it was . . ." He grimaced. "I don't remember . . . Some French dish. It was in a foam box, like you get at restaurants. I teased her that I was paying her too much if she could afford restaurants like that and she blushed. Said she hadn't paid the check herself. Ian teased her about having a boyfriend and that made her really mad."

"Why would a twenty-two-year-old girl be upset over having a boyfriend?" Emma asked. "Especially one that took her to fancy French restaurants." She looked at Harris shrewdly. "Why do you ask, Detective?"

"When she disappeared yesterday I went back to check my notes from my interviews with her after Darrell's death. She'd been home sick the night before. It struck me as a little coincidental that she'd be sick the night he was killed." Harris shrugged. "Coupled with the fact that her ID had been used to enter the lab when the vandalism was done a month ago . . . It didn't add up. I asked her aunt how she got home that night, when she was sick."

"Tanya didn't have a car," Christopher said numbly. "She used the bus."

"That's what her aunt said. But somebody dropped her off that night. Her aunt remembered hearing a car door slam just before Tanya staggered in. She had a high fever that night, but the next day was fine."

"Food poisoning?" Emma asked.

"Maybe. The ME's doing a tox screen, but if it was garden-variety food poisoning, it won't show up. Regardless, somebody brought her home. Somebody she trusted. She didn't call anybody to take her home from your phone here. I checked the LUDs. I'm pulling her cell phone LUDs so we may get a lead there. She was shocked to find Darrell had been murdered on Sunday, Professor. You weren't looking at her face, but I was. If she knew something, suspected someone, she may have confronted them."

"And they killed her." Christopher slowly stood up. "Like they killed Darrell. What about my other students, Detective? Will you have them protected?"

"I've got unmarked cars sitting outside both Ian and Nate's residences."

Christopher shook his head. "I hope Ian doesn't see them. He's so damn sure you're going to deport him, this will just underscore his paranoia."

"Why is Ian so afraid he'll be deported?" Emma asked. "What has he done?"

Harris waved his hand. "Some protests back in Scotland when he was just a kid. His record's been clean ever since. I'm not INS. I'm not going to deport him. I just want to know who killed two people. Now we know someone stood to gain or lose financially from you analyzing those soil samples, but we still don't know their connection to this lab or to you. Someone followed you this weekend, saw you pass what they thought was information to you, Dr. Townsend. We still need to know who that person is."

"Because that person probably killed Darrell and Tanya." Christopher's voice hardened.

"That's my thinking, Professor. Now I'm going to see if I can find somebody who can get into state building permit records after closing hours. I'll call you when I know something. For now, go home and get some rest." With a nod of his head, he was gone, leaving Emma and Christopher staring at each other.

"I'm sorry, Christopher," Emma said quietly. "I'm so sorry."

"Why?" Megan asked from the doorway, taking her headphones off her ears. "Who was that guy that just left?"

Christopher sighed. "That was the detective working Darrell's death, honey. I don't know how to tell you this . . . so I'll just tell you. Tanya's dead."

Megan's composure crumbled. "Oh, Daddy, no." She rushed into his arms, tears coursing down her face, and Christopher rocked her. Emma stood to the side, feeling like a third wheel and ashamed of herself for feeling so. They were grieving. They needed each other. Then Christopher met her eyes over Megan's head and the sorrow in his gaze made any feelings of isolation disappear. *He needs me, too.*

"Let's go home, Punkin," Christopher murmured. "You need to sleep."

Tuesday, March 2, 11:35 P.M.

As she had the night before, Emma stood at the spare bedroom window, watching for Christopher to appear in his room. The trip back from the lab had been tense, to say the least. Megan, still weeping, had pushed past Emma to climb in the front seat, next to her father. Christopher had opened his mouth to tell Megan to move, but Emma shook her head and took the backseat, listening to Megan's sniffling the whole way.

She had no doubt that Megan was devastated over Tanya's death. According to Christopher, Megan was close to all his students, so she had a real right to her grief. But Emma was equally positive that Megan had seen this as an opportunity to insert herself between Emma and her father, an adolescent attempt to sever a relationship of which the young girl didn't approve. So while annoyance tickled at the back of Emma's neck, compassion for the girl overwhelmed. Her life had been turned upside down, as had Emma's and Christopher's. But adults had the maturity to deal with such upheaval. A thirteen-year-old girl did not.

When they'd arrived back at the house Christopher had tucked his daughter into bed, rubbing her back as she cried herself to sleep, and once again Emma had felt out of place. In the way. Christopher and Megan had lost two people they'd loved, two people Emma would never know. Helpless to comfort either of them, Emma made herself a cup of tea and went to her room. Stood at the window. And waited.

The sounds of the shower running were followed by various soft bumps and thuds as he prepared for bed. Emma stood there, drinking in the sounds after so many months alone, remembering what it felt like to wait for Will as he got ready for bed. Watching as he'd gone through his regular little routine, knowing that in a few minutes Will would be next to her in their bed, holding her tight. She craved that now, that closeness, the knowledge that she wasn't alone. Craved the feeling of a man's arms around her. Christopher's arms.

Eventually the light switched on in Christopher's room and once again, he began to pace. But he covered the breadth of his room only once before leaning his forehead against his window, his shoulders sagging. Then heaving. Again and again.

He was crying. Soundlessly weeping. The sight broke Emma's heart. Her feet moved and she made no move to stop them. Carefully she opened his bedroom door and slipped inside. He still stood at the window, shirtless, head bowed, his arms crossed hard over his bare chest, the corded muscles of his arms and back clenching with each shuddering breath he drew. She pushed away the tug of desire at the sight of him. He was grieving and with this she was trained to deal. "Christopher."

His back went ramrod straight. He kept his face carefully averted. "Did you need something?" The tears had thickened his voice and he cleared his throat.

"Is Megan all right?"

"She's upset, afraid. She's worried that I might be next."

An icy fist gripped her gut. "I've thought of that," Emma replied, her voice certainly more controlled than she felt at the moment. "Haven't you?"

"Let them come," he said with barely restrained fury. "I'd welcome the chance to do to them what they did to Tanya. She was too small to fight back. I'm not."

Emma pursed her lips, hard. "Don't talk like that. Whoever is behind this has killed twice, Christopher. Tanya may not have been able to fight back, but Darrell was a healthy young man. Don't you think he fought for his life?"

His shoulders sagged. "I haven't been able to think of anything else."

"None of this is your fault, Christopher," she said quietly.

"I know," he said bitterly. "But that doesn't give much comfort to their parents."

Tentatively she approached, close enough to smell the soap from his shower. His sagging shoulders straightened as if he'd been electrocuted. Perhaps he had. God only knew her skin was almost painfully sensitized. "You'll help find the person who did this. That will bring resolution to their parents. Comfort will come. In time."

Lightly she ran her hand across his bare back and he sucked in a breath. Gritted his teeth. "Emma. Please. Go away."

The muscles in his back quivered under her palm. "Is that what you want?"

He turned his head then, his face hard, his cheeks streaked. His eyes wet. Yet still they burned. "You know it's not."

Gently she pried free one of his hands. Cupped his palm against her cheek and kissed his hand. Then slid it lower to cup her breast through the modest cotton sleep shirt she wore. Waited, breath pent until his hand took her, greedily kneading, his thumb flicking against her rigid nipple. The breath she held rushed out in a gasp of pleasure.

"You're sure this is what you want?" he whispered fiercely.

"Yes." She clamped her teeth over her lower lip, biting back the moan that surely would have echoed off the walls. "Please."

No sooner had the plea passed her lips than her nightshirt was on the floor and she was in his arms, scooped up effortlessly, held tight against his thundering heart. Then she was laid down on his bed, so reverently she wanted to sigh.

He stood at the edge of his bed, his bare chest rising and falling with the silent, labored breaths he drew. He stared down, those wonderful blue eyes nearly black with passion. His eyes traveled the length of her body, taking in her breasts, making them tingle in anticipation. He ran a finger down her stomach, lightly, making her nerves quiver and jump. He hooked that finger just inside the elastic band of the plain white cotton panties she wished were lace instead. Then she didn't care what they were made of because the finger dipped lower, questing.

Finding. She arched her back, pressing closer to the finger that seemed to know exactly how to touch her, and watched his powerful body shudder. With need. *For me.*

She reached up, cupped his rigid erection through his jeans. His head fell backward when she wrapped her fingers around him, touching him for the first time. She leaned up and tugged at the snap of his jeans, then slowly pulled at the tab of his zipper, feeling him throb beneath her fingertips. Then reached inside his briefs. He was hot and hard and silky. Ready. God, he was ready. *For me.*

She was touching him. *Finally.* It was heaven. Hell. And everything in between. A surge of lust barreled through him with the force of a hurricane, snapping his body into motion. Jerkily he pushed his jeans to the floor and yanked her panties down her legs. And stared. She was exquisite. Better than any fantasy his mind had ever conjured, every one of which was tumbling through his mind. He wanted them all, knew he'd have them all. She was here, in his bed, looking up at him with raw hunger that literally brought him to his knees, and he knew which fantasy he'd have first.

Kneeling by the bed he scooped his arms beneath her back and lifted her, repositioning her. Slipped her smooth thighs over his shoulders. And felt her entire body jolt when he kissed her hot wet heat. Heard her muffled whimper when his tongue delved deep. Felt his own climax inexorably building when she arched and bucked and thrashed beneath his mouth, driving him even deeper. Then her body went completely stiff, her thighs closing hard, bringing him even closer, and he rode the wave of her orgasm until she collapsed, panting, gasping, her thighs trembling as he feathered kisses across her skin.

Carefully, very carefully, he stood and clenched his teeth against the vicious need to take her. He'd hurt her if he

wasn't slow, if he wasn't careful. She was lying limply on
his bedspread, one arm flung above her head, her hand
open, twitching still. The other hand was fisted against her
mouth and her eyes were closed. She looked . . .

Like every dream he'd ever had. He'd slip into her now,
he thought, fighting the urge to thrust himself inside her.
He'd gently rock her to another orgasm. *Then I'll let myself
come. That's what I'll do.* He leaned forward, meaning to
press a soft kiss to her shoulder, when her eyes opened,
dark and brown and turbulent.

And hot. God, she was hot. *For me.* Slowly she moved
the hand that covered her mouth. "Christopher." She
mouthed his name, no sound emerging. "Please."

And his control snapped. Frantically he pulled her to the
middle of the bed, shocked when she dug her heels into
the mattress to help him. More shocked when her small
hands pulled him down on her, grabbing his buttocks, pulling him closer.

"Dammit, Emma." His breath was hot in her ear, his
harsh whispers thrilling her. "I need to go slow."

She shook her head, her whisper desperate to her own
ears. "No, you don't. I need you now. *Now, Christopher.*"
And she couldn't stop the small cry of satisfaction when
with one hard thrust he was inside her. Filling her. He
felt . . . so good.

He pushed his body above her, his biceps cording as he
held himself still. His eyes were closed, his expression . . .
reverent. He shuddered once. Then began to move. Slow
and hard, his face set with an almost grim resolve.

She could feel him, every stroke of his hips stirring embers of sensation that had been dormant too long. She
arched, drawing him deeper still, and he groaned.

"I wanted to make this last. But I can't." His thrusts
took new power and the bedspread scratched her back as
the force of his thrusts moved her up the bed. She was
climbing again, unbelievably. She'd thought herself emptied
after the first climax, but it wasn't so. The second peak
took her by surprise and she cried out, his hand covering
her mouth to stifle the sound as she shuddered. His thrusts
grew frantic and fast. Then he stiffened, his chest ex-
panding, his teeth bared as he spilled himself deep into
her body.

Then collapsed against her, shaking. "My God," he breathed. "My God. Emma."

She pressed her lips to the side of his neck, hot and sweaty. So strong. And she said nothing. There were simply no words.

Still shaking, he rolled them to their sides, his hands on her butt, his body still buried deep inside hers. She wondered if, after all those years, it had been what he'd hoped. She didn't have to wonder long.

His lips grazed her ear, vibrating gently as he hummed in completion. "That was more than I ever dared to hope for."

She said nothing and he leaned back, anxious to see her face. Wondering if he'd hurt her. Afraid he'd see regret in her eyes. But it wasn't regret. It was awe. And intense satisfaction. The worries he'd harbored, worries that he wouldn't be able to please her as her husband had, just disappeared. She stared at him, as if stunned. Maybe she'd never come twice before. But Christopher was wise enough not to ask. He'd pleased her and that was all that mattered. And if he had his way, he thought, pulling the blanket around them, he'd please her again before the night was over.

Chapter 8

He waited in the shadows of the trees, dreading what was to come, knowing he would be unable to stop it. The crunch of gravel was like ground glass in his gut. Andrews was here. The heavy footsteps behind him stopped and there was a scratch of a match, the flare of a flame. Andrews took a long drag on his cigarette, blew it out.

"Walker was up at the site today."

Nausea rolled through him. "I know."

"If Walker doesn't know now, within days he will. It's just a matter of time."

"I won't kill him," he hissed. Vehemently.

Andrews just chuckled, sending the chill of wet sweat dripping down his back. "You know, for a man who can be tied to two murders . . ." Andrews took another deep drag on the cigarette, making him wish for one of his own. "One phone call from me and you'll be locked up tight. And Walker would still die if I wanted him to."

"If Walker dies, it will all come back to you. Your company will go under."

"If Walker dies, yes, that's probably true, especially now that you killed the Meyer woman." Cold fury edged Andrews's voice. "I never told you to kill her. Why did you?"

"Tanya suspected. I had to." He was trembling now, the vile memory of choking the life out of Tanya's body rising above his fear of Andrews. "The night Darrell . . ."

"The night you killed Darrell Roberts," Andrews supplied acidly.

He swiped the sweat from his forehead with his sleeve. "I

tried to get him out of the lab, tried to get him to go drinking with me, but he insisted he had to work. And if he worked, Tanya would be with him. It's Walker's rule. Nobody works alone. I needed to get her out of there, so that night before she went to the lab I made her dinner. She's allergic . . ." *Dammit. Was.* "She was allergic to cinnamon. It made her nauseous. I made spicy chili, added the cinnamon in so she wouldn't taste it, but she did anyway. I told her she was imagining it. When she called me to come get her later that night she told me she knew what it felt like when she ate cinnamon. I denied it again. I told her I didn't even keep cinnamon in my kitchen. But Sunday, Harris came to the lab, proved Darrell had been murdered. Tanya came to my apartment, went straight to the kitchen."

"Where she found the cinnamon because you were too stupid to throw it away."

Stupid was exactly what he'd been. "Yes. She remembered me asking questions about Darrell's work. She was so angry. She accused me of poisoning her, too. She said she was going to Harris with what she knew. I didn't have any choice. I killed her." He gritted his teeth. "But no more. I can't do it again. Not Walker."

"No, we won't kill Walker. We'll just convince him it's in his best interest to forget about all of this. You'll see that his new girlfriend disappears. Make it look like she went home. Then make sure Walker knows she didn't. If he cooperates, his girlfriend will be the only one who disappears. If he doesn't, that pretty little girl of his will be next."

Wednesday, March 3, 5:15 A.M.

Emma opened one eye to squint at the alarm clock next to Christopher's bed. It would be dawn soon. She needed to be getting back to her own bed before his daughter woke up. Gingerly she swung her legs over the side of the bed, only to be pulled back, his arm snaking around her waist.

"Not yet," he murmured. "Stay a little longer. Please."

He'd snuggled up against her, his lips grazing her hip. His eyes were closed but he was very much awake. "That's what you said the last time I tried to get up."

One corner of his mouth lifted in a smug smile. "It worked, too."

She had to smile back. "That it did." It worked. *She*
worked. It hadn't been until after she'd climaxed in his
arms that she'd admitted that she'd been afraid her body
wouldn't function. That she'd never again feel that incredi-
ble rush, that explosion of feeling. But feel it she had. Several times during the night, as a matter of fact. But now it
was morning and they had to face the ramifications of what
they'd done. Sobering, she frowned slightly. "Christopher,
what happened here—"

She was silenced by his fingertips on her lips. He sat up
and she averted her eyes from his chest, every square inch
of which she'd savored during the night. He was too tempting, she knew. A look would become a kiss, which would
become a caress. And she wasn't certain her body would
allow any more of what would follow that. She was sore,
inside and out. Even so, she wanted more.

"Don't say you're sorry," he warned, his voice low, his
blue eyes intense.

Gently she pulled his hand away from her mouth, entwin-
ing their fingers. "I wasn't going to because I'm not. I
needed you last night and I think you needed me."

"I did. I do."

She brought their joined hands to her lips. "What I was
going to say is that we shouldn't assume that what happened here last night . . . well, it may be the start of something permanent and it may not. Either way, this has been
a night I'll never forget. You gave me back myself, Christopher. For that I'm grateful."

He let out a heavy breath. "Are you finished?"

He was hurt. She hadn't meant to hurt him. "Yes, but—"

"Emma, please. I know this is happening fast for you. I
know you didn't come down here with the intent of sleeping with me, but I'm damn glad you did. Last night may
have been the first time, but it won't be the last. Wherever
we end up."

"Will you be able to live with whatever happens? Even
if it's not permanent?"

He threaded his fingers through her hair and pulled her
against him for a soft kiss. "Whatever happens, we will
have had the dance, Emma."

"That song again. It was years before I could listen to it

without wondering where you were. I thought I'd scared you away because I'd danced too close . . ."

He pulled back far enough for her to see his grimace. "I gave up a whole music category," he said darkly and she chuckled. "It's true. It was like some cosmic bad joke. Every time I'd let the radio station land on a country station, that song was playing. And I'd think of you, and wonder if you were happy. I wanted you to be happy, Em," he whispered. "Wherever you were."

She looked into his eyes, seeing so many things. Her old friend, the boy he'd been. Her new friend, the man he'd become. Her new lover. It was overwhelming. "There were times I thought I knew you better than I knew myself," she murmured. "Why didn't I see how you felt?"

"You were so shy about certain things," he murmured back. "Anything academic was a breeze for you. But anything that had to do with yourself, your self-confidence . . ." He shrugged. "I was afraid to push. Afraid I'd run the other way and I'd lose your friendship. Then that night of the junior prom, I don't know what came over me. I took a chance. Asked you to dance. You were so scared at first, I could tell. But you relaxed and laid your head against me and I thought my heart would beat right out of my chest. I thought: *This is the time. Make your move.* But I guess I was shy, too. It was always easier to write letters to you than to talk to you about things like that in person."

"They were lovely letters, Christopher. You should have been a poet." His cheeks darkened and she smiled, delighted. "You do! You write poetry, too?"

"Not very good poetry," he admitted. He tilted his head, his eyes suddenly very serious. "We were careless last night, Em."

Emma caught her breath. They'd made love three times and not once used a condom. That wasn't careless. That was insane. Gathering her thoughts, she sought to reassure him as best she could. "Will was the only man I'd ever been with. There were no others after his death. But I'll get a test if you want."

"That's not necessary, Emma. And I did get tested when I found out Mona had cheated. Luckily I was clean. I was thinking more about pregnancy."

Oh, Lord. Rapidly she counted days in her mind. "It's dicey, but probably okay." A shadow of disappointment crossed his face and she blinked at him. "You wanted me to be pregnant? *Christopher.*"

He slid back down to the pillows and closed his eyes. "I always did. Do you remember that project in Mr. Bell's health class where we got a pretend spouse and had to take care of a doll for a week as our pretend kid?"

"How could I forget?" she grumbled, still reeling. "I was 'married' to Skip Loomis."

A smile flitted about Christopher's lips. "I wanted to kill him because he thought the project gave him a right to touch you."

Emma shuddered. "Don't remind me. You got hooked up with Bethany Rigonelli who left your doll at a pot party," she said smugly. "I hated her."

Christopher chuckled. "So did I. I had to explain to Mr. Bell why my doll smelled like the child of sixties flower children. I wanted so badly to be your husband then. I'd watch you carry that doll around like it was real and I'd wish it *was* real. And mine."

"Oh, Christopher, that's so sweet."

"Emma . . . Why didn't you ever have children with Will?"

Emma hesitated, then shrugged. "He couldn't. He'd had mumps when he was a little boy and it left him . . . You know. We were planning to adopt a child. We'd even filled out the initial paperwork. And then he was killed."

His eyes opened, regarding her intently. "If we made a baby here, we get married."

She sighed, unable to think that far ahead at the moment. "Why don't we cross that bridge when we get there? For now, I just need to get back to my room before your child wakes up. She doesn't like me as it is. I don't want to add fuel to the fire."

"I'm sorry, Emma. Mona should never have told her those things. I've got to think of a way to undo that damage."

Emma slid off the bed and pulled on her nightshirt. "Counseling will help her, Christopher. But I say we get through this current crisis before we tackle any new ones. Will you send Megan to school today?"

He frowned. "I think she's as safe there as anywhere, as long as she doesn't leave the campus. I'll drop her off, then go see Tanya's parents."

"Megan may not want to go to school today," Emma said gently. "Someone she was close to is dead. She's going to need time to deal with that." She kissed his forehead. "Sleep. We've got a few hours before she has to wake up and decide."

Christopher watched her go with a sigh. He'd been careless on purpose, he admitted to himself. At least the second and third times. The first time he'd needed to be inside her so badly, everything else just seemed irrelevant. He had a whole box of condoms in his nightstand. They'd use them next time. And the time after that. He'd give her all the time she needed to come to terms with her own feelings, but when all was said and done, they'd be together. He just knew it.

"*Christopher!* Come here! *Now. Please.*"

He bolted upright at the sound of Emma's panicked cry. Pulling on his pants, he ran to her room, only to find her standing in Megan's open doorway. Megan's room was empty and Emma held a note. His heart was pounding, so hard he thought he'd pass out. "Where is she, Emma? Where's Megan?"

Emma's face was tight with fear. "She's run away."

"Why? She just wouldn't run away! Dammit." He grabbed the note and read it in disbelief. *Dear Daddy. I got up for a glass of water and found your houseguest's door open and her bed empty. How could you? I won't stay in the same house with that woman another minute. I'll come home when she's gone. Megan.*

Emma stared up at him, her brown eyes pained. "You call her friends. I'll call Detective Harris. We'll find her, Christopher."

The fear that gripped them both went unsaid. *Before somebody else does.*

Wednesday, March 3, 7:15 A.M.

"He's gone."

Megan slid out from under her friend's bed. "Thanks." Debbie sat on her bed with a frown, her arms crossed over her chest. "I don't feel right about this, Megan. I just lied to my mother and your father."

Megan's jaw set. Her friend had denied having seen her, but this wasn't Debbie's problem. *It's mine.* "I'm sorry."

"Your dad's so worried, Megan. You need to call him, let him know you're safe."

"When that bitch leaves, I will."

"How will you know she's gone?"

"I'm going to go back to my house and watch from across the street. I only came here last night because it was too cold to sleep outside. The bitch'll be going home soon," Megan said with satisfaction. "Dad won't make the same mistake twice."

Debbie bit her lip. "Doesn't sound like he really made a mistake the first time, Meg. You said he didn't cheat on your mother with this Emma person."

"No, I said *he said* he didn't cheat with this Emma person," she said with contempt, narrowing her eyes at her best friend. "Promise me you won't say a word. *Promise.*"

Debbie nodded miserably. "I promise. Call me later. Let me know you're okay."

"I will." Megan stuck her head out of Debbie's bedroom window and looked both ways. "Coast is clear. I'm gone."

Keeping to back yards, Megan made her way home. She'd never left the house in the middle of the night before. Never skipped school for that matter. It was all Emma's fault. When *she* was gone, everything would be back to normal. She and her father did fine on their own. Besides, if *she* lived with them, her mom would never come home.

Her father's old car was gone from the driveway. He'd be making the rounds to her friends' houses. All would say they'd never seen her. She stood in the shadow of her neighbor's garage, the morning sun growing bright enough to make her easily seen. *So I'll stay out of sight.* Her teeth grated when the front door opened and Emma came out, clutching the cordless phone in one hand, shielding her eyes from the sun with the other. *She's watching for me. Wearing a sweatshirt that belongs to my father.*

To Megan's surprise a strange car pulled in the driveway and the man who'd come to the lab last night got out. Detective Harris. What was he doing here? *Oh my God,* she thought, horrified. *The bitch has called the cops on me.*

He went inside the house with her. A few minutes later he came out, giving her shoulder a squeeze. *Like she cares,* Megan thought sardonically. *Like she gives a shit about me or my dad. If she did, she wouldn't be here.* The cop drove away slowly, checking out the street.

I can't stay here. He might come back. She couldn't go to her friends' houses—they'd all have left for school by now and their mothers wouldn't go along with her plan.

Then a few minutes later salvation arrived. Uncle Jerry's SUV pulled into the driveway. She'd go with him. He'd understand. He was her father's friend, but he'd been her mother's friend first. Her mother had told her so. Megan bit her lip. Her mother had told her a lot of other things that she didn't want to think about now.

She frowned. Jerry was taking a long time to get out of the SUV. He sat there, his hands clenched on the wheel. Finally he got out and slowly walked up to the house and let himself in the front door. Her frown deepened. Uncle Jerry never looked old to her before, but this morning he walked like an old man. She'd make sure he was eating right, just like she did for her dad. No more KFC for Jerry.

But for now, he was her escape. *He's my godfather. He'll understand. He'll let me hang with him until she's gone.* But just to be safe, she'd hide in the back seat until he got far enough away from the house that she could explain without being taken immediately home. Looking both ways for that detective, Megan sprinted across the street. Luck was with her and he'd left his door unlocked. Quickly she climbed in and over the back seats, hiding in the cargo area. She pulled a blanket over herself and waited.

Emma's head jerked up when the door opened. "Chris—" His name went unfinished because it was Jerry who stood in the foyer, a haunted expression on his face. Of course, Christopher had called him. He was Megan's godfather. Of course he'd be worried. She stood up, uncertainly. "Jerry. Christopher isn't here. Megan is—"

"You have to come with me," he said heavily. She studied him with a frown. It wasn't intoxication that made his speech slow. It was dread.

Suddenly his dread became hers. "Why are you here? Everyone else is—"

"You have to come with me," he repeated, drawing a semiautomatic pistol from his coat pocket. "Don't make me use this, Dr. Townsend. Please."

Emma's eyes darted side to side. The cordless phone was . . . on the coffee table. Just out of reach. But her cell phone was in the pocket of her jeans.

"Dr. Townsend, please. I will use this, I can assure you. Don't even think about touching that phone. And give me the cell phone in the pocket of your jeans. Let's go."

"Why?"

Jerry shook his head. "Just go."

She didn't move a muscle, just stood her ground. "It's you, isn't it? Darrell and Tanya? You killed them. Or you know who did."

For a bulky man he moved quickly. In a split second his hand was tangled in her hair, lifting her to her toes. The back of his other hand crashed into her cheek, making her cry out. "I said, let's go." He forced her to the door, the gun jammed against the small of her back. "I'm going to let go of your hair and take the phone from your pocket. Then you're going to walk quietly to my car. If anyone sees you, you will smile and say 'Hello' as will I. If you scream, I will shoot you and any innocent bystander that sees us."

Her heart pounding in her head, Emma did what he said, stumbling as she was forced to his SUV. He opened the back passenger door and pushed her. "Climb in," he said softly. "Don't try anything stupid. I really don't want to kill you."

She climbed in, her lungs pumping. She had to think. *Think.*

He slammed the door and walked around to the driver's side. Emma grabbed the door handle and pulled, but nothing happened.

"I have the child locks set on both doors," he said, climbing into the front seat. "Now get down on the floorboards and don't move."

Helplessly Emma did what he said. "Where are you taking me?"

"Shut up."

"If you're going to kill me, I at least have a right to know why." She knew why. Jerry was the connection between the lab and whoever had falsified those soil tests. But she wouldn't let him know. Feigning ignorance might be the only thing that saved her life.

"Shut up."

"But—"

"Dr. Townsend, I don't want to hurt you anymore than I wanted to hurt the others. But I will if I must. Now shut up."

Emma tried to control her breathing. "Are you the one that broke into my house?"

The SUV made a right turn, slowed, then stopped. Jerry's arm came whipping over the seat and grabbed her by the sweatshirt. They were in an alley, between two buildings, not a window or person in sight. "I said shut up." His fist slammed into her other cheek, the pain shocking her. Rage and pain erupted and she stared him down in contempt. Blood filled her mouth and she spat it at him. Furiously he stared down at the stain on his white shirt and cuffed her on the side of her head. Stars twinkled before her eyes and she moaned.

"Now you'll shut up," he growled and threw her back down to the floorboards.

Clenching her teeth against what would have been a whimper of pain she was quiet, wondering how this man had become involved in such a mess. He was a physics professor, for God's sake. Christopher's closest friend.

Christopher.

"What will you do to Christopher?" she asked, her speech now slurred. Her tongue felt swollen and her jaw ached along with her head. He said nothing and she knew. Panic gripped her. He was planning to kill Christopher, too.

Wednesday, March 3, 9:45 A.M.

She wasn't here. He'd called to talk to Emma, to see if Megan had returned, but the phone rang and rang so he'd raced back home to find her gone, too. Christopher ran from room to room, retracing his steps, checking every closet, under every bed.

They weren't here. He punched in Harris's number on his cell, jumping when the doorbell rang. It was Detective Harris himself, holding his ringing phone, looking grim. His stomach roiling, Christopher disconnected his cell and stepped aside to let Harris in.

"Megan's still missing. I've been to every one of her friends' houses, her school, the mall, *everywhere*."

Harris nodded. "I know. I was here earlier talking to Dr. Townsend. Where is she?"

"I was hoping you could tell me. Because Emma's gone, too." He could hear the hitching panic in his voice and was powerless to stop it.

"Maybe she went out somewhere."

"She didn't have the car. I had the car." Shaking, Christopher pressed his fist against his lips. "She wouldn't just leave, Detective. She was staying here in case Megan came home. Something's wrong." He frowned. "If you're not here about Megan, why are you here?"

"I just got Tanya's cell phone LUDs. Here's the number she called when she left the lab Thursday night, when she was sick. It's a disposable cell." Harris held out a piece of paper with a number scrawled across the top.

Christopher shook his head. "I don't recognize it."

"Do me a favor," Harris said evenly. "Call it."

His palms sweaty, Christopher complied. And his heart dropped from his chest to his gut like a rock as his phone's display listed the name that went along with the number. "That's not possible. It's Jerry's cell."

"Is he answering it?"

"No. It's still ringing." Dazed, Christopher sank to the arm of the sofa. "He called me once and I asked what number this was because it wasn't his normal cell. He said it was a new phone, so I stored the number. This isn't possible. Jerry didn't even know Tanya that well." He blinked at Harris. "But you're not surprised."

"No. After I left you and Dr. Townsend last night I went by Tanya's aunt's house and searched again. This time I went through the dirty clothes in the laundry room. In the pocket of her jeans, I found a matchbook from a place called Le Panoramique."

"I've never heard of it," Christopher said, still staring at his cell display in disbelief.

"It's not around here. It's up past Madeira Beach. I drove up there last night, got there as they were closing. Showed them Tanya's picture. The bartender remembered her because he thought she had an illegal ID when he carded her. She looked younger than twenty-two, he said. He remembers her showing her University ID, which annoyed her companion. A bulky man in his forties with a black beard."

"Jerry and Tanya?" Christopher whispered. "My God. That's against the code of conduct. He'll lose his tenure." He closed his eyes. As if Jerry's breaking University rules was their only problem. "I'm sorry, that was a stupid thing to say."

"No, Professor, it's not. That's why Tanya never told anyone about her boyfriend. It could get Dr. Grayson fired or at least harshly reprimanded. I'm afraid we need to find him, bring him in for questioning."

"But why would Jerry be involved with Tanya? Why is he involved in any of this?"

"I don't know, Professor. But we'll find out."

The doorbell rang and Christopher bolted. *Megan.* Then exhaled in disappointment when he saw his elderly neighbor standing on his doorstep. "Mrs. Hewett, have you seen Megan?"

Mrs. Hewett's face fell. "Megan's not home yet? I hoped he'd brought her home."

Christopher straightened slowly. "Who, Mrs. Hewett?"

"That friend of yours. The one who drives the big black Expedition."

Christopher's heart stopped. "He was here?"

Mrs. Hewett started when Harris stepped out from behind the door. "Who are you?"

"I'm Detective Harris, ma'am," he said, showing her his badge. "What time was the black Expedition here?"

"It was daylight," she said. "Maybe quarter to eight? He didn't stay long."

Harris wrote it down. "You're sure?"

"Yes. My husband had just left for work. Chris, your guest from up north went with him," she said and looked over at Harris. "She got in the backseat, not the front."

Christopher steeled his body to stay upright even though every drop of blood had drained from his head. "He's got her, Harris. Just like Tanya."

"But now we know who we're looking for, Professor," Harris said. "I'll put out an APB for Dr. Townsend. I want you to focus on finding your daughter."

Chapter 9

Wednesday, March 3, 11:00 A.M.

The gravel crunched under her shoes as Jerry dragged her. She was blindfolded and her hands were bound in front of her. They had driven for hours, she thought, but she didn't know how far she was from Christopher's house. Jerry had made a lot of turns before arriving here. Wherever "here" was. She was dragged up three steps, then pushed through a door into a stuffy room. Pushed into a chair, her feet bound to the chair legs. Someone else was here. They were smoking, but didn't speak. Finally Jerry pulled the blindfold from her eyes and Emma looked around.

It was a small trailer, dingy and hot. A large man with a nasty sneer was looking her over, head to toe. A shiver of fear ran down Emma's back, which seemed to amuse the man. "So you're the famous Dr. Townsend," he said sarcastically, taking a drag on his cigarette. "What took you so long?" he snapped to Jerry. "We're only a half hour from Walker's house. You drive around for hours, losing your nerve?"

Jerry said nothing and Emma felt a spurt of hope. Jerry was weakening. Maybe she could use that to her advantage.

"Why am I here?" she demanded with far more bravado than she possessed.

"Because your boyfriend can't keep out of matters that don't concern him. I know you were at the Costaine construction site yesterday, gathering samples."

Emma did her best to appear confused. "We were at so many sites yesterday. I'm not sure which one you mean."

110

Then she cried out when the man struck her, harder than Jerry had.

"Maybe you'll remember now. It's a pretty little place. Two big condos. One enormous medical center." Her eyes must have flickered, because he grinned. "Good. Now we're speaking the same language. Did you analyze the samples you took?"

She said nothing. His lip curled. Another blow knocked her to the floor, chair and all. "Don't even consider lying to me," he said quietly. With one hand he jerked the chair back up and Emma felt a sob build in her chest, but ruthlessly battled it back.

"What does it matter what I say?" Emma said, her breath hitching. "If I say we found nothing, you won't believe me. If I say we found something, which we didn't, you'll kill me."

He shrugged. "I'm going to kill you anyway. I just want to know how much damage control I have to do. What did you find?"

She looked into his stubbled face, at his hard jaw, his crooked nose, and knew he spoke the truth. She was seeing his face. There was no way he'd let her live. Panic welled, but like the sob, she battled it back. At this point, all that mattered was protecting Christopher. "We found nothing. We were only able to test about half the samples. We hadn't gotten to the samples from that construction site yet." She narrowed her eyes. "You can believe me or not. It's the truth." Carefully she turned her head toward the door where Jerry stood, pale, his pipe clenched between his teeth. Ignoring the pain shooting down her spine, she shook her head. "How could you?" she asked. "Christopher is your best friend. How could you betray him this way?"

"Money is a powerful motivator," the man with the crooked nose said, humor in his voice. "Professor Grayson here has a bit of a gambling problem. We offered to help him out of his dilemma in exchange for a small favor."

"You betrayed your best friend," Emma said quietly. "You killed Darrell and Tanya. Will you kill Christopher too?"

Jerry flinched. "I brought her to you, Andrews. I fulfilled my end. Let me go."

Andrews stood abruptly when the door opened. Filling the opening was yet another thug, this one older and balding. But it wasn't his receding hairline that had both Emma and Jerry gasping. It was the young girl whose shoulders he held in an iron grip.

Megan.

"She was in Grayson's SUV," the man said, his voice raspy. "She was trying to sneak away."

"Megan," Jerry whispered. All the color had drained from his face. "What—"

White-faced, Megan said nothing, just stood looking at all three men. And Emma. Andrews made the floor creak as he crossed to her. Ran a fingertip down her cheek. "Pretty," he murmured mockingly.

Emma lunged to her feet, bringing the chair with her. "Don't you touch that child," she snarled and Andrews just laughed.

"My taste doesn't run this young," he said, his voice back to amused contempt. "But I know lots of people who would pay good money for a girl this pretty."

As if the words were a whip to her back, Megan began to frantically struggle.

The man holding Megan shoved her at Andrews and with excessive force pushed Emma back down, her teeth jarring in her head as her chair made contact with the floor. Horrified, she could only sit there and stare at Andrews. "You monster."

Jerry put his pipe in his pocket, his hands shaking. "Surely you can't be serious," he said, trying for calm reason even though his voice was shaking nearly as badly as his hands. "She's just a child."

Andrews shrugged. "Then kill her. But she's not leaving here free." He flicked a finger at Jerry's shirt, bloody where Emma had spat on him. "Kill her or I'll sell her. I like the second one because it makes me a profit. But I'll let you choose. I have to go deal with Walker. With his daughter gone, we'll have no leverage, so he'll have to go, too. He's got an old car, doesn't he? Too bad about old cars. Their brakes go bad."

"No," Megan whispered harshly. "Uncle Jerry, please. Don't let them hurt my dad."

"You don't think anyone's going to notice all these missing people?" Emma asked derisively. "You don't think anyone will figure all this out?"

"Probably," Andrews said smoothly. "But none of it can be linked to me. Grayson will go down for all the murders."

Jerry made a choking noise. "But—"

Andrews just smiled. "Never forget, Professor, when you gamble, the house always has the advantage. Always." He grabbed Megan by her arm and forced her into a chair. "Sit down, Princess. Your uncle's about to decide your future. Wait outside the door," he said to the balding man. "Don't let him leave unless Townsend is dead. Then bring the girl to me. If he doesn't come out in twenty minutes, go in and kill him and Townsend yourself." He smiled. "Then bring the girl to me. I have some calls to make."

The door shut, leaving Emma, Megan and Jerry alone.

"You can't kill her," Emma said, her voice husky with fear. "You can't. You are her godfather. You vowed to care for her. You promised, Jerry. Kill me if you must, but you have to get her out of here alive."

Wide-eyed, Megan sat and cried quietly.

"You don't understand," Jerry said pathetically. "These men are powerful."

"For God's sake, Jerry," Emma exploded. "Be a man, dammit. You've got a gun. Use it on them."

"You think it's just the two of them?" Jerry laughed hysterically. "There are ten men out there. Even if I kill Hudson out there on the stairs, two more will take his place. I'll be dead. I can't run. They can get to me anywhere. They got to you in your own house, a thousand miles away. They'll kill me."

"You are an adult, Jerry," Emma said levelly. "You made choices that brought you here. Megan did not. You have to find a way to get her out of here and keep Christopher safe. You owe that to them, Jerry. Whatever the cost to yourself."

"What about you?" Megan whispered, her voice small.

Emma turned to her, saw the girl wince at the bruises on her face. "I don't want to die, Megan. I'll fight to live. But you're a child. Adults . . ." She glared at Jerry. "Good, responsible adults care for children. You are important to your father. He's important to me. I don't want to see either of you hurt."

Jerry pulled his pipe from his pocket and tried to light it, but his shaking hands extinguished every match he lit. Finally he sank into the chair at Andrews's desk and covered his face with his hands. "I don't know what to do," he murmured.

"Yes, you do," Emma said, injecting into her voice all the authority she could muster. "Untie me, Jerry."

"Please, Uncle Jerry," Megan sobbed. "Please don't do this."

He dropped his hands and looked at her sadly. "I'm sorry, Megan. I'm so sorry."

Wednesday, March 3, 11:00 A.M.

Harris slipped his cell phone into his pocket. "Do you know a soil testing firm by the name of Seymour and Elliot?" he asked Christopher, who sat in a chair at the police station, numbly watching the activity. All available personnel had been put against finding Jerry. And Emma.

Jerry. There was still a piece of Christopher's heart that refused to believe his friend could be involved. *I've known him for fifteen years.* Since before Megan was born. Since before he'd married Mona. The Jerry Grayson he knew could never do something so vile. But pictures didn't lie. While the surveillance cameras in the chemistry lab had been disabled, the cameras in Jerry's condo complex had not. There was proof in black and white that Tanya had visited Jerry the afternoon she disappeared. Right after two big men wearing baseball caps had visited Jerry. Harris was circulating photos of the two big men, but held little hope as their caps hid their faces.

"Professor?" Harris snapped his fingers under Christopher's nose. "Seymour and Elliot. Have you heard of them?"

Christopher shook his head to clear his thoughts. "No. Should I?"

"According to the state records department, they're the testing company that gave that contaminated land the thumbs up. We'll check their records, find out who knew what and when. A land management company in Atlanta holds the title, so they're suspects as well. A company named Costaine is managing the construction at the site you took the samples from. Owner's name is Andrews. We'll audit his records, too."

Christopher blanched. "Now?"

Harris's mouth quirked in sympathy. "Not now. Maybe tomorrow or the next day."

"When Megan's home," he murmured. "And Emma." His cell phone shrilled and with unsteady hands he answered it. "Hello?"

"Chris, this is Stella." Debbie's mom. His heart started to race.

"Does Debbie know where Megan is?"

"Not directly, no. I just got a call from Debbie at school. She promised Megan not to talk, but her conscience has been bothering her all morning. She lied to both of us, Chris. Apparently Megan was hiding under her bed all along. When you'd left, Megan told Debbie she was going home. That she'd watch your house from across the street to know when Emma had gone home. She left here a little after seven fifteen. I don't know where she is now. I'm so sorry, Chris."

"I've got to go," he murmured, the implications already flashing through his mind.

"Chris, call me when you find her, please."

"I will." Slowly he hung up and looked at Harris. "Megan left her friend's house after seven this morning, headed for home. She would have gotten there right about the time Jerry did." Numbly, he rubbed his face, barely feeling the stubble scratching his palms. "Last night she said she wanted to stay with Jerry. If she's with him . . ."

Harris sighed grimly. "Shit." He stood up and shouted for the attention of every other detective in the room. "Walker's thirteen-year-old daughter may be with Emma Townsend and Jerry Grayson," he said. A ripple of discussion moved through the room. "How close are we to tracking his vehicle through GPS?"

Christopher's head jerked up. "GPS? You know where Jerry's SUV is?"

"Don't get your hopes up," Harris said gently. "Even if we find the SUV, it doesn't mean your daughter and Dr. Townsend will be inside. Phillips, have you found it?"

Detective Phillips was on the phone and held up one finger. "Almost. Another minute." After another minute that felt like a day, Phillips aimed an encouraging smile Christopher's direction. "Here it is, Harris. They're at 1298 Milliken Road, east of town. I'll call all available cars to that location."

"Sirens off," Harris ordered. "Silent approach, everybody wears a vest. Walker, you stay here."

Christopher waited until most of the detectives had cleared the room. Then calmly rose and exited the building. Found his car and turned the ignition. And followed them.

His daughter was in danger. As was his . . . what was Emma? he wondered as he pointed his car in the direction of Milliken Road. He was feeling strangely calm, surreally so. So what was Emma? His lover? After last night, yes. His girlfriend? So high school. How appropriate. The woman he'd loved the better part of his life? Perhaps.

All Christopher knew for certain was that he'd have nothing left to live for without Megan. Without Emma he'd survive, but at what cost? He prayed that would be a question forever left unasked and unanswered.

Please. I swear I'll ask for nothing else for the rest of my life. Let them be alive. Please.

"Don't do this, Jerry," Emma said, her voice cracking. He'd risen from the table and, hand shaking, held his semi-automatic pistol to her head. If she was dead, there would be no one to protect Megan for Christopher. "Please don't do this."

"Uncle Jerry." Megan was sobbing, begging pitifully. "You're not a bad man deep down. Don't kill us. Think of Dad." She drew a ragged breath. "Think of my mother."

Emma strained her peripheral vision staring at Jerry's face. Guilt was stamped there, indelibly. But more than that, Emma saw a stunned paralysis in the man's eyes. She'd seen this before in patients she'd counseled. Faced with an untenable choice, he'd frozen. He was incapable of making a decision either way, but in less than twelve minutes it wouldn't matter. The balding man named Hudson would barrel through that door and kill her and Jerry. And take Megan. *Over my dead body. Bad metaphor.*

Think of my mother, Megan had said, and that had triggered Jerry's response. She looked at Megan, the girl's dark eyes weary and ancient as tears poured down her face.

What else did this child know? What strength did she possess, both physical and emotional? It was time to find out. "Megan, I see Jerry's penknife on the desk over there next to his pipe. I want you to get it and bring it to me." She gave a nod of encouragement. "It's all right. Just do it."

Sniffling, Megan got the knife and held it uncertainly.

"Cut my ropes, Megan."

Her eyes narrowing in trepidation, Megan obeyed, sawing the rope until Emma's hands and feet were free. As she'd expected, Jerry never moved. Just stood in his guilty paralysis, holding his gun. Emma slowly rose to her feet and gently pried the gun from Jerry's fingers. He never put up the minutest of struggles.

She put her finger over her lips, signaling Megan to silence. "We need a diversion," she breathed. "For now I want you to continue begging for Jerry not to kill you."

But Megan just looked at her wide-eyed and silent. They now had ten minutes to plan before Hudson came in. Fewer if he got impatient or suspicious at the silence.

"Dammit, Jerry," Emma said loudly. "She's your godchild. She trusts you." Megan stared at her as if she were poleaxed. "You changed her diapers for God's sake. You can't let Andrews have her. You can't." With that she moved to Andrews's desk. There was no phone.

Phone. Jerry had taken her cell and put it in his pocket. Emma plunged her hands in his jacket pockets as he looked at her with all the life of a mannequin. Triumphantly she found her phone and dialed 911 and told the operator everything she knew. Then she handed the phone to Megan. "Just hold it. Hopefully they can trace us here."

Returning to Andrews's desk, she cautiously opened a drawer to find a pair of mud-covered shoes and a set of rolled-up blueprints. Another drawer yielded pencils and pens. Damn, she thought. It was a construction site. Was it too much to hope for a few sticks of dynamite? But realistically, those would be locked up, she knew. There had to be something here she could use. *Something.* She slid open the final drawer, exposing a nearly full bottle of vodka.

Very good vodka. Absolut. One hundred proof. And very flammable. She remembered the gravel that crunched under her feet. Given the proper propulsion, the gravel would blow like leaves under a leaf blower, and when it came down, it would rain like hail. Hopefully it would be enough to distract the ten men Jerry said were outside with Hudson and Andrews. Emma grabbed Jerry's shirt and sliced a long thin strip with the knife. Even then he said nothing. It was almost as if he was beyond consciousness.

Carefully Emma doused the strip of cotton with the vodka, then just as carefully threaded the strip into the mouth of the bottle. Jerry's matches were still on the desk and she grabbed them, her tool set complete. She gripped Jerry's gun in her right hand, her makeshift Molotov cocktail in her left.

Megan was watching her, a light of cognition in her eyes. "You're going to light it and throw it," she breathed.

"And hopefully buy us some time. Your job is to hold on to that cell phone. Don't let it get hung up. And if it does, redial. Understand?"

Megan nodded. "I understand."

"And Megan. If something happens to me, you keep running, you understand me? Run and use that phone to call for help."

Megan drew a breath. "I understand."

"Then let's go. Jerry, are you coming?"

He blinked. Just blinked. Emma sighed. "Then it's just you and me, Megan. Stay behind me and when we get out, you run like hell."

Quietly Emma pulled the door open an inch. Hudson stood with his back to the door, staring at the trees that lined the gravel. There was another trailer next to this one. A Jeep was parked about ten feet away, between the two trailers. She couldn't see Jerry's SUV. She'd handled guns before, tagging along when Will had taken up target shooting as a hobby. But shooting a paper target was different from a breathing man. She'd never shot anyone before. Never even considered it. Well, except for meting retribution on the punk that killed Will. But that was a revenge fantasy. This was very, very real. There would be emotional fallout, she knew. Taking the life of another . . . But she'd cross that bridge when she came to it.

Praying for calm, she leveled the gun at Hudson's back and quickly pulled the trigger. Once, twice. Three times. The shots cracked like cannon. In seconds they would be overrun. Andrews would come back. *Hurry, Emma, hurry.*

Hudson managed to turn after the third shot and lunged. Her fourth shot hit him squarely in the chest. Gurgling, he dropped to the ground, his body covering the wooden stairs.

"Megan, run!" Uncertainly, Megan stepped over Hudson. "Dammit," Emma hissed. "Run, girl!" But Megan stared, the cell phone clutched in her hand. Her own hands shaking, Emma trapped the gun under her arm and lit the match. Held it to the vodka-soaked cotton, waited a full second.

Then aiming at the Jeep parked just outside the trailer, threw it with all her might. The bottle shattered on impact. And Emma grabbed Megan's hand and ran like hell.

Andrews emerged from the other trailer, and Emma might have enjoyed the look of stunned shock on his face had she more time. The gun in her hand again, Emma dragged Megan as shouts filled the air, shouts to *get them, get them*. They'd gone about fifty feet when a huge explosion rent the air. She tackled Megan, knocking her to the ground, covering Christopher's daughter with her own body, wincing as debris showered down, pelting her back. Gravel stung, hot metal burned, but they weren't dead. "Do you have the phone?"

"Yeah," Megan grunted.

"Then get up and run!"

"I don't think so, Dr. Townsend." The shout stopped them both in their tracks.

Emma rose, turned and found herself staring into the barrel of Andrews's gun. It was a .38, much bigger and more powerful than her .22. She pulled Megan behind her, but the girl was already half a head taller than she was, so the gesture meant little.

"Drop your gun, Dr. Townsend. *Now*."

Harris grabbed his radio at the dispatcher's call. He was less than a mile from the site where Grayson's SUV had been tracked. "Harris."

"A 911 call has been received from the same coordinates as the tracked SUV. It's Townsend and Megan Walker is with her. We've heard gunfire and an explosion."

Harris surveyed the sky. "I see the smoke. How many units are here?"

"Ten. Five more are on their way. Sirens silenced." ·

"Thanks." Harris hooked his radio back in its bracket. He pulled his car alongside the line of radio cars that had responded to the call. "What happened?"

A county cop came forward, frowning. "We don't know. We just got here when something through those trees just exploded."

Harris spotted Phillips and beckoned him over. "Is the SUV still in position?"

"It's there. Whether the lady and girl are with it, that's anybody's guess. We called the fire department, Wes. If this fire gets going, it could spread to all these woods and the winter's been so dry . . . This whole area will go up like a tinderbox."

Harris raised his hand, getting the attention of all the responding officers. "People! If you see fire coming your way, don't go further. The last thing we need is to send the fire department in to rescue trapped law enforcement. You're looking for a woman and a little girl. Thirty-four and thirteen. The girl's name is Megan and she's probably scared stiff. The lady's name is Emma. Be careful and let's go."

Christopher brought his car to a stop at the tail end of a long line of police cars. Common sense told him to stay put, that he was more likely to get shot by a cop than to do any real good. He stared at the thick black smoke, his heart going a mile a minute.

My baby's in there. Megan.

Emma.

He pulled his shirt over his mouth and moved toward the trees.

Emma drew a labored breath. Thick black smoke rose from the burning Jeep, burning her lungs, but the discomfort was nothing compared to the sight of Andrews and his gun. If the call to 911 worked, the police could be on their way by now. If not, she was on her own. So to his demand to drop her gun she said, "No."

Andrews's brows rose. "No?"

"I said no. You'll kill me either way, so I'd be insane to give up my only hope of escape." She clutched the gun in her hand, feeling its weight. "I killed Hudson. I don't have anything to lose. So, no, I won't drop my gun. You'll have to shoot me."

He lifted his hand and she could actually see his fingers squeezing the trigger when a dark blur came from the right, barreling into Andrews, sending him flying to his back.

Jerry stood before him, chest heaving. "You will not touch that girl," he hissed.

Fury on his face, Andrews stared up at Jerry. And pulled the trigger.

Jerry dropped like a rock and Emma cried out, covering Megan's eyes with her hand. Megan's scream rent the air.

"*Jerry. No.*" She tried to pull out of Emma's arms, but Emma held her firm. Turned her the other way. And pushed with all her might.

"*Run, Megan.*"

She could hear Megan stumbling behind her, moving away. She wasn't running yet but Christopher's daughter was at least moving. Andrews was struggling to his knees, shaking his head. Jerry must have knocked the wind out of him. *Well, I'll knock out the rest.* She pointed the gun straight at his chest and squeezed, catching her breath at the crack of the bullet. At the rapidly spreading red stain in the middle of his chest.

With a roar of indignation Andrews lurched to his feet, stumbling a few steps closer. Emma backed away, matching his pace. *He'll fall down soon. He's bleeding. Why isn't he falling down? Why isn't he dead?*

She fired again, flinching at her gun's recoil that hadn't hurt the first few times, but her shoulder was now sore. Then the soreness in her shoulder was simply eclipsed by the ripping, excruciating burning in her gut. She looked down at her stomach as her legs buckled. She was on her knees, staring at her own body. At Christopher's sweatshirt. Christopher's sweatshirt was growing wet and dark. Blood.

He shot me. God, it hurts. Nausea roiled and she fought it. Because he was coming closer. Andrews was coming closer.

Christopher was running, his eyes scanning the ground for some trace of them. Some sign they'd been there. *My baby. Jerry has my little girl.*

Jerry. His heart threatened to break even as it pounded against his ribs. His foot caught on a root, sending him crashing to the ground. Not stopping, he forced himself to his feet, skidding along the pine needles.

His rampaging heart nearly stopped when he saw her. *Megan.* She was thrashing, pulling herself free from branches that tangled in her hair. Sobbing, panting. Breathing.

Alive. He ran to her, grabbed her in his arms. Was shocked when she fought him, clawing and screaming. "Baby, baby, it's me. It's me. It's Daddy. Megan, it's me." He rocked her in his arms. Felt her stiffen, then sag as she recognized his voice. He supported her as she crumbled, sobbing wildly.

"He's dead. Jerry's dead. He shot him. He's dead."

He. "Who, baby? Where's Emma?"

"He's got her. He'll k-k-kill her."

Christopher stilled. "Jerry has her?"

"No!" Megan screamed. "Didn't you hear me? Jerry's dead. I saw him. He shot him and he died." Her fists pounded his chest and Christopher held on. "She's still there. She made me run. I was so scared, Daddy." She convulsed into a terrifying spasm of sobbing and Christopher grabbed her shoulders and pulled her face back.

"Megan, listen to me. *Listen.* Is Emma alive?"

Megan shook her head, gasping for air, her body shaking with the force of her weeping. "I'm sorry, Daddy. She made me run. I couldn't do anything."

Christopher gut turned to water. "Stay here." He pulled her behind a tree, made her lie flat on her stomach. "Stay here. Don't move, Megan. I'll be back." He dug for his cell phone and dialed Harris. "Where the hell are your men?"

"Where the hell are you?" Harris shot back, breathing hard. He sounded like he'd been running. *Run faster.*

"I'm at the south end of the woods. Back from the line of police cars." Christopher squinted at the sun, high in the sky, but not straight overhead. "A quarter-mile southwest of the road. My daughter is here, Harris. Emma Townsend is still inside."

"Walker, stop right there."

But the crack of gunshots tore the air and Christopher

was running again, following the path of broken branches Megan had left behind. His heart in his throat.

Andrews was coming closer. On his knees, crawling. One hand clutching his chest, the other his gun.

He'll kill me now.

It hurts. She wanted to curl up and cry. But she didn't. She wasn't dead yet. But neither was he. She wouldn't give up.

"No." Saying the word aloud gave her strength when she would have sworn she had none left. Hands shaking, she lifted the gun. It was heavy. God, so heavy. *It must weigh a thousand pounds.* The thought was airy, it echoed in her mind.

I'm losing blood. I'll die here. She gritted her teeth. *Then so will he.* Closing her eyes she squeezed the trigger. And felt nothing. Heard nothing but an empty click.

Andrews laughed, his breath wheezing from his chest. Rattling. "Next time you steal a gun . . ." He drew a labored breath. "Make sure it has a full . . . magazine. Like mine."

Slowly he extended his arm. His whole body shook, but at this range, he couldn't miss. *Megan, please get away. Please.* She could only watch, unable to move, unable to look away. Then Andrews crumpled into a heap.

Emma blinked, her limbs heavy. *He finally fell down.* It was getting dark. *It can't be dark. It's only noon. Dammit.*

Christopher threw the rock to the ground and wrested the gun from the unconscious man's fingers. He was bleeding badly, whoever he was.

But so was Emma. She'd collapsed just as he'd run up behind the man with the gun. Now she lay on her side, his gray sweatshirt dark with blood. She was so pale. *The blood is hers. My God. She's been hit.*

He dropped to his knees by her side, gingerly rolled her to her back. "Emma. Dammit, wake up." His breath hitched in his chest, a terrified sob building. Gritting his teeth he forced it back, forced himself to breathe. To remember basic first aid. Harris was coming. He'd call an ambulance. *I just have to make her hold on till they get here.*

Trembling, he tore his shirt open, buttons flying. He shrugged out of the shirt and ripped a three-inch-wide strip. Gingerly lifted the hem of the sweatshirt.

Gritted his teeth again to choke back the bile in his throat. It was bad. Really bad. She might die. Oh, God, she might die. *Not if I can help it.* "Come on, Emma," he growled, carefully tucking the strip of cotton against the gaping hole in her stomach. "You didn't find me after all this time to die on me now. Stay with me. You stay with me."

"Walker!"

Christopher didn't turn around, intent on pulling his belt from his pants. "Did you find Megan?"

"She's with a policewoman. She's fine." Harris dropped to his knees between Emma and the unconscious man as two uniformed officers skidded to a stop behind him. "Radio for a bus," he barked. "Tell 'em we have two coming in. GSWs. Both unconscious." He frowned at Jerry's body. "Your friend—"

"He's not breathing," Christopher said flatly. "I don't know who this other guy is, but Megan said he shot Jerry. Help me lift Emma up." Harris tilted Emma's body, allowing Christopher to thread his belt beneath her back. His hands shaking, he fastened the belt over the makeshift bandage, just tight enough to put pressure on the bleeding wound. "Emma, stay with me! Listen to my voice. Lift her legs, Harris."

"I know," Harris snapped. He glanced around, then pulled Jerry's body closer, lifted Emma's legs and propped them on Jerry's chest. Then Harris yanked at his jacket. "Put this under her head. Move over, Walker, you look like you're ready to pass out."

Christopher sat back on his heels, breathing in, out. Trying to stay calm. *Be all right, Emma. Please.* He took Emma's hand in his, so gently. Her hand was so cold. "Emma, hold on. Just a little longer. Megan's fine. You saved her. Thank you." He brought her hand to his lips, a shudder wracking his body. "Thank you."

Chapter 10

"Daddy?"

Christopher woke with a jerk. Megan stood in the doorway of Emma's room in the ICU. He pushed himself straight in the chair and opened his arms. "Baby. I thought they wouldn't let you in because you're not sixteen."

Megan slid onto his knee and pressed her face into his neck. "Detective Harris told them to let me in." Harris had been waiting for Andrews to regain consciousness after his surgery. *If Harris is back at the hospital, that bastard Andrews must be awake.* Fury blazed through Christopher, making his body tense. "Daddy, I'm so sorry."

"You didn't do this, baby," he murmured. "Andrews did." Harris had identified the man that owned the construction company building on the contaminated land in the area Darrell had labeled "Number Seven." The man who'd killed his best friend. The man who'd threatened to . . . to *sell* his child. His stomach rolled at the thought. The man who'd damn near killed the woman he'd waited for more than half his life.

Touch and go, the doctor had said. But Emma was a fighter. They'd nearly lost her on the operating table, but she fought back. Her heart kept beating. Now she lay still as death, tubes running from her body. But the monitor continued to beep as her heart continued to beat. The next twenty-four hours would be critical, the doctor had said when he came out of surgery. It had already been twelve and Emma wasn't yet awake.

"No," Megan whispered. "I meant I'm sorry about the note I wrote. I wanted to hurt you. I'm so sorry, Daddy."

Christopher brushed a kiss across his daughter's hair. She was cleaned up, her minor cuts, bruises and scratches attended to. Her friend Debbie's mother had come, taken her to their house, let her shower and sleep. While he sat, keeping vigil at Emma's side. "I know, Megan. You were hurt. I understand that. You never should have been told any of this to start with. Your mother should have come to me, never to you. I'm sorry you've carried that burden all this time." He lifted her chin with a gentle forefinger. "But honey, I never, ever was unfaithful to your mother, no matter what she thought or believed. I need you to believe me."

She nodded, shakily. "I do." Her eyes darted to Emma. "Mother hated her."

"I never knew," Christopher said simply. "Once I decided to marry your mother, I didn't look back. I may have thought about Emma from time to time, but it was more with . . . wistfulness. I may have occasionally wondered about what might have been, but I loved your mother, Megan. She gave me . . . you."

Megan swallowed hard. "She . . . Daddy, she wasn't."

Christopher's brows snapped together. "She wasn't what, Megan?"

Megan closed her eyes. "Faithful. To you."

Christopher dropped his head back against the chair, closing his eyes on a soft groan. "Dear God. She told you that, too?"

"You knew?" Megan's voice was slightly accusatory. "You knew?"

"She told me." Christopher opened his eyes with a sigh. "I never knew who."

Megan shifted uncomfortably. Looked guilty. And said nothing. Christopher rubbed the bridge of his nose. *Mona, how could you?* "But you do?"

"Jerry."

It was barely a whisper. Christopher's eyes widened. His heart stuttered. He'd thought it couldn't get worse. "Jerry?"

Megan was pale. "I'm sorry, Daddy."

He pulled her to his chest, enveloping her in a hard hug.

"It's all right, honey. I guess I never really knew him. Do you know why he did all this?"

"No. He just kept saying he was sorry. He tackled that man, Andrews. He may have saved our lives."

No, Emma did that. But Christopher gritted his teeth, knowing his daughter needed some part of her childhood to hold on to. Her mother had abandoned her. The uncle she loved had been killed before her eyes. "Maybe he did at that, honey."

She was quiet for a long, long moment. Then she sighed and pushed back, sitting on the edge of his knee again. "No, Daddy. Emma saved us. She shot the man outside the trailer. She made that bottle bomb and blew up the Jeep."

A Molotov cocktail. Christopher's heart had burst with pride when Megan had first told the story, hours ago now. His Emma thought on her feet.

"She made me run," she whispered harshly. "She pushed me, made me go."

Christopher swallowed. *Thank you, Em.* "She's a good person, Meg."

Megan's eyes filled. "I said terrible things to her."

"She understood."

His daughter blinked, sending a stream of tears down her face. "I'm sorry."

"She'd understand that, too."

"When she wakes up, I'll try . . . I really will."

Christopher hugged her hard. "I'd appreciate it, Punkin."

"Are you coming home tonight?"

"No, baby. I want you to go home with Debbie's mom. I'll call you when she wakes up." *Please wake up, Em. Please.* He walked Megan to where Debbie's mother waited. Kissed her on the forehead and watched her walk away. At the end of the hall Megan turned and ran back, throwing her arms around his neck. "I love you, Dad."

Christopher held on, rocking her, overwhelmed once again by what might have happened, so grateful it had not. So grateful that his child was unharmed. Untouched. Wanting to make that bastard Andrews pay for laying a single finger on his daughter. Wanting to kill him for what he had planned to do to Megan. The very thought made his blood run cold. Christopher laid his head on top of Megan's head. His baby was safe. "I love you, too, Megan. I love you, too." With difficulty he let her go and met Debbie's mother's understanding eyes.

"I'll check on her every hour, Christopher," she murmured. "Come on, Megan. Debbie's waiting out by the candy machine with a roll of quarters. She said she was getting enough chocolate for you two to make yourself sick on the way home." She put her arm around Megan's shoulders and walked her out.

"She'll be okay, Walker."

Christopher turned to find Harris leaning against the wall. "I know." He had to believe that. It was the only thing to keep him going. "So Andrews is awake?"

"He is. We're going to transfer him up to Tampa General when he's stable. I don't want you to have to risk running into him as Dr. Townsend goes through her recovery."

"Thanks. Do you know why he did this?"

"It's what you thought, Professor. Andrews's company had a lot riding on the construction up north. Two condos, a medical center." He lifted a shaggy brow. "They didn't own the land, but they'd lose the building contract if the soil contamination became known. His business was nearly bankrupt. He needed the money from the medical center to keep himself afloat. He convinced one of the chemists at Seymour and Elliot to falsify the records."

"When will you arrest the chemist?"

"We won't. He died in a car accident six months ago." Again the shaggy brows went up. "Dry day, no tire wear, and the guy's car skids off the road and into a tree."

"Andrews?"

"I'm going to try to prove it, but it'll be tough."

"I don't understand. This would have come out sooner or later. Who was Andrews trying to fool?"

"I think he was buying time. If he could keep it quiet until the medical center was built, he'd still get paid. When you guys started taking samples, he panicked. I'm guessing he talked your friend Grayson into helping him figure out how much you knew. That's why Grayson got involved with Tanya."

Christopher felt light-headed. "I still can't believe Jerry killed Darrell and Tanya."

"I found several transfers into Grayson's bank account.

I'll trace them back to Andrews if it's the last thing I do. Grayson had paid money out to a local bookie."

"He gambled? I never knew he gambled. How could I not know this?"

"He bet the ponies. He still had a lot of Andrews's money in his account, though."

Christopher closed his eyes. "He said he had rainy day money set aside. He offered to give it to Darrell's mother. Sonofabitch."

Harris's chuckle was mirthless. "I don't know if it was guilt or chutzpah. I imagine a bit of both. Professor, you look beat. Why don't you go home and get some sleep?"

"No, I want to be here when Emma wakes up."

"She's a strong lady. Tell her I said so."

Christopher walked to Emma's room and sank into the chair at her side. "Emma, I'm back." She didn't move, didn't flicker an eyelash. "Harris said to tell you you're a strong lady." He settled into the chair. "Remember back in high school? Remember Elton Jacobs, the kid that everybody said would either be a garbage collector or a politician? Well, he's a TV news reporter so I guess that puts him somewhere in between. He heard about this and remembered us and wants to interview you. So you have to wake up. I also got a call from Kate. She'll be flying down later this morning." He leaned forward and took her hand. And prepared himself to talk until his voice gave out. She could hear him, he was sure of it. And he wasn't letting her go.

Friday, March 5, 1:00 P.M.

The bed was hard. And her head hurt. Her body hurt. It felt like she'd been knocked flat by a Mack truck. Cognition slowly returned and Emma was convinced there might be one toe on her right foot that didn't hurt. She was cold. Except for her left hand. It was warm.

Because Christopher held it. She blinked, trying in vain to bring him in focus. Someone had removed her contacts and everything was a blur. He sat next to her bed, his clothes rumpled, his face dark with a new beard. *That's no five o'clock shadow,* she thought. *I've been here a while.* Tenderness clutched her heart. *So has he.*

"Christopher." Her voice sounded like a stranger's, raspy and croaky. His eyes flew open and he was on his knees beside the bed before she could blink again. "Don't move so fast. You'll make me sick."

"You're awake."

She tried to smile. "So it would seem. Megan?"

Tears filled his eyes. "She's fine."

Emma breathed again. "I'm glad."

"How can I ever thank you, Em? Megan told me what you did."

"You would have done the same for me," she murmured, tired already. "How long have I been here?"

"Two days, give or take."

"You stayed with me."

"I told you, Emma, I waited for you seventeen years. I'm not about to lose you now."

"When can I go home?"

"The doctor says you can't fly for a few weeks at least. You'll have to stay with me."

Her lips curved. "That's what I meant."

He smiled back. "Good, because I hadn't planned to let you go anyway." He pressed his lips to her forehead. "Thank you."

"You said that already."

"You heard me?"

"Snippets. I remember you reading me letters."

He grimaced. "Poems."

"You read me poems you wrote yourself?"

"I did, but only because the circumstances were extreme. I'd run out of things to say and you wouldn't wake up. Now the poems go back in the vault." He brushed a kiss against her lips. "Welcome back, Em. Don't ever leave me again."

"I won't. You're stuck with me."

"And glad to be."

Epilogue

Friday, August 6, 6:30 P.M.

Emma slid the glass door closed, shuddering as she blocked the sound of seven squealing fourteen-year-old girls. Christopher sat outside in a chaise lounge with a cold beer in his hand and a smirk on his face.

"I told you to only let her invite three girls," he said. "But you said, no, a girl only turns fourteen once. So *you* get to deal with them all."

"I was insane, obviously," Emma said dryly and sat down on the edge of his lounge, making him scoot over. "I'll remember this when she's fifteen."

"Uh-huh." He sounded unconvinced. "You spoil her."

She kissed his nose. "I didn't have anybody to spoil for so long. I'm catching up."

"So what are they doing in there?"

"Watching a horror movie and seeing who can scream the loudest. I say we stay out here until it's over."

"I say you're right." He scooted a little lower in the lounge, looking at the new boat tied to their dock. "I like my birthday present, by the way."

Emma grinned down at him. "Which one?" They'd celebrated his birthday the month before, with a sail on his new boat and a sail in his bed later that night.

He chuckled and pinched her butt. "The boat's nice, too. Seems to me you have a birthday coming up."

She grimaced. Her own birthday was less than two months away. "Don't remind me. Thirty-five is a milestone, then it's downhill to forty." But she had to admit that

131

thirty-five was looking pretty damn good. She was happy again. She'd just finished writing *Bite-Sized II* and no longer did she feel like a hypocrite, running from her own grief. She'd met it, dealt with it. And a few days out of every month shared her experiences with auditoriums full of others. But each time she came back to Christopher. Each time he met her at the airport with a bouquet of wildflowers to welcome her home.

"You'll look as beautiful at forty as you did when you were seventeen," Christopher said and she had to kiss him for being so sweet. One kiss became two, then three and when she pulled away they were both breathing hard.

"No fair turning me on with guests in your house." She was still technically a guest herself. After getting out of the hospital, she'd slowed their relationship down a bit. She'd needed a place of her own, and despite Megan's turn-around, the girl had needed time to get used to the idea of another woman in her father's life. So Emma had leased a condo on St. Pete Beach, less than a mile from where they'd first kissed that first night. That particular patch of sand held fond memories and they'd returned to it often.

Things had settled down after her release from the hospital, five months ago now. Christopher had grieved Darrell and Tanya. And Jerry. Despite everything Jerry had done, he'd been Christopher's friend. Andrews was in prison, awaiting trial and Emma hoped he had suffered the same fate he'd planned for Megan. There were nights she woke from the nightmare where Megan hadn't gotten away. But it was just a dream.

She'd returned to Cincinnati a month after "that day" to find Kate had reboxed all of Will's things and given them away. Emma had walked around the empty house and felt peace, knowing that Will would have wanted her to go on, to be happy. So she'd sold the house and put the proceeds of the sale in a fund for Darrell Roberts's mother and brothers. Properly invested, the money would support the Roberts family for years to come. Will would have wanted that, too.

Megan had come around. Months of counseling had helped her to sleep at night. Helped her to accept Emma as a part of her father's life. Helped her realize Emma could never take the place of her own mother, nor did

Emma plan to try. Mona had breezed in for Jerry's funeral, then was gone once again, leaving Megan with the too-adult understanding of the kind of woman her mother really was.

Another loud round of squeals from inside the house made Emma wince, but Christopher seemed oblivious to the sound. He hadn't moved his gaze from her face and her pulse kicked up a few beats. His blue eyes flashed, surprising her with their sudden intensity. "Make this your house, too, Emma. Move in with me. Us."

She drew a careful breath. "Christopher—" He put a finger over her lips.

"We said you would move in when we were sure this was going to last."

She couldn't look away from his eyes. So it would be tonight then. The question that had been so long in the making. "That's true."

His mouth didn't smile. "So are you sure?"

She'd been examining that same question with great frequency over the last five months, and came up with the same response each time. "Yes."

He reached blindly to the table beside him, then opened his hand before her eyes. On his palm lay a ring. "Then marry me, Emma."

She'd been anticipating this question as well and once again, the response was always the same. "Yes."

Again his eyes flashed, more intensely than before. With hands that were absolutely steady he slid the ring on her finger. "I love you."

"I love you, too." They'd grown into it, this love of theirs. It was so much more than an attempt to recapture their youth. True, it was inextricably connected to their past, but it was grounded in their present and it was, quite simply, their future.

He tilted her face up, covered her lips with his. Kissed her thoroughly, making her wish they were alone in her condo instead of a glass door away from seven squealing teenaged girls. "You'll stay with me tonight?" he murmured, his voice husky.

She smiled at him. "Nope. I'm sleeping in a bag on the floor with the girls. Megan's friends promised to give me a pedicure if I make French toast in the morning."

His lips twitched. "I'll give you a pedicure."

"No you won't. You always say you will, then you get distracted by other parts."

"I like your other parts."

"You can like them tomorrow night." She rested her forehead against his. "So we're getting married. Kate will finally stop asking me if you've proposed yet."

He leaned back, his grin very satisfied. "Yep. And it's no fake high school health project either. I get true husbandly privileges unlike that poor sap that you got paired up with back then. Skip Loomis can just eat his heart out."

She lifted one corner of her mouth. "You get those privileges now."

His grin faded, his eyes sobering. "I'm not talking about sex, Emma. I want to wake up with you every morning. Hold you every night. And I don't want any fake dolls like we had in that high school project. I want a real baby with you. Maybe two."

The thought of Christopher holding their babies made her eyes sting. "At least. We'll have to get started soon. I'm ticking, you know."

"You could sneak out and meet me on the boat later tonight. I'll play our song and we can dance," he added slyly and she laughed.

"Tomorrow, Christopher." She leaned down and kissed him softly. "And every night after that. For the rest of your life."

NECESSARY BETRAYALS

Annie Solomon

Chapter 1

At two A.M. Sal's was still going strong. Behind the bar, Francesca Bern rubbed one foot against the other, pulled the handle to dispense the Bud, and wondered why the hell everyone didn't go home. Yes it was Saturday night, yes it was Sal's in Baypointe, that happening little corner on Long Island Sound, but the band had left an hour ago, and even though Sal had cranked up the music, it was only Jimmy Buffett whining about wasting his life again.

She set the beer in front of the customer, caught a wave from the crowd at the other end of the bar: some guy holding up his glass. What had he been drinking? Oh, yeah, shades of Buffettville. Tequila shots. She slid down to him, poured two more, and made sure the lime and salt were in easy reach. He winked at her with two bleary eyes. She smiled—better tips that way—but rolled her eyes when she turned her back.

"Hey, Frannie!" Sal was waving the phone over his head. His sixty-year-old's paunch hung over the waistband of his pants, but his hair was still greased back in the ducktail of his youth. "Keep it short," he added when she grabbed the phone, his pencil mustache twitching, and she mouthed the words in her head because he always said the same thing.

Thinking it was her nightly call from Brucie Kiel, a bar regular who'd made it his mission to walk her home Saturday nights—a little piece of chivalry he always wanted to turn into something more—she said, "Look, Brucie, I'm beat—"

"Frannie? Oh, God, Frannie, can you hear me?" Her little sister's voice gulped and stuttered, full of panicked tears.

Frannie's pulse leaped into the stratosphere. "Gina? What's the matter?"

"Frannie, I—" Static intervened.

"Where are you? You're breaking up."

More static. Then Gina's voice, still full of fear. "Oh my God, Frannie. Someone just"—the voice broke up again, then one word got through— "Calvino."

"Gina? What about the Calvinos? Where are you?" She waited, heard nothing. "Gina? Gina!"

Faster than she thought possible, Francesca punched in her phone number. It was two in the morning. Gina was fifteen. She was supposed to be home. In bed. If that little brat had snuck out again . . .

She listened to the endless buzz indicating the phone was ringing on Gina's nightstand. Francesca disconnected, a cruel chill crawling up her back.

Gina had sounded terrified. She'd been on a cell phone. She didn't own a cell phone. She either wasn't home or couldn't answer the phone, and worse, she'd said the one word calculated to scare the shit out of Francesca.

"Hey, Frannie," Sal said. "You got your love life straightened out, there's drinks to pour." Sal tried to take the phone away, but Francesca had it in a death grip.

"Go away, Sal." Leaving Sal openmouthed, she scurried into the back room where the swinging door deadened the scream of the music enough so she could hear herself think.

Calvino.

That name hadn't passed her lips in five years. Not since the day her father had gone to prison.

She looked down at the phone. Her hand was shaking. With slow, deliberate thought, she dredged up the phone number. Her stomach knotted as she waited for someone to pick up on the other end. But like the call home, this one also went unanswered.

Everything tightened around her. The room grew smaller, the air colder.

Someone was *always* at the Calvino compound. The phone never rang unanswered.

The door swung open. Francesca jumped out of her skin.

"Frannie! We got customers."

"I—I gotta go, Sal." She shoved the phone at him, grabbed her purse from a hook by the employee entrance, and ran out.

"Hey!"

She was leaving him short—hell, she'd probably just fired herself—but what could she do? It was Gina.

She raced to her car and fumbled with the keys, dropping them once before getting the right one inserted. Tires squealed as she backed out, and the car bucked as she sped through the parking lot entrance.

It took twenty minutes to get to the aging neighborhood where she and Gina had lived for the last five years. Built up after the second World War, it was filled with tiny clapboard homes on postage stamp lots. A far cry from where they used to live, but it was all she could afford. As it was, she'd used almost every cent her father had left to buy it.

She zipped into a parking space in front of the house, leaped out, and raced across the grass to the front door. When she got hold of that kid . . . Hands shaking, she inserted the key in the lock and opened the door.

"Gina!" She turned on the hall light and looked up the steps to the darkened second floor. "Gina, are you home?"

She took the stairs two at a time, flung open the door to Gina's bedroom and yanked up the light switch. Swirls of black and color screamed back at her from walls covered with Gina's artwork. She stared at them for a moment, disturbed as always by their angry intensity. Tearing her gaze away, she rifled through the week's worth of clothes strewn over the floor, searched the unmade bed. No clue as to where Gina had gone.

She ran to the dresser, scavenging through the junk on top: stickers and earrings, a black bra, a dried up paint brush, a photo strip of Gina in various incarnations, all of them with heavy eye makeup and orange hair that stuck out all over her head in short, witchy spikes.

Gina's words from earlier that evening echoed in her mind. "You're not my mother! You can't tell me what to do!"

And her own, as she snatched Gina's purse out of her hands. "I can and I will, and you're not going out unless you tell me where!"

But Gina had only crossed her arms and glared at her.

A familiar fury shook Francesca. Why couldn't Gina be neater? Less angry? Why did she have to make everything so hard? Even when Francesca was fifteen, she'd never dyed her hair or walked around looking like a vampire. And her room had never looked like World War III had been fought there.

Then again, neither had Gina's; the cleaning lady had picked up after them both.

Growling in frustration, Francesca wheeled around and bolted out the door. "Gina! Don't do this to me!" She ran down the stairs, checked the kitchen, the TV room, the basement. All empty.

By the time she finished, a thin film of dread coated her stomach. Inside her head she heard that name again. *Calvino*.

Returning to her car, she sped from Baypointe, where people like her hung out—people who worked for a living—to Old Baypointe—where people like Arturo Calvino lived off what other people did for them.

She saw the blue lights almost before she saw the gates to the Calvino estate, which were wide open and unnaturally welcoming. If she wasn't scared before, she was now. Blue lights and Calvinos weren't a normal combination. The last time she'd seen them together had been the day of her father's arrest. Now, as then, something was terribly wrong.

A cop car and requisite uniform blocked the entrance.

"Move along." He gestured up the road with an orange light.

She lowered her window and called out. "What's happened?"

"Read about it tomorrow. Keep moving."

"Look, I need to go in there. I got a call from my sister. Something about the Calvinos."

The cop came closer. "Who's your sister?"

Before she could answer, a second cop ran up. "Trouble?" he asked the first guy, who shrugged.

"Says her sister called about the Calvinos."

The second cop peered into the window. A look of recognition crossed his face. "You're Francesca Bern."

She stilled. There was a time when it seemed that everyone on the planet knew who she was. But that was a long time ago. "That's right."

"Too bad about your dad."

She gave him a cold look. "Shit happens. Can I talk to someone? I think my sister, Gina, might be in trouble here."

The two cops exchanged a look. "Pull the car over," the second cop said, "and come with me." He waited until she'd turned off the engine and got out, then he escorted her through the gates and into the chaos beyond.

More cars with flashing blue lights, men and a few women scurrying back and forth, some in blue, others in suits, more guys huddled in small groups, talking low. A scrawny woman in a maid's uniform sat hunched by herself on the low stone wall that bordered the place. She looked like she was crying—shoulders shaking, tissues crumpled in one hand.

A van with CSU scrawled over it was parked on the lawn, an ambulance next to it. Francesca refused to draw conclusions, refused to even think that Gina might be inside it. But her mouth was dry, her palms sweaty.

Her escort led her to a tree just inside the gate. "Wait here," he said. "I'll tell the lead and when he's ready, he'll come talk to you. Don't touch anything."

He stalked off toward a huddle and spoke to one of the men. As if he'd been told a ghost had appeared, the man whipped around, and she saw his face.

Whatever blood her elevated pulse had been pumping fled in an instant. It was a warm August night, but she went cold, then hot, then cold again.

The man came forward, and every instinct inside Francesca cried "run," but her feet wouldn't budge.

His cool, assessing gaze flicked over her. She was wearing her bar clothes—tight white blouse and clinging black pants, because a bit of cleavage and a curve of ass was another help in the tip department—and looked nothing like the private school girl he once knew.

Thinking about that other life started a slow fury building. She tamped it into hard embers and examined him right back. She'd forgotten how tall he was. His big shoulders seemed to envelop the space around him. His thick blond hair used to have waves in it, and he'd push it off his forehead with a lazy grin. Now it was skinned to military correctness, which only made his face more sculpted, his mouth more sensual. She remembered that mouth and a sudden pang of pain and longing cut through her anger.

"Hello, Francesca." His voice, deep and gruff, seemed to match the gray suit he wore.

"Quinn."

The exchange was short and stiff—enemies meeting to discuss a temporary truce.

"Brody says you want to talk to me."

Not you. Never you. "It's about Gina."

"What happened to Gina?"

You put her father in prison and he died there, she wanted to say, that's what happened to Gina. "She called about half an hour ago. From a cell phone. She kept breaking up, but she was crying, and she said something about the Calvinos." She drew a breath, forced the quiver out of her voice. "Is she here? Has . . . has something happened to her?"

"No." The answer was quick and decisive, and for half a second, her knees wobbled. She stumbled, and Quinn caught her, propping her up against his shoulder. "It's okay. She's not here, Francesca."

She nodded, swallowing hard. "For a minute, I thought—"

"No. Don't go there. She's not here. Look, sit down." He led her to a cop car, opened the door, and guided her inside. "Brody! See if you can find a cup of coffee or a glass of water."

She didn't want something to drink. She didn't want anything from Quinn Parker—God no, he wasn't Quinn Parker, he was Quinn Parker Lewis, Detective Quinn Parker Lewis. But she perched on the seat, legs outside

on the ground, while he loomed over her. Dully, she
asked, "What happened here?"

"Someone killed Arturo Calvino." No hesitation, no
cop bullshit. At least he'd given her that.

Then the implications of what he'd just told her sank
in. The head of the Calvino mob, dead. No wonder there
was a swarm here. The anthill had been overturned.

Not that she'd grieve. They could rot in hell for all
she cared. Except that Gina had spoken that hated name.
She shuddered again. Where was her sister?

"When's the last time you saw Calvino?"

She looked at him. Saw the implications in his face.
As if she and Artie were friends. Maybe even more than
friends. She raised her chin. "Five years ago. I'm sure
you remember."

If he flushed, she couldn't tell in the darkness. "You
haven't seen him? Not once in five years?"

"You think I'm lying? I don't lie. That's your department."

He ignored that. "Arturo Calvino was very close to
your father. I can't imagine he'd make no effort to
help you."

"I didn't say he didn't try. I said I haven't seen him."
She glanced away. "Look, I came here about Gina. If
you can't help me, maybe someone else can." She got
up, and he blocked her way.

"Tell me again about the phone call."

Quinn watched her as she repeated what she'd already
told him. Truth was, he didn't listen. It was just an excuse
to look at her. After all this time, he would have thought
she couldn't rattle him, but the sight of her.

Christ, the sight of her.

Her dark hair, which had been long and flowing and
lit with streaks of red gold, was now clipped short. Did
it still smell like summer flowers? Did he even have the
right to wonder?

And the clothes. When he knew her, she'd worn skirts
and tailored slacks, pretty things, but classic. Never anything that hugged her body. Now, she not only looked
older, but harder, and something inside him twisted. How
much of that had been his fault?

"What's her cell phone number?" he asked, as much to avoid answering his own question as anything else.

"Haven't you been listening? She doesn't have a cell phone. I wouldn't even have guessed she was calling from one, except that the line kept breaking up. I don't know where she was calling from."

He thought of the ten-year-old Gina, the one who liked ice skating and marshmallows in her hot chocolate, and wondered what she was doing wandering around at two in the morning. "Who was she with?"

Francesca's face tensed. "I don't know. She wasn't supposed to be with anyone. She was supposed to be at home."

He frowned. "By herself?"

"She's fifteen. She's not supposed to need a babysitter anymore."

It hit him then, the vast gulf between then and now. Gina had been a child, now she was a teenager. And Francesca. She had whispered his name, kissed his mouth. Now she was a stranger.

"What about your aunt?" Francesca's mother had died in a car accident just after Gina was born, so Bruno's sister had come to help out after his arrest. It had given Quinn a bit of peace to know that if Francesca wouldn't lean on him, at least she wouldn't be alone.

"She died, okay? And there wasn't a long line of volunteers waiting to take her place. I'm doing the best I can, but Gina's never been the same since . . . "

Since he put her father in jail.

"And lately . . . " She pressed a hand to her forehead. He noticed it trembling.

"Lately what?"

She flashed him a defiant look. "She's been sneaking out. Running away a lot."

He nodded, tried not to let the concern show on his face. "So maybe that's all this is. She ran away again. Did you say something to upset her? Have a fight? Kids can go off at the slightest—"

"That's not what happened."

"Did you have a fight with her, Francesca?"

The angry slam of the front door echoed in her head. She closed her eyes. "Yes."

"So it's possible—"

"She called me in tears! She said Calvino's name!"

"Okay, okay. I didn't say we wouldn't check it out."

Brody came with a plastic cup of water. He handed it to Francesca, but she shook her head and rose. "I didn't come for a pat on the shoulder and a little 'there, there.' I came to find Gina."

"If she's here, we'll find her," Quinn said, doing his best Dragnet imitation.

Francesca wasn't buying it. "Have you searched the mansion, the grounds?"

"We're working on it."

"What does that mean?"

"We're still working the scene."

"Then how do you know she's not here?"

"All I mean is we didn't find her with Calvino."

Beyond her, Quinn saw Al Stellman giving him a heads-up. Older than Quinn, he was stoop shouldered and shuffling, but not nearly as decrepit as he liked to make out.

"I'll be right back," Quinn told Francesca and stepped away.

"Two more bodies inside," Stellman said in a low voice.

Quinn froze. A picture of Arturo Calvino flashed in his head. He'd been shot, then his throat slit and his tongue cut out. Quinn could barely entertain the thought of Gina in similar straits. "Who?"

"Calvino's guys. Tommy Pelotti and the other one. Paul O'Neil."

"No girl?"

Stellman frowned. "Girl?"

"Gina Bern is missing." He nodded over his shoulder at Francesca. Stellman saw her, whistled low, then peered at Quinn closely.

"Oi, boychik. I'll bet that set you back." Stellman had been Quinn's partner since he'd transferred to homicide, but before that, he'd been a family friend. He knew all about Francesca.

Quinn shrugged and lied. "I'm fine."

Stellman nodded as though he didn't believe it any more than Quinn did. "So the little one's gone?"

"Not so little anymore. She's fifteen." Briefly, Quinn filled him in.

"Kind of a coincidence, the kid mentioning Calvino the same night Artie Calvino gets drilled. What'd you tell Francesca?"

"Nothing. She's halfway to hysterical already."

"You thinking there's another body we haven't found?"

Bile rose in Quinn's throat. "I hope to God not. How far have you got in the house?"

"Not very. I wanted to let you know about the two skells."

"Anyone else living there?"

"Couldn't get much out of the maid. English isn't too good. I got Nuñez talking to her. I think she mentioned someone named Tony."

"Calvino has a nephew, Tony. His sister's kid. See if that's him. And if it is, get a line on the sister. See if she can locate him."

Just then there was a commotion by the gate. Quinn turned to see a man charging in, two uniforms blocking the way.

Out of the darkness, the little Honduran maid who'd made the panicked phone call to Joey Zachariah leaped up. "Señor Z! Señor Z!" She was wringing her hands and screaming at the intruder in a mixture of Spanish and English. "*No llamé a la policia.* I no call them. I no call them!"

Quinn and Stellman exchanged looks. The maid was right: she hadn't phoned the police. But the call to Zachariah telling him that Arturo Calvino was dead was made on one of the house phones.

"Thank God for wiretaps," Stellman said.

Francesca saw and heard the disturbance, too. It had been a long time since she'd seen Joey Zachariah, but he'd been her father's close friend, and she'd known him for most of her life. All of a sudden he was a welcome face among strangers.

She ran over to where he was wrestling with a couple of cops. "Uncle Z!"

He wasn't a big man, but age had been kind to him.

Even in his late fifties, he still had a thick head of dark hair, and though a bad case of teenage acne had left its mark on his craggy face, he'd retained much of the casual good looks he'd been born with. His strong chin was balanced by a jutting nose, both of which were raised in anger at the cops holding him back. "Hands off!"

"Uncle Z!"

His still-powerful arms bulged, but he stopped struggling when he finally noticed her. His eyes narrowed, then bugged out. "Francesca?"

"Yeah, it's me."

"What the—honey, what the hell are you doing here?"

"It's Gina. She's in trouble. I need help."

"What?" He tried to pull free. "Take your damn hands off—"

Quinn appeared, apparently finished with his private little chat. "It's okay," he told the uniforms. "Let him go."

Immediately, Uncle Z opened his arms and she sank into them. "Now, what's this about Gina?"

For what seemed like the hundredth time, she replayed her conversation with her sister. He listened closely. "Okay," he said, "not to worry. Uncle Z has it covered."

But Quinn grabbed her wrist and tugged her away. "She doesn't need your help. If Gina is here, we'll find her."

"You couldn't find the nose on your face." Joey spit, underlining the point. "What happened to Artie? Where is he?"

"Out by the pool," Quinn said. "And I do mean out."

But she didn't want to think about Arturo Calvino or what had happened to him. She wanted to find her sister. She jerked free of Quinn's hold and turned to Uncle Z. "Have you seen Gina?"

Sadly, Joey laid his palm over his heart. "Francesca. You wouldn't let me. I haven't seen her since they closed the doors on Bruno. What would she be doing here anyway?"

She looked around helplessly. "I don't know. I only know she said something about the Calvinos. And Uncle Z, she sounded terrified."

"Look, honey, I gotta see about Artie." He chucked her lightly under the chin and gave her an encouraging smile. "You stay here. We'll talk."

He started off, but Quinn blocked his way, slapping a hand against Z's chest. "You're not going anywhere. Where were you tonight?"

Joey gave the hand a look of cold disdain, then stepped back, neatly dislodging it. "With friends. I got friends, detective. Which is a helluva lot more than I can say for you."

Quinn didn't rise to the taunt. "And these friends. You were with them . . . where?"

But Francesca had had enough of the Quinn Parker Lewis cop show. "If Artie's dead, he's dead," she said to Quinn. "It's Gina you should be worrying about." She turned to Z. "Can you help me find her?"

Z put one of his massive arms around her shoulders and squeezed. "Sure, honey. We'll find her. I'll get Tommy on it." He took out his phone and started punching in numbers.

"Forget Tommy," Quinn said. "He's inside. As dead as Artie."

Joey Z's face tightened. "What?"

"And O'Neil, too."

Francesca's stomach flopped. Someone had taken out Artie and his thugs. Had Gina been caught in the cross fire?

Desperate, she turned to Quinn. "What about Gina? Did you . . . Is she?"

"No," he said quietly. "I told you. No." Then more harshly, "What's going on, Zachariah? Arturo going to war?"

"No!" Z's black eyes flashed. "Artie was keeping the peace."

"He wasn't a peaceful kind of guy," Quinn said dryly.

"He was young, maybe a little full of himself. Maybe he made a few mistakes, but—"

"Mistakes? Like your brother? Where is Mike, by the way?"

With frightening swiftness, Z's face churned into hatred and he lunged at Quinn, crushing his suit lapels in a vicious grip. "You leave Mike out of this." They were nose to nose, and Quinn the taller, but Z didn't seem to notice or care. "You lied to him, you tricked him. He brought you in and—"

"Calvino killed him for it." With a jerk, Quinn freed himself from Z's hold.

Breathing hard, Z glared at Quinn. "You want to know who's breaking the peace?" He stabbed the air. "It wasn't Artie."

"So, who do you make for this?" With frigid calm, Quinn straightened his tie. "Volkov?"

Another name from her father's past that sent a shiver down Francesca's back. There had been trouble between Volkov's Russians and the Calvinos since before Arturo took over.

Joey Zachariah's hard face reflected that tension. "Ask that son of a bitch yourself."

"Oh, we will. In the meantime, no one goes in until we're done here."

Francesca's chest tightened. She thought she was through with names like Calvino and Volkov. Thought she'd never have to see another cop or made man. And now, as if a bad nightmare was coming true, they were wrecking her life all over again. And she was sick of it.

She turned on Quinn. "You don't get it, do you? I'm not sitting here while you and your buddies talk and poke and twiddle their thumbs. I want to look for Gina. Let me search the house. I know it. I practically grew up here."

"It's a crime scene, Francesca. All of it—the mansion, the grounds. We'll be going over every inch. Trust me, if she's here, we'll find her."

"Trust you?" Joey scoffed. "She wouldn't trust you with a goldfish. Come on, Frannie." He pulled her away. "Let's talk."

Quinn watched them go. The mobster and the mobster's daughter. It made his skin crawl to see them together again. Joey Z had been a fixture in the Bern house. Both kids from the neighborhood, he and Bruno had grown up together. Joey and his brother, Michael, had gone the muscle route; Bruno had become an accountant. But both of them had ended up in the same place: the Calvino organization.

It had killed him when Francesca had refused to see him, but at least she'd also cut her ties with the Calvinos. He didn't like to think that anything could bring them together again.

But Gina had. And murder.

Just then a woman in uniform ran up. Her name tag read Nuñez. "Detective Stellman asked me to give this to you." She handed him an evidence bag. Inside was a zippered canvas case. "What is it?"

"CD holder. Got slots inside to hold discs."

He examined the case through the Baggie by the glow of car headlights. Someone had used it as a doodle pad. Loops and swirls, cartoons, initials. Several TGs and lots of GBs. His throat closed up.

"Where'd they find this?"

She gestured toward the east side of the property. "Inside the pool house."

"Okay. Thanks."

Nuñez nodded and jogged off.

Quinn turned to where Francesca and Joey Z had their heads together. Slowly, he made his way over to them.

Francesca looked up, her face cold, wary, and fearful. He could still remember when she'd looked at him altogether differently. But he didn't waste time reminding her. Get the bad news over fast.

He thrust the Baggie at her. "Recognize this?"

She peered at the contents. "Oh, my God." She glanced at Quinn, stricken. "It's Gina's. Where was it?"

"Inside the pool house. Ten feet from where Arturo was killed."

Chapter 2

Francesca felt as though her body were slowly turning to ice. Horrified, she stared at the CD case, which was covered in Gina's crazed designs, and refused to believe what her eyes were telling her. "No." She shook her head and backed away. "It's not possible. There must be another reason. Someone took it. Stole it." She looked for help, for confirmation, and found none in either Quinn or Z. "She wasn't here," she pleaded. "She wasn't—" Her voice broke and she clamped a terrified hand over her mouth, looking wildly around for a place to run. Hide. Escape.

She was heading into a panicked free fall, and all of a sudden, Quinn was gripping her shoulders. "Francesca! Look at me. Look at me!" He shook her, his hard command compelling her to turn to him. He held her with a piercing gaze. "She called you when?"

It took a moment for her to focus. "A-around two."

"Calvino was killed closer to midnight. That's two hours earlier. She's alive, Francesca. Alive." He shook her again so the word would penetrate. "I think she saw what happened and ran."

Uncle Z patted her back. "See? It's gonna be fine, honey."

She looked from him to Quinn, who nodded encouragingly. His hands still held her, and all at once she remembered why she shouldn't take comfort from him.

Pulling away, she turned to Z. "Then why didn't she come home?"

"She's a kid," Z said with a shrug. "A mystery. Who knows what they'll do?"

She looked into Z's streetwise face, saw his thick neck and bulldog stance. Everything about him said Calvino. What wasn't he saying? Had Gina been kidnapped? Forced to come here? But why? What would the Calvinos want with her? Bruno was dead; Gina knew nothing about his business. And if the Calvinos *had* taken her, where was she?

God, why oh why didn't Gina tell her where she was going tonight?

The answer rose up from deep inside like an unwelcome prediction. *Because she was coming here.*

No. Absolutely not. She refused to believe it. Instead, she yanked her purse open and scrabbled for her phone. "Maybe she did go home. You know, after I checked. Maybe she's there now." With dreadful hope, she punched in her home number, fingers flying over the keys. Quinn stood silently, and she turned around so she wouldn't have to see his blank face.

The call rang and rang and rang. Quinn had to pry the phone out of her hand. She let it go with a little yelp of defeat.

"We'll find her," he said.

"Not if you're on the job," Z said, then to her, "She's gonna be fine. I'll put some people on it."

She nodded stiffly, but Quinn said, "No, you won't. You stay out of it, Z." He retrieved the evidence bag, dragged her a few feet away, and held it out to her. "Any ideas who TG is?"

"TG?"

He pointed to something. "The other set of initials."

Grudgingly, she looked at what he indicated. Amid the swirls and fantastic designs were several baroque initials. She stared at them, puzzled. "She has a friend, Tammy, but her last name is Levison."

"What about boys?" He turned the Baggie over. "See here? She's got the initials in a heart."

A heart. "I . . . I don't know. If she had a crush on someone, wouldn't I know?" She turned to Z, pleading with him to agree, to tell her of course she'd know because she was doing a fine job with Gina, and her sister wouldn't keep secrets from her.

But the truth was, her sister *was* a secret. A hard little

ball of angry inscrutability that Francesca constantly struggled to penetrate.

As if Z understood, he strolled over, shook his head. "Like I said, doll, a mystery."

Quinn handed her back the phone. "Call around to her friends. See if they can tell you anything."

She took a breath and nodded. It was almost three, but she punched in the Levisons' number first. There was no answer.

"I think Gina said they were on vacation."

"All right. Try someone else."

She woke up four sets of parents, who in various forms of grumpiness agreed to let their children talk. No one had seen Gina that night. Most hadn't seen much of Gina for the last month.

"She has a boyfriend," one said, as if that explained Gina's disappearance from her friend's life.

"A boyfriend?" The information rocketed through Francesca. How could Gina have a boyfriend and Francesca not know?

"Some older guy."

Francesca's stomach clenched. "Older? What do you mean? How much older?"

"I don't know. A senior or something."

Thank God. For a minute she was afraid older meant thirty-five. "What's his name?"

"She wouldn't tell me. She had this big secret and liked it that way."

Yeah, tell me about it.

Discouraged, she thanked the girl for her help, disconnected, and relayed the information, finishing just as an older cop came up to Quinn. He introduced him as Detective Stellman.

Stellman was a rumpled sad sack with a face like a punched-down ball of dough. "We found Calvino's sister," he told Quinn. "Angie Giamatti. She wasn't too happy about being woken up, then went to pieces when I told her about Artie."

"You should have left that to the family," Uncle Z snapped.

Neither Quinn nor his colleague responded.

"What about the nephew?" Quinn asked.

"Family's divorced. She wanted to give Tony a male role model." Stellman rolled his eyes. "He's been spending the summer with his uncle Artie."

She remembered Angie. Lots of platinum hair and low-cut sweaters. The last time Francesca had seen Angie's son, Tony, he'd been a tall 13-year-old with Travolta blue eyes and a head of thick black hair. A heartbreaker even then. Absently, she did the math. He'd be nearly eighteen now.

"She have any idea where Tony might be?" Quinn asked.

"I got the feeling she never has much of an idea about anything," said Stellman.

But all of a sudden Francesca did. "Wait a minute," she said nervously. "Let me see the CD holder." Quinn handed it to her. "The initials. TG." She looked at Uncle Z. "Could they be Tony Giamatti?"

Z shrugged, took a moment. "Maybe," he said slowly. "I heard the guys teasing him about some girl. They caught him making out with her in the"—he glanced from Francesca to Quinn and back again—"pool house."

Francesca stood there, stunned. It couldn't be. It couldn't.

"How old is Tony?" Stellman asked.

"He's a kid," said Z. "How old is that? He's supposed to go to college next year, so he's what—seventeen, eighteen?"

"There's your older man," Quinn said.

Oh, God. Gina and Arturo Calvino's nephew. Francesca's stomach lurched. She wanted to scream. She wanted to wring her sister's skinny little neck. No wonder Gina never said anything.

"If Gina's with Tony, she'll be okay," Z said. "That kid's always disappearing. Artie put a watch on him last month, and the kid managed to give him the slip."

Not exactly what Francesca wanted to hear. "But if Gina was with him in the pool house, and they saw who killed Arturo . . ."

Z nodded. "Yeah, I could see why she was upset."

Understatement of the year.

"And maybe why you haven't heard from her," Stellman said.

"If Tony's running the show, he'd know to lie low," Z said. "The kid's no dummy."

She bit her lip, looked anxiously at Z. "Would he . . . would he hurt her? I mean, what's he like?"

"Hurt her? Nah. Why would he? He'd a good kid." He shrugged. "More or less. I mean he's had a few dustups, maybe, but then what kid doesn't? It wasn't nothing serious. Artie was sending him to Fordham next year to study business."

No need to mention what kind of business.

Once again, she wished she had Gina there so she could rattle some sense into her. Oh, God. The Calvinos were famous for making people disappear. Not even Z's brother, Michael, had been immune. Tony was a Calvino. What if she never saw her sister again?

"Where would he take her?" Quinn demanded of Z.

Z threw up his hands. "Hey—I'm no babysitter."

Quinn's jaw tightened. "Who did Artie put on his tail?"

"I don't know. O'Neil got someone."

"O'Neil is dead," Quinn said flatly, his eyes locked with Z's.

"So that leaves you," Stellman added.

All she needed now was the three of them brawling. She put a calming hand on Joey Z's arm. "Can you call around? See if you can find out who was watching him?"

Z dragged his black gaze away from Quinn. "Sure, honey. For you? Absolutely." He took out a phone and stepped away.

"In the meantime," Quinn said to her, "where would Gina go if she was by herself? You and I could start there."

She looked at him coolly. "You and I?"

"Quinn," said Stellman in a low voice. "We got a mess here. Send a uniform."

"CSU has hours yet. I got a neighborhood canvass going, and I got you." He checked his watch. "Ortiz and Stepanski should be here soon, so you'll have help. If Gina and Tony were here, they're our best lead."

The other cop nodded sagely. "Let's talk." He nodded over his shoulder.

Quinn put up his hands. "Al. It's okay."

Al shook his head. "It's poison, boychik, and you know it."

She had a feeling he wasn't talking about the case, and she couldn't blame him for the warning. The thought of going anywhere with Quinn tightened an already taut thread inside her.

But instead of responding to Stellman, Quinn turned to her. "Do you have a picture of Gina?"

She nodded. "In my wallet." She dove inside her purse. "School picture. It's a couple of years old but . . ."

She showed it to him, realizing it wouldn't do much good. In the snapshot, Gina's hair was long and light brown, her eyes clear and free of makeup. She looked so innocent, so young. Francesca swallowed hard. "Her hair . . . it's different now. Shorter. And it's . . . it's orange. She's got it in these"—she flicked her fingers around her own head to demonstrate—"little spikes."

Quinn raised his eyebrows. "Orange spikes?"

She resented the way he said it, as though it was her fault her sister looked like a freak. But she wasn't going to replay for him the huge battle she'd had with Gina when she came home from Tammy's looking like that.

Z came back from his phone call. "Okay, I got a line on Tony's watcher and called him. Says Tony liked to hang out at Rudy's." That was an all-night diner between Baypointe and Old Baypointe. All the high school kids used to hang out there. Did they still? "And he went to Hadley Park a lot. He liked the rocks."

Quinn and Stellman exchanged looks. Stellman mimed inhaling a joint. "Favorite spot."

Quinn frowned at Francesca. "Gina do drugs?"

She was insulted. "Of course not!" But Quinn kept staring at her, and she had to look away. "I don't know," she admitted unhappily. "I don't think so, but . . . I don't know."

Quinn turned on Z. "What about Tony? Weed? Ecstasy? Meth?"

The names swirled in Francesca's head, one more fear she didn't want to face.

"How should I know?" Z said with belligerence. "I only said what my guy said. The kid went to the park a lot. You don't like it, stay home."

Again, Francesca got between the two men. "Thanks, Uncle Z."

Z was glaring at Quinn, and Quinn was glaring right back. "You're welcome," Z said.

Quinn held out a hand to Francesca. "You coming?"

Did she have a choice? She could search by herself, but Quinn would only follow. "If Uncle Z comes, too."

Quinn's jaw tightened. "We should keep this simple. Small. Too many people tramping around could scare them off."

She turned to Z, knowing she was using him as a barrier between her and Quinn as much as she wanted his help finding Gina. "Uncle Z?"

"If it means watching your back while you're with that son of a bitch, yeah, sure. I'll meet you at the park."

In the car, Quinn turned to her. "How can you trust that guy? You gotta know what he does. He doesn't have those arms for nothing."

"He never lied to me. Never came into my house, pretended to be my father's friend, pretended to love me—"

"I wasn't pretending."

"No?" She laughed curtly. "It was all a lie, Quinn. How am I supposed to separate one part from the other?" She looked out the passenger window so she wouldn't have to look at him. "Besides, it's done. Over. It was years ago. My father's dead, and we can all move on. I don't want to talk about it."

"Fine," Quinn muttered. He jerked the car into gear and pulled out of the estate, heading east.

"I thought we were meeting Uncle Z at the park."

"Uncle Z can go fuck himself. We're going to Rudy's first."

She shot him a look of pure resentment, but if he saw it, he didn't say. She sat stiffly, a prisoner in his car until Rudy's big sign came into view.

As always, the place was lit, its pink, green, and blue light making the chrome around the diner's foundation a wash of neon color.

It was after three, but groups still sat in the fake leather booths and at the counter, where chrome-wrapped stools swiveled. A glass case near the cash register was stuffed with mounds of baked goods: huge yellow cookies studded with massive chocolate chips, outsized danish that oozed red filling, and her favorite, the giant black and whites iced half in chocolate and half in vanilla. She hadn't been here in years. In high school she used to watch the kids from public school come here on dates, the girls laughing into their boyfriends' faces. She'd gone to an all-girls school and never came here with a boy. Quinn had rectified that by taking her once. He'd bought her a black and white and teased her when she devoured every crumb.

She cut him a sideways glance. Did he remember?

The girl behind the hostess stand had a name tag that said Kimberly. She looked as though she was in high school herself. Thin and long-haired with black raccoon liner encircling her eyes, she took a couple of menus off a pile. "Two?"

Quinn shook his head. "Something to go."

Francesca looked at him. They hadn't come here for food.

"A black and white and two coffees," he said.

Sudden heat suffused her face, and she turned away so he couldn't see it. So he did remember.

When the hostess left to get the coffee, Quinn leaned in. "Look around. Anyone you recognize?"

She scanned the place carefully. "No."

He nodded toward the back. "Check out the ladies'."

He disappeared into the men's room while she scouted out the women's restroom. A couple of girls in low-slung jeans and halter tops were giggling inside. She took out the picture of Gina.

"I'm looking for my sister," she told them. "Have you seen her?"

They glanced at the picture, and both shook their heads.

She met Quinn back at the checkout counter. The hostess had returned with his purchase in a white Rudy's bag, the name scrawled gaily in red.

He handed her some bills and gestured with his chin toward her name tag. "Kim, right?" She nodded. "You been here all night?"

"Since twelve." She rang up the sale with a bored expression.

"We're looking for someone. Fifteen, short red hair."

"It's more orange really. Very short. Spiky." Francesca didn't bother with the picture, it was so out of date.

"She might have been with a guy," Quinn said.

"Dark hair, blue eyes. Very cute," Francesca added.

Kim's face lit up. "Oh yeah, him." She nodded. "Yeah, they were here. Also wanted something to go. They ordered at the counter."

The two waitresses behind the counter confirmed. "He kept looking over his shoulder," one of them said.

"She asked to use the phone, and he told her to wait until later," the other one said.

"What did they get?"

"Sheesh, that was a couple of hours ago," said one.

"Two burgers, two club sandwiches, two large Cokes," said the other. "Oh, and a chocolate chip and a linzer cookie." She winked. "Bad with names, great with orders."

"Linzer cookies are Gina's favorite," Francesca murmured. "She loves raspberry."

Quinn thanked the waitresses, then he and Francesca left. "Gina a big eater?" he asked as they got in the car.

"Not big enough to eat all that in one sitting."

"Sounds like they're stocking up."

"Which means what?"

"They've got a plan. A place to go."

"So they'll be okay?"

"They're making moves. Thinking. That could be good, because it'll keep them safe. But it could also be a pain in the butt if it makes them harder to find."

She nodded, uneasy. She wished she knew more about Tony Giamatti. Had he given Gina drugs? What else had he done to her?

Quinn cut into her anxiety by handing her the cookie and a cup of coffee.

"I'm not hungry."

He put his own coffee in the holder and drove off. "It's not for hunger. It's to keep your energy up."

"I'm fine."

"And to help you remember the best night of my life."

Mine, too, said a traitorous voice in her head before she drowned it out.

He shot her a crooked grin. "Not that I need much help remembering."

"I thought we weren't going to talk about it."

"Your rules, not mine."

Quinn let her stew on that for a moment. Closed up in

the car like they were, he could smell her, even with the coffee steaming. She smelled sweet, like those summer flowers. Like the past.

He glanced over. Her face was a mask.

"I didn't intend to hurt you," he said softly.

"You think sending my father to prison wouldn't hurt me?"

"Your dad worked for bad men. He helped them do bad things. Someone had to stop him."

"You stopped him all right."

"I didn't kill him, Francesca. Artie did that. Or had it done." Her father had been stabbed in the shower, assailant unknown to this day.

"Then why didn't you arrest Artie?"

"You know why."

"Oh, yeah. Same reason why my father was left to hang by himself. Artie covers his tracks. He was good at that."

The radio barked and he reached for the dash where it lay against the windshield.

"Hey, boychik." It was Stellman. "Just thought you'd like to know. We woke up everyone at the Volkov place. The big guy's out of town."

"That's a surprise."

"Yeah, what I thought, too. Perfect timing. A little too perfect."

They were at the park now, and as he pulled into the parking lot, he saw Joey Z pacing at the north end. Quinn parked the car.

"Keep me posted," Quinn said, and disconnected.

Then Joey Z was pounding on his window. "Where the fuck you been?"

And Francesca was out of the car soothing him. "We went to Rudy's. They bought a ton of food there. Quinn thinks they're holed up somewhere."

"Yeah? Well, what does 'Quinn' think about this?" He gestured out to the park.

"Quinn thinks you should go home," Quinn said.

"And leave you alone with her? Not likely."

"Look, let's do what we came here for," Francesca said, and with grumbling agreement, Z nodded.

Quinn organized them into a long, spaced row, and they tramped over the grounds in a disciplined rank. They checked the locker room at the pool, the restrooms by the ball field, and the one on the other side by the picnic tables. They found no trace of the teens.

The rocks were last. This was an area of large flat boulders that tumbled against one another in uneven clumps leaving crevices to hide in. Local kids hung out there, smoked a little weed, and made out. Uniforms did a weekly sweep of the area that never seemed to clean it out. He'd hoped someone would be there tonight, someone who might have seen Tony or Gina, but for once the place was deserted.

They started on ground level, finding the spots where the rocks left enough room for two people to take cover. Quinn couldn't imagine anyone using them as a permanent hideout, but Gina and Tony might have stopped there temporarily to plan or think or just breathe before moving on to something more secure.

"You ever come here as a kid?" he asked Francesca.

"No, I was too much of a lady then." She scrambled over ruts and stones, none too careful about getting hands or anything else dirty. "Now I'm not so fastidious."

"You still like those big words, though."

She shrugged. "Not much chance to use them in Sal's."

"Sal's? In Baypointe?" He knew that place. Hell, everyone knew that place. Live music, alcohol, a couple of fights a week.

"I pour drinks there. Seven to closing."

He paused to look at her. Never in a million years would he have pictured her in a place like Sal's. "What happened to Stony Brook?" She'd been a second semester freshman when they met, a rising junior when her father went in. She was studying chemistry, had talked about going to medical school.

She shrugged. "Life happened."

But he heard what she hadn't said: he'd happened.

When they didn't find a trace of Gina or Tony at ground level, Quinn began climbing. The rocks were flat and sloping—not hard to scamper over, but he offered Francesca a hand up, which she refused. Joey Z he let roam at will, but always where he could keep an eye on him.

Ten minutes into the search, Z called out. "Hey, doll, come here!"

Quinn followed Francesca to an opening in one of the rock formations. Joey Z had a paper wrapper in his hand. A smattering of white powder and what looked like jam. Quinn ran a finger over the specks and tasted them.

"Raspberry."

"The linzer cookie." Francesca's eyes lit up with hope. "That means they were—"

CRACK!

The rocks exploded around them.

A shot. Someone was shooting at them.

Quinn dove for the ground, taking Francesca with him.

Joey Z was already down. He groaned. "I'm hit."

"Oh, my God," Francesca said. She put her head up, but Quinn pulled her down.

"Don't move!"

He yanked out his service weapon and took a fast look around. They were on top of the rocks, a perfect target if they stood. The shot came from behind, but he couldn't see where. Francesca was half covered by his body, but still exposed. She was trembling. Her skin was cold and covered in goose bumps. Zachariah was a few feet away.

Quinn spoke fast and low. "Listen, I'm going to get you inside the rocks here. Okay?"

"What about Uncle Z?" she said in a strained voice. "He's hurt."

"He's also over there. You're here. It'll be easier to get you safe, then come back for him."

She seemed to see the sense of this, albeit reluctantly. "Okay."

"Go as fast as you can, but keep yourself glued to the rock. Don't give the shooter a target. I'm right behind you. Okay? Go!"

She slithered backward and he guarded her with his body and his gun. Tense, he waited for more shots, but none came. When she was ensconced between the rocks, he went back for Zachariah, keeping his head down and dragging the older man by his feet until they were shielded by the rocks.

Zachariah was alert and cursing. Quinn ripped open his shirt. The wound was in his arm. "Looks like you'll live."

"Don't sound so happy," Z said through gritted teeth.

Quinn fashioned the remnants of Z's shirt into a thick

pad, which he placed over the wound. "Hold this tight. You'll need pressure to stop the bleeding." He slapped Z's free hand over the pad. "Any idea who's out there?"

Zachariah sucked in a breath. "Volkov is top of my list. That bastard's been after Calvino's operation for years."

Quinn used his cell phone to call Stellman for backup and an ambulance.

"Z," he said. "You carrying?"

"I might be."

"Keep it handy." He edged out of their hiding place.

Francesca leaped to pull him back. What was he doing? "Where are you going?" The question came out in a tight, fear-drenched squeak.

"Seeing if I can catch the guy."

"What?" Her pulse shot up. She heard the shot again, saw the blood on Z's shirt. What if the same happened to Quinn? Or worse? "No! You can't—"

"Stay here."

"But—"

And he was gone.

She stared at the opening into which he'd disappeared. Vacant blackness stared back at her.

She didn't care, she told herself. Let him get shot. He deserved it.

Then why was she trembling? Why did her skin feel like it was coated in frost?

And why, why, why was he taking so long to come back?

"Hey, doll!" Z's pain-filled voice stopped her silent argument. "Can you come here and hold this a minute?"

Outside, Quinn ducked onto the rocks. Keeping low, he skittered over them toward the sound of the shot. His chest felt tight. Any minute he expected a bullet to tear through it.

But none came.

By the time sirens screamed into the night, he'd found an empty shell casing caught between the rocks, but no other trace of whoever the shooter had been.

He got Z squared away with an EMT, then took Francesca aside. She hadn't said much since the shooting, but an unnatural pallor told him she was shaken up.

"It's time you go home. I'll request a uniform to go with

you. Whoever took out Arturo is a serious guy. He wants everyone dead. You'll be safer at home."

Her face grew stubborn. "I'd also go insane."

"Better insane than dead."

She paled even more, but the look she gave him was resolute, chin raised, dark eyes steely. "Damn you," she said softly. "Gina is all I have left. I won't let you shut me out."

If her family had been decimated she had no one to blame but her father. Yet his own part in her isolation sat heavy with him, as it always had. He looked around at the two cop cars, one of which was already heading out, and the ambulance. The night was getting away from him.

Against his better judgment, he nodded. "Okay."

"Thank you."

"Just stick close. And do what I tell you."

"No."

He gaped at her. "No? What do you mean, no? If you don't—" Her hand on his arm shut him up fast. He looked down. She was touching him gently, not in anger. He met her gaze.

"I mean no, you don't understand." She hit him with a small, tender smile. "The thanks is not just for letting me tag along. It's for saving my life. And Z's."

The expression on her face had gone soft and was suddenly so familiar he ached with the recognition. "You're . . . you're welcome." He looked away so he wouldn't drown in it. "So . . . " He cleared his throat, which had all of a sudden jammed up. "Any ideas where to go next?"

"Maybe."

His eyes widened; he hadn't expected her to say that.

"I've been thinking about where Gina might go, and there's one place . . . " She took a breath. "She used to play there as a kid and once when she ran away, I found her there."

Something about the roundabout way she was getting this out made him uneasy. As though bad news was coming.

"Is it far?"

She shook her head. He waited.

A resigned look crept over her face. "Oyster Cove," she said at last.

He stared at her, and she dodged his gaze. The name echoed in his brain, a ghost returning to the haunt.

Was it true or a trick? Was she doing this to hurt him, to twist the knife a little deeper?

But her face looked as haunted as he felt, and he knew going there would be as hard for her as it was for him.

He didn't like it.

But if it meant keeping Gina safe, he'd do whatever he had to. Even take a painful trip down Memory Lane.

Chapter 3

Francesca sat still and silent in the car as they headed for Oyster Cove. It had been years, but she didn't have to remind Quinn how to get there. The car seemed to go there on its own, as though called by some urgent voice. *Find me, find me.*

She concentrated on the words, hoping they'd prove prophetic, and Gina would be at the cove, whole and undamaged.

But the crack of a gun echoed in her head. Did whoever shot at them at Hadley Park have Gina? Had he hurt her? A current of fear blazed through her, and she glanced at Quinn. He seemed so solid beside her. His jaw was taut, the lines clean and firm. A face made for touching, though she clamped her hands together so she wouldn't.

She should be through with Quinn Parker; hadn't she consigned his memory to the Dumpster long ago?

But those few moments at the rocks when he'd disappeared had been among the longest in her life.

What if he hadn't come back?

Why did she even care?

She didn't want to. Didn't want her heart to thump when she looked at him. But attraction was a powerful thing, and below her carefully nurtured contempt that familiar pull was still there.

So much had happened since they'd been together. Her father gone, her aunt, too. Gina grown wild and difficult. A flare of resentment burned through Francesca. She could have been in medical school by now. She should be starting a life of challenge and purpose. She'd gone from pampered rich girl to working stiff, and the trip had been quick and necessary, while he . . . he was still a cop, still doing what he wanted to do.

Yet new lines had formed around his eyes and mouth. What had put them there?

"Quinn . . . what happened to you?"

It was the first personal question she'd asked, and he shot her a surprised and somewhat confused look. "What do you mean? When?"

"I thought . . . well, when I did think about you, which trust me wasn't much, I assumed you'd still be . . . undercover."

"Still lying, you mean?"

The question was said lightly, but she didn't miss the bitterness underneath. It generated an unwanted jolt of compassion, and to dispel it, she acknowledged the accusation with a small shift of her shoulders.

"It's what you do best, isn't it? And yet . . . here you are. In a suit. You never used to wear suits. And your hair." She couldn't help the wistful look she gave his buzz cut, remembering how the sun used to streak his hair gold.

"Easier to keep this way," he said gruffly, then added, "And no reminders."

"Reminders?"

"Of that other me. Of you. What happened."

She understood that. The effort it took to forget. Start over. She and Gina were still struggling with it.

"But still obsessed with the Calvinos, I see. Like a dog with a bone."

His hands tightened on the steering wheel. "I work homicide now," he said bluntly. "It was my shift. I caught the case. Coincidence."

She gave him a swift, startled glance. "Homicide? No more deep cover?"

Quinn cut her a glance, then looked away quickly. It was an expression of what? Shame? Avoidance? He didn't explain, merely said, "I got transferred."

She searched his face. "That's it?"

"That's it."

Disappointed, Francesca turned to gaze out the window at the passing street lights. So while her life was shattered, his just . . . went on.

The realization powered a jolt of anger that left her

seething. She wished he had suffered. Wished he had burned and twisted with it.

God, she hated him.

And yet . . .

She looked down at her hands as though the answers to her feelings lay there. All she saw were her fingers, as tangled with each other as her thoughts.

When she looked back up, he was pulling onto Cliff Road, which would eventually lead down to the private beach. She hadn't been here in five years and now twice in the last six months. Both times to find Gina.

Like the last time, the trip was full of memories. They passed the house in which she grew up. The people who had bought it had sold it again, and the new owners didn't seem to be gardeners. The rose bushes climbed over the front wall, wild and untrimmed.

She couldn't see her favorite side of the house. It was too dark and the house blocked the back view. But she remembered the way the bay looked from her bedroom window, the sun shimmering the surface and white sails dotting the water.

She looked away. It hurt to see the house. She knew now they should never have lived there. Knew every inch of wood and molding, every article of clothing and scrap of food had been bought with someone else's pain. But it had been her life and she'd lived there innocently, believing her father to be what he'd said, an ordinary businessman. If she'd had suspicions, they'd been easy to dismiss. He was her father, and she couldn't help trusting him.

But, like Quinn's, her father's life had been a lie, and she hadn't forgiven him for it. He'd died naked and humiliated in a prison shower with her anger in his heart, and she'd regretted it ever since.

She glanced at Quinn. He walked a dangerous path. Would she repeat the same mistake?

The car began its descent, traveling the steep hill toward the shore. Circling the cliff that overlooked the bay, the road twisted into the inky night. Occasionally, a street light appeared, casting distorted shadows of lamp and tree that did little to illuminate the way. She shivered. Was it because she didn't know what waited for her at the bottom or because she did?

If only Gina would be there. She pictured the reunion, Gina running into her arms. She would take her sister home and pretend all this had never happened.

Quinn parked near the boat launch and they sat there, neither one reaching for the door. Outside, a dock light showered the pier with a dim glow. Beyond it, the night bore down, black and oppressive. Quinn gripped the steering wheel as though anchoring himself there. As for herself, she seemed to have lost the ability to move.

Finally, he gave the wheel a light tap with his fist. "You ready?"

How could she be? But she gave him a tight nod. "Ready or not . . ."

"Okay. Slide down in your seat and wait for me."

Before she could protest, he'd drawn his gun and slipped out of the car into a crouch. Slowly, he stood, inched away, and disappeared into the darkness.

What was he doing?

She could see little from her lowered position. As in the park, her body tensed, waiting for the crack of a shot or the sound of a lethal struggle.

Again, she imagined a world without Quinn, and again, grief and loss welled up, as real and present as they were unexpected and unwanted.

Half an eternity later, her door opened and Quinn stood there. "Okay. Looks quiet. You can get out."

Okay? Why was he doing this to her? First he broke her heart, then he scared her half to death.

She slid out into the shelter of his body and realized that, once again, he was prepared to protect her. But more than bullets were out there, and no way could he keep her safe from the other pain.

She gave him a swift push in the chest. "Don't do that again."

He grabbed her wrist and scowled at her. "Do what?"

"Leave me alone while you go off into the night like Dudley Do-Right."

"Look, I have the gun. That means I take point."

"Whatever." She dismissed his explanation with a flap of her hand. "Just don't play the big hero with me."

His mouth tightened, but all he said was, "Stay behind."

Positioning himself half in front of her, he led her down to the shore. Water lapped quietly against the sand, a small but constant rhythm. The bay had a distinctive odor, part fish, part decaying greenery, part fresh air, and the familiar smell took her back.

She'd spent half her life there. As a kid, the hot summer sun had baked her golden. Later, she'd learned to enjoy the night, too, laughing around bonfires her friends built.

Later still, there'd been moonlight. And Quinn.

She blocked a dart of pain and followed him down. Oyster Cove was a private beach for the homeowners on Cliff Road. Steep stairs led from the homes to the shore. Some ended in docks and boats at anchor. It was a good five-minute walk east from the boat launch to the back of her house. She could still tick off the intervening homes in her mind.

But Quinn put his back to what used to be her home and turned west instead. Up against the cliff wall the tide had deposited shards of shells and pebbles, and the path was rocky. Closer to the water it was smoother, but Quinn stuck to the cliff, moving them forward in a careful, sliding crawl. Gun still drawn, he stayed vigilant, scanning all directions. The weapon, the caution, all helped distance her from the past, when they had run barefoot down the sand.

But nothing Quinn did could make her forget altogether. Just as it had then, the moon gilded the bay. And just like then, her heart thumped along with her footsteps, though this time it was from danger of a different sort.

Or maybe not so different. They passed the Rotiers' place, at least she still thought of it as the Rotiers' place though she had no idea if the Rotiers still owned it. In her mind it was forever theirs, the place where Quinn had pulled her beneath the wooden stairs and kissed her until she thought her legs would melt and wash away in the tide.

She threw him a quick glance. Was he feeling the same? If she reached over, placed a hand on his arm, turned him and lifted her head, would he kiss her? Would it taste the same? Would her blood fire and her heart detonate like it had then?

With an effort, she forced herself to remember why they had come. Not to revisit the scene of Quinn's crime, but to find Gina.

Find Gina.

Francesca picked up the pace, anxious to have this over and done.

"Whoa." Quinn pulled her back. "Hold on. I told you to stay behind."

She tried to shake him loose, but his grip was firm. "While we shuffle along Gina could be scared and alone in there."

"And she could have company."

In her mind, the shot in Hadley Park rang out, and she ceased struggling with him.

"We go in slow," Quinn said. "Carefully. No running off."

Chastened, she stepped back, and they continued their deliberate progress forward. Quinn kept close, too close. She could lay her hand on his back, feel those hard planes once more. It was wicked of him to tempt her, wicked of herself to be tempted.

Ahead of her, he continued to examine their surroundings for signs of attackers. But no one jumped out at them, nothing blasted into the quiet. Sadly, some despairing part of her wished it would. Then she wouldn't have to think about anything but physical survival.

But too soon the cliff wall gave way to a long line of boulders that plunged into the bay. On the other side, she knew the rocks formed an opening in the wall, a small cave with room enough for two.

Quinn scrambled up and over, keeping watch as she followed. The last time they'd done this he'd been shirtless, his broad shoulders tanned brown by the sun. Now he stood suited and somber, and held out a hand to help her over.

For half a moment she ignored it, afraid his touch would explode something inside her, something she wanted to keep dammed up. But her feet slipped on the rocks and she was forced to grab onto to him. He braced himself in the sand while she tumbled into his arms. They hung there, clinging to each other. The smell of the bay, the sand, her hand on his shoulder all combined to merge past and present, and she looked into his eyes and saw the boy she thought had loved her.

For one heart-stopping moment, his face moved toward hers, his mouth moved toward hers. She forgot where she was and why, and knew only that Quinn was going to kiss

her. Again. His arms would go around her and she would
feel as though she'd come home.

Then a voice hissed in her head.

Look at who you're with.

Remember what he's done.

All elbows and arms, she extricated herself with awkward
but chilled precision.

But the feel of him lingered, snaking around her like
smoke from a distant fire, beckoning, seducing.

A pulse hammered in her skull. If she didn't get away,
break the connection, put air between them, she'd be lost.

She dodged past him toward the cave, crying, "Gina?
Are you there?" but he yanked at her arm, shoving her
into the corner between the rocks and the cliff.

He closed his hand over her chin, shutting her mouth.
His fingers were strong and possessive on her face, and she
struggled not to like the feel of them, but it was a losing
cause. Desire shot through her, making her knees wobble.
Then his lips moved across her temple to her ear, and she
shuddered involuntarily, closing her eyes.

"Sshh." His whisper was rough as sandpaper, his mouth
warm against her skin, his taut body close and alluring.
"Do you want the whole world to know we're here?"

She swallowed, praying silently.

Please make him let me go.

Please let him touch me again.

She opened her eyes to find his gaze boring into hers,
carrying its own warning. *No sound.* Slowly, she nodded,
and, as if in answer to her first plea, he released her.

Positioning himself in front with his back to the wall so
he could keep watch, he took her hand and sidled toward
the mouth of the cave. She didn't know which frightened
her more—what they'd find in the cave, or the thrill she
couldn't quite suppress from feeling his hand wrapped
around hers.

He signaled for her to stay; then, gun high and aimed,
he charged the entrance, and her lungs clogged in hope.
Was Gina there? A flashlight she didn't even know he'd
brought switched on. She could see the rim of light as it
moved over the cave's interior.

With a jerk of his hand, he motioned her forward.

"I'm sorry," he said with compassion. "It's empty."

Her heart nose-dived, but she refused to give up. Maybe he'd missed something. Maybe she was hiding. Maybe—

She pushed past him and penetrated deeper until they both stood in the small sandy area hidden by the curve of the rocks that formed the cove. She glanced around, still clinging to the possibility that Gina was there, somewhere. "This is where I found her last time," she said.

But no one was here tonight.

Quinn skimmed the ground with his light. Indentations in the sand might have been footprints, but if so they could have belonged to anyone. There were no telltale food wrappers. No convenient notes scrawled in lipstick on the rocks. Nothing.

"I'm sorry," Quinn said quietly, squeezing her shoulder.

She emitted a pitiful sound—half moan, half sob—and sank onto the sand.

Someone must have called Quinn, because suddenly he fished out his cell phone and spoke into it. "Lewis." His name hung in the darkness. "Okay. Keep trying. Let me know if you get something." He knelt down beside her. "That was Stellman. He got Tony's cell, but no one answers."

More bad news. She wanted to lie down and sleep for a week. She couldn't handle much more. "What does that mean?"

"His phone could have run out of juice, or he could just be ignoring it."

The truth slapped her in the face. "Or someone could be preventing him from answering." Or worse.

He looked away as though he didn't want to admit that possibility, then back at her as though he had to. "Yeah. That, too."

He set the flashlight on a ledge, and leaned against a rock jutting out from the cave wall. He'd left his jacket in the car. Now he rolled up his sleeves and loosened his tie. In the dim light she couldn't see his face, but his body drooped as though he was bone tired, too.

Dread surged through her. "She's not dead."

The words seem to galvanize him. His head snapped up. "I didn't say she was."

"You didn't have to."

He grabbed her by the shoulders. "We'll find her." His grip was tight. "I promise."

She swallowed, wanting to believe and not quite making it. "Oh, God. What if . . . " She couldn't say the words. "If anything happens to her . . . " And suddenly it was all too much to bear. The fight with Gina, the phone call at Sal's, the dead bodies, the shooting in the park, Gina still missing, and Quinn suddenly back in her life—it all swelled inside her, a massive buildup that choked her. She pressed her hands against the sand in a desperate effort to block it. She tried to breathe and sobbed instead.

"It won't." He pulled her toward him, enveloping her in his arms. "It won't. I swear it." She clung to him like a lifeline and he held her tight enough to crush her.

"God, Francesca." His hands were in her hair, stroking it away from her face. "We'll find her. We'll find her." Then he was kissing her face at the hairline, and then her cheek and jaw, and then his mouth was on hers.

Heat melted pain and, for one staggering moment, cut into her moorings and set her free. She opened her mouth and tasted his warmth, let herself feel everything she'd tried to bottle up. Heat shimmied through her, a panting shivery wind. She wanted to sink into his arms, melt into his mouth. Her eyes closed and the world narrowed until it was just her and the magic of his hands, the remembered strength of his body.

"Francesca. God. God, I'm sorry, I'm so sorry."

His voice was wracked with pain, and the sound penetrated her thick wall of grief.

It wasn't just Gina he was talking about.

Immediately, she scuttled away. "Don't . . ."

He stared at her. "Don't?" He was breathing hard, his face twisted in a frown. "Don't what? Touch you? Try to get through to you? Tell you what I've wanted to tell you all these years?"

She rose, but he tugged her back down.

"Let go of me!"

"No, you're going to stay here and listen." He had an iron grip on her arm. "Yes, it started as a lie. A job. I'm a cop. I catch criminals. Yes, I arranged to meet Michael Zachariah in prison, I became his friend, and when we got out I used that friendship to insinuate myself into the Calvino organization. Yes, I lied. But never once, never once about you." He released her to cup a hand around her face. "Never once." He gazed at her so intensely, and she felt as though he would pull her soul out of her body. "The first time I saw you, at that barbeque Artie threw . . ." He shuddered, as though the memory was a sledgehammer pounding him. "God, I thought time had stopped."

She remembered that day. That moment. She had just come down from the house with Gina, who was already in her bathing suit and who jumped in the pool with such ferocity she splashed Michael Zachariah and the man beside him. Both men leaped away, and the stranger, that blond god with the sun-kissed hair, looked up, laughing.

And her breath had caught. She remembered it exactly. The air inside her lungs seemed to disappear.

Somehow she managed to apologize.

He accepted.

But his grin had faltered as he did so. Something shifted in his eyes.

And the universe took a wide turn and left her behind.

Now, the universe had taken a different turn. Gina was missing, and everything he'd done was between them.

"God, Francesca . . . "

She heard what he didn't say, heard the plea in his voice. *Forgive me.*

But she couldn't. Not here. This was where he took her body, where they'd become one creature with one flesh. This was where he'd perpetrated his greatest betrayal on her, and she didn't want to forget. Or forgive. He had cut her to the bone, and they could never come together like that again.

So she stood and coolly dusted off the sand. "We should go."

As if the fates agreed, the sound of a boom box drifted in from a distance.

He rose and they stood there unmoving. He held her gaze, his stony face shuttered, the expression a rebuke. Every nerve ending ached to reach out to him, while at the same time the chugging rap beat grew obscenely loud, as loud and insistent as the voice in her head telling her not to.

"Stay here," he said at last. "I'll get rid of them."

She nodded, relieved to have a moment to herself. It had been a mistake to come here. Had she seriously thought Gina might be here? Or had that been a thin excuse to get them out here? Some sick, sad, misguided wish to recover what they'd lost?

She watched him scurry out, his hands scrubbing at his face, and refused to admit what that meant.

It didn't matter how sorry he was. Nothing he did or said could change what happened. They couldn't start over again, even if she wanted to. It would be like stomping on her family's grave.

Outside, the music reached its peak, then cut off abruptly. She could hear the rumble of voices, but not what they said.

Closer, another sound penetrated. Her cell phone. Instantly, her heart sprang for her throat. She dug the phone out of her pocket, fingers so excited she almost dropped the thing before fumbling to punch in the right key. "Gina? Is that you? Are you all right?"

"She's fine, Frannie." Her heart flipped over. Not Gina. A man's voice. "Just do what I say and she'll keep on being fine."

Her blood froze. "Who is this?"

"If the cop is with you, smile and say, 'Hi, Uncle Z.'"

Uncle Z? It wasn't Z on the phone. The voice was . . . familiar, but not one she could place. "Do you know where Gina is? Is she all right?"

"I take it the cop is not with you."

"For the moment."

"Good. Here, someone wants to speak to you."

A shuffling ensued as the phone was passed.

"Frannie? Frannie, I—"

"Gina? Gina! Where—"

"That's enough of a reunion for now," the voice said.

"Where is she?" Francesca demanded. "What do you want?"

He laughed. "Oh, I want a lot of things. A big house with a pool, a silver Porsche, a steak at Peter Luger's. Right now I'll settle for Quinn."

"Quinn? Why? What for?"

"You tell him Uncle Z called and knows where Gina is. You take him there. You get him to go in unarmed and alone. One walks in, another walks out. Simple. But you bring friends, cops, negotiators, stuff like that, your little sister won't ever walk anywhere again." He paused for a breath. "So . . . Frannie . . . we got a deal?"

"I . . . I don't know."

"What don't you know? That scumbag put your father in jail. He fucked you and then screwed your whole family. What do you care what happens to him?"

"I—"

"He who hesitates, Frannie."

In the background, Gina started screaming. "Don't. Don't!"

"What are you doing? Leave her alone!"

"You have ten seconds or she's a stain on the wall."

"All right! All right! Whatever you want. Just don't hurt her."

"Can't promise, Frannie. I'm in a mood tonight. You better get over here." And he gave her an address.

Her brain went haywire. Gina's screams melded into the disembodied voice. *One walks in, another walks out.*

Quinn. He wanted Quinn.

As though to point it up, Quinn hurtled back, gun at the ready. "What is it? Who were you talking to? Is it Gina? Is that her?"

She couldn't think. Couldn't think. "Uncle Z," she said lamely.

"Z? What did he want?"

The choice was there in front of her. Gina or Quinn. Nothing was simpler. *He fucked you and then screwed your whole family.*

Her stomach shifted. She wanted to throw up. "He . . . he says he knows where Gina is."

Chapter 4

Excitement warred with suspicion in Quinn's face. "How did he find her?"

She blanked, panicked, then blurted out the truth. "I don't know. I . . . I didn't ask. I couldn't think." God, that was true.

His eyes narrowed. "He's playing you. He wants something. Guys like that never do anything without a what's-in-it-for-me."

"Don't confuse your agenda with his."

He took that like a slap, and she had the grace to feel ashamed. But she didn't apologize. She couldn't. If a single soft word left her mouth, the lie would come tumbling out. And she couldn't let that happen. "Let's just go get her."

She turned to leave, but he grabbed her arm, pulling her back. "Why doesn't he just bring her home himself?"

"I don't know!" Questions. Too many questions! She couldn't think fast enough, lie fast enough. Her skin was like ice, her stomach twisted around itself. She had to get to Gina, and all he did was ask questions. She wrenched her arm away. "I'm not standing around while you grill me. If you won't take me, I'll take myself."

She stormed out of the cave, and he followed. "You don't have a car."

"I'll call a cab." Stomping back the way they'd come, she scrambled over the wall of boulders and took out her cell phone. She began to punch in numbers, and she had to concentrate hard because her hands were shaking.

"All right." He grabbed the phone out of her hand. "All right. Where are they?"

Oh, God. Stall or tell? Which was better?

Control. She had to maintain control. That meant keeping him in the dark, right?

She avoided his eyes and continued tramping over the shore. "He . . . he didn't say exactly."

"Jesus Christ." He started to key in a phone number.

She stopped short. "What are you doing?"

"Calling for backup. This stinks."

"No!" She made a grab for the phone, but he snatched it away.

"No? Why not? What's the matter with you?" The expression on his face said he thought she'd lost her mind.

She licked her lips, wracked her brains to give him a plausible reason for her behavior. "It's just Uncle Z. We don't need a platoon with us."

"I don't trust him."

"Your opinion doesn't count. We do this quietly. No trigger-happy goons along for the ride."

"Uh-uh. None of this adds up. You're hiding something."

"Don't be ridiculous." She started forward; he blocked her way.

"What else did Z say?"

She avoided his gaze; she couldn't bear to face him. "We have to . . . " She steeled herself, raised her chin. "We have to come alone."

For half a second he just looked at her. Then he threw up his hands. "It's a setup, Francesca. Joey Z is setting you up."

"For what? Why?"

"I don't know, but the whole thing sucks. Did he give you an address?"

She shook her head. Why couldn't he just shut up and do what she wanted? "Directions." She started to scamper over the sand again, needing to get away from his penetrating gaze.

He stood planted. "I'm not taking any chances. I call for help, or we don't go."

She rounded on him, fear and nerves coming together in a rush. "You self-righteous son of a . . . haven't you done enough?" The words tumbled out, faster than she could stop them. "You destroyed my family. Broke my heart. You put everything ahead of me—your job, your orders, your career. Fine. Your decision. But don't think I'm going to let you do it again. I will not let you put Gina's life in danger the way you did my father's. I will not let you take everything away one more time." Angry tears stung her lids, but she ignored them. "You want to make it up to me? Back there"—she gestured wildly behind her toward the cave—"you seemed awfully eager to make it up to me. Was that another lie?"

He was white-faced and tight-lipped.

"Was it?"

"No."

"Then I'm asking you. Now. If you've never done anything for me before, do this. Let me go by myself or shut up and come with me. Either way, no backup."

She thought her chest would implode with misery. What was she doing? And more important, more sickening: was it working? Would he walk away? If he left her, Gina was dead.

But he didn't disappoint her. He gave her a long, cold look, then nodded once—a short stiff bow of his head—and gestured for her to precede him.

The address the man on the phone had given her was off Northern Boulevard, so she directed him there. Except for her voice telling him to go left or right, they made the trip in silence.

But inside her head other voices screamed at her.

You can't do this.

You have no choice.

You can tell him the truth.

You can't risk it.

By the time they found the address, her brain was battered by the argument, a meat cleaver hacking away at her conscience.

The location turned out to be a construction site, a new office building, as if the world, not to mention Long Island, needed one. Not surprisingly, the sign guarding the site said CC CONSTRUCTION. The double C stood for Calvino Corporation.

A few lights had been set up, and she eyed the half-finished building in the dim glow. Dingy plastic wrap hung from a beam, shielding the interior and creating skeletal shadows that danced with the night breeze. She shivered at the death's head images, and forced herself out of the car.

A wire fence wrapping the entire area stopped their approach.

"Z!" Quinn's voice cut into the night. "Joey Z! You in there?"

The answering silence was unnerving.

Quinn turned slowly, scrutinizing the location. "You sure this is the right place?"

She nodded.

He called out again. "Zachariah!"

This time, the call was answered by a scream. Francesca's head snapped toward the sound.

Three stories above, an upside down Gina dangled off a beam on the top ledge, hands tied behind her, her bottle-orange hair hanging in spiky ropes. A cord around her ankles was the only thing keeping her from falling.

Francesca sucked in a breath and clutched at Quinn, crying out her sister's name. "Gina!"

"Frannie? Frannie, is that you? Are you there?" Her voice strained, desperate hope rising through panic.

The sound galvanized Francesca. She would have climbed the fence if Quinn hadn't held her back. Instead, she gripped the wire and shouted, "It's me, Gina. I'm coming. You're going to be all right."

"He shot Tony!" From behind the plastic sheets that hid the building interior, an invisible something—hand, foot or . . . God, was that a two-by-four?—pushed Gina in the back, and she screamed, swaying helplessly in and out of the light. "Don't. Don't! All right. All right, I will!" She gulped back tears. "He says . . . he says to look to your left. There's an opening in the fence."

Swiftly, Quinn ran left and found it. He nodded at Francesca.

"Okay!" Francesca said. "We see it." Francesca's fingers tightened around the fence, the wire cutting into her hand. "You're going to be okay, Gina. I promise!"

"He says . . . he says the cop comes in alone."

He shoved her again, she squealed again. "No gun!" Gina shrilled quickly. "He has to leave his gun. We have to see him leave it." Another push and Gina swung even

farther out, then back, a limp, powerless rag doll. "Oh,
God. Please do what he says. He says . . . he says he'll cut
the rope if you don't."

Quinn was already taking off his suit coat, revealing a
holstered gun at his hip. He removed the gun and held it
above his head for a few seconds.

"That isn't Z in there, is it?" he said in a low tone
pitched for Francesca's ears alone.

She hesitated a fraction, then crumbled. Tears thickened
the back of her throat. "No."

With slow, deliberate caution, he stooped and laid the
gun on the ground. "Who is it?"

"I . . . I don't know."

He looked up at her from the ground, his expression
clearly disbelieving.

"Truly, Quinn. His voice sounded familiar, but I . . . I
couldn't place it."

"But you knew he had Gina."

Her chest constricted with guilt. "Yes."

"And he told you to come alone."

She nodded, the words drying in her mouth.

"What else did he tell you?"

A scream from above. "What's taking so long? Please,
oh God, please hurry."

Grimly, Quinn repeated his question.

Francesca looked desperately from Gina back to Quinn.
"He said you . . . you had to come unarmed."

"Me? Or whoever was with you?"

"He . . . " Her breath wedged in her lungs. Ashamed,
she pushed out the words, "He mentioned you by name."

It was all out in the open now. How she'd manipulated
him here and betrayed him into danger. Not some cop, but
a trap set expressly to catch him. Quinn. She watched for
his contempt and anger, but his stoic face revealed none of
that as he rose slowly and raised his hands high in the air
to show they were empty.

Gina moaned as she was jerked in the air again. "No,
no! Not on the ground! Give the gun to Frannie, so he can
see you don't have it."

Francesca swept the gun up and held it above her head.
"I've got it! Leave her alone, you bastard!"

"Pull her in!" Quinn shouted. "Pull her in or I'm not coming!"

For a moment, the only thing that moved was Gina, the only sound the creak of the rope as she swung in the night. Then, slowly, her body began to move toward the plastic sheets and the building interior. Quinn began walking through the opening in the fence at the same time.

The reality of what was about to happen slammed into Francesca. Quinn was walking into a deadly ambush, one he might not survive. One she'd set up.

"Wait!" She ran after him and reached out to stop him. "Don't go!" Immediately, the invisible arm pulling Gina to safety also stopped, leaving her suspended once more.

Quinn gave her a soul-searching look. "Don't go? Isn't that why we came here?"

"Yes, but . . ."

"Isn't that why you lied to me? So I would do what I'm doing and go in there?"

Shame seared her.

"What's happening?" Gina screamed, panic in her voice. "Why are you stopping? Please, just please . . ." She began to moan.

"What happens to Gina if I don't go?"

Francesca looked desperately from the horrible picture of her upside-down sister to Quinn, quietly standing there waiting for her response.

"I . . . oh, God, I don't know. I can't choose. Don't make me choose."

"You already did, Frannie," he said softly, and he gently tucked a stray strand of hair behind her ears. "You lied because you had to. It was a hard choice, but you made it." Abruptly, he leaned over, kissed her lightly on the mouth. "Gotta go." And he walked toward the building.

In a few seconds the plastic sheeting had swallowed him up.

"Zachariah!" His disembodied voice echoed from inside the building, and Francesca's heart thudded dully at the sound. "Zachari—"

And then silence.

Dark, motionless, endless silence.

What was happening?

She strained her ears, heard nothing.

A moan surged up from deep inside and she pressed a hand to her throat to stop it.

Was he already—?

No, she hadn't heard a shot. She hadn't heard anything. Not from Quinn or Gina. Maybe they were still alive. Maybe there was still a chance . . .

Her fingers clawed at something, and she looked down. Her hands were clenched around Quinn's gun. She stared at it.

Quinn's gun.

He might not be armed, but she was.

She was.

The thought exploded in her brain. Could she get inside without whoever was there noticing?

But she'd never touched a gun before. Hadn't a clue how it worked.

Just pull the trigger. How hard could that be?

The lights were trained on the half-finished building, but here, by the fence, she was more or less in shadow. She closed her eyes, took a breath for courage, and tightened her grip on the weapon. Then she began to sidle along the fence, hoping whoever was inside the building would be busy with Quinn.

Busy with Quinn.

She couldn't think about what that meant.

Turning the corner, she stopped to take stock of her position. She was out of sight of the front; was she out of sight period? She could only hope.

The distance between her and the building was maybe fifty yards of open ground. Could she make it without detection?

Only one way to find out.

Before she could think too hard about it, she dashed forward. The building yawned ahead, dark and furtive, and with every step she took it seemed to retreat two more.

But no one called out, no shots pinged.

She slipped through the plastic and halted, gulping air. While she waited for her heart to slow down, she looked up at the second story. Steel beams and girders crisscrossed overhead, leaving holes that would eventually be filled in with flooring. Since she'd circled around she was now on the east side of the building. Gina had been suspended from the west. Not only couldn't she see her, Francesca couldn't see a way of getting to her. There had to be ladders, a make-shift elevator, some way of getting up to the upper story, but none of those options were visible.

Something sounded to her left.

Voices?

She was wearing her bar shoes, which meant the rubber soles would absorb her footsteps. She crept toward the noise, and as she got closer the sounds resolved themselves into words.

". . . all make choices." That was Quinn. She inhaled a shaky but relieved breath. "A man takes the consequences."

"Yeah? Well, that's nice and philosophical of you, Quinn." That was the man on the phone. His voice still sounded so familiar. She wracked her brain trying to place him, but couldn't come up with a name.

"Tell you what," he was saying. "Since you're so fond of choices, you can choose this one last time." The tone hardened. "Stand or kneel? Back of the head or do you want to see it coming?"

Her heart nearly stopped, and for a minute, she couldn't go on.

"First, I want you to let Gina go. That was the deal, Michael."

Michael.

The name echoed in her head like a shock wave. Everything made clear and sudden sense.

Michael Zachariah, Joey's brother.

Michael Zachariah, who had disappeared—killed, everyone assumed, by Artie for sponsoring Quinn. But there he was in front of her, very much alive.

No wonder his voice had sounded familiar.

No wonder he wanted Quinn up close and personal.

Michael Zachariah must think he had a lot of payback owed him. Quinn had tricked him, lied to him, used him.

A stack of wood covered by a tarpaulin lay to one side. Pushing herself to move, she crept toward it, but her body was quaking so much she was afraid she'd knock some of it over.

She stiffened her shoulders, forced herself to more or less calm down and peek out.

Michael had most of his back to her. From her angle,

she couldn't see his arm, but she could see the huge black gun in his hand. The gun aimed squarely at Quinn.

Michael said, "I control the deal this time, not you."

Oh, God. She was going to throw up. She was going to throw up all over everywhere and they would hear her. And Michael would shoot Quinn and then her and then G—

Stop.

Okay. Okay. She could do this. She could . . . do . . . this.

Gritting her teeth, she shoved back the nausea and heard Quinn say, "Then keep your promise. Those girls have been lied to enough."

"I'm not the liar here."

Quinn's hands were in front, but tied. Despite the danger, he seemed calm. Relaxed even. How did he do that? Whatever the trick, she took strength from his seeming composure and managed to get her breathing under control. Slowly, she inched around the wood for a better look.

Michael was as thin as she remembered, thinner even, as though eaten up by something from the inside. Five or six years younger than Z, he'd never had Z's sharp good looks, but she didn't remember him being downright scrawny. He still had Z's hair, though. Black and longer than it should be. And greasy, as though he hadn't washed it in a while. A pair of jeans drooped loosely on his hips and his T-shirt was rumpled and stained. She could see the outline of a pack of cigarettes in the shirt pocket. He'd had a habit of hitching up his pants, and he did that now, automatically, as if the clothes were running away from him. He'd been a bit player in the Calvino organization, the guy who fetched and carried out the orders, but never issued any.

He was issuing plenty now.

"I gave you a choice, Quinn." He sniffed loudly, rubbed his nose with the back of his wrist. "Now I'm choosing for you. Down on the ground like the cockroach you are."

Heart in her throat, she watched as Michael forced Quinn to his knees.

"Your brother let you live, didn't he," Quinn said, a statement more than a question.

"Leave Z out of this."

"He's going to be pretty pissed that you're throwing away his gift."

"Gift? Oh, yeah, Z let me live, if you call that living,

away from everything and everyone." With his free forearm, he wiped his nose again. Then he shifted his stance. His shoulders twitched. It was as though he couldn't stay still for more than a minute. But he'd always been hyper, out of control. Or at least, that's what she gathered from things she'd overheard her father saying.

"You know what shit is?" Michael said. "Working for a living. That's not a life. That's what guys like you do."

"Z disobeyed Artie's orders, didn't he? He put himself on the line for you."

"So what? Artie's in hell where I hope he burns for eternity, so he can't do fuck all about it."

"Did you put him there?"

Michael shrugged. "Maybe."

"Nah, I don't think so. You're too much of a screwup. Z must've done it."

"I did it. Me! Now shut up!" He shoved the gun into the side of Quinn's head.

Francesca covered a gasp and raised her own gun, not sure what to do with it, especially since she couldn't keep her arm steady.

Quinn's calm voice droned on. "What about the two women? You going to take care of them, too?"

"I told you to shut up! Shut the fuck up!"

Francesca didn't even know when she'd made her decision. She only knew she had. Briefly she closed her eyes, then tightened her hold on Quinn's gun, and darted forward. Before she could breathe, she pressed the trigger.

Nothing happened.

A little cry escaped her. What was wrong? Why didn't it fire? She pressed the trigger again, but by now Michael had heard her.

"Get out of here, Frannie!" Quinn cried. He lunged at Michael, who easily sidestepped him. Before she knew what was happening, Michael had grabbed her, disarmed her, and shoved his gun at her head.

With a brutal tug around her throat, Michael said roughly, "You ever shot a gun, Frannie? First you gotta take the safety off."

Quinn half rose. "Let her go!"

Michael kicked him back. "Stay there, you fuckhead. Don't move."

He was squeezing her neck, his arm pressed against her windpipe. Grunting, she tried to twist out of his grasp, but Michael only held her tighter, squashing her painfully against him. His face was close; she could smell his sour cigarette breath. "After what he did, how can you care what happens to him?"

"Leave her alone!"

"Answer me!" Michael shook her so hard her teeth rattled. "How can you give a fuck about this piece of shit?"

Her eyes locked with Quinn's. She could barely breathe, let alone talk. "I don't know," she choked out. "I just do."

With a vicious shove, he heaved her roughly to the ground. "You think he's worth saving, you deserve whatever he's got coming."

He kicked her weapon away. It slid over the ground, bounced against a beam, and tumbled out of sight on the other side, disappearing into the darkness between the beams and the wall. She watched it vanish with a sick feeling.

Michael's hate-filled eyes turned to her and her mouth dried up. She began to quiver uncontrollably.

"You don't want her, Michael. You want me." Quinn crawled away from her, stopping just short of Michael's feet.

"You got that right." A satisfied smirk crossed Michael's face as Quinn knelt before him. "You gonna beg now? Ooh, I'd like that." He started pacing in front of him, a drill sergeant surveying a single troop with tense, jerky steps. "Yeah, I'd like that almost as much as killing you." He chuckled, the tone a sneer. "Almost."

Quinn scurried on his knees, following the other man's movements. "Yeah, I'll beg." He was being shamed and degraded, and she could barely watch. But each time he moved away he went a little further, so she had a clear view of his humiliation. Tears blurred her eyes.

"I'll do whatever you want. Just let Francesca and Gina go."

"I can't hear you," Michael said in a sing-song voice. "Go ahead." The smirk on his face widened in scorn. "Beg."

"Please."

"Please what?"

Francesca couldn't bear it. "Don't, Quinn." She thought of her father and how he'd died shamed and alone. Her voice cracked. "Don't do it."

"Come on," Michael mocked, "beg real nice and maybe I'll shoot her before I shoot you." He backed Quinn up, forcing him to scuttle like a beetle until he was pressed against the wall beams. "Say it, you fucking traitor. Please don't do what?"

"Please don't"—in one breath-clogging acrobatic twist, Quinn ducked, reached behind the beams with his tied hands, came up with his gun, and fired it—"shoot me."

Francesca screamed, and Quinn dove in front of her.

Michael staggered, fell to one knee, and raised his gun. Quinn shot him again.

Francesca flinched, then gaped in openmouthed horror as Michael looked down at his chest, where dark stains were already spreading.

"You fucking asshole," he said, and fell over with a horrifying thump.

Chapter 5

Francesca stared at the lifeless form on the ground. Her brain was on stop, her body on freeze. But not Quinn. He shoved Michael's gun away, then checked his neck for a pulse.

"There's a knife in my right front pocket. Get it out."

Michael's eyes were open and glazed over. Francesca gaped at them, repelled and fascinated.

"Frannie," Quinn said, and she heard his voice from a distance. "Frannie!" He took her chin in his tied hands, turning her toward him. "Look at me. Look at me!" She obeyed, and forced to concentrate on his face, his dear, alive face, the world came back into focus. "You with me now?" he said.

She nodded.

"Get the knife out of my pocket and cut the ropes."

She followed his instructions and freed his hands. He took out a cell phone. While he punched something in, he looked wildly above him.

"Gina!" he shouted. "Gina! Where are you?"

"Here!" came her sister's weak voice from somewhere above and to the left. "Up here."

He shoved the phone at Francesca. "Tell Stellman what happened, where we are, and that Michael Zachariah is dead." Then he disappeared around a corner.

Francesca heard a thud and scrabbling sounds. Then Stellman answered and she was too busy talking to hear anything more. Finishing quickly, she followed Quinn and found him on the second story, holding the top of a ladder while Gina climbed down.

A cry, and then her sister was in her arms.

"Toss me the phone." Quinn was on his stomach, hands reaching down at them from the opening above. He caught the phone and disappeared.

"Oh, God, are you all right?" Francesca did a minute inventory, examining Gina with frantic hands. "What did he do to you?"

"I'm . . . I'm okay."

"Sure?" They were both crying and shuddering, clinging to each other with desperation.

"I was so scared," Gina said through sobs.

"Me, too," Francesca said. "But it's over now. We're okay. We're all okay."

"Francesca." Quinn was calling her. She glanced up, but couldn't hear him over the sound of her own and Gina's tears. Taking a deep breath, she ran a hand over her sister's hair. "It's all right. Ssh, you're okay. Let me talk to Quinn for a minute."

Gina nodded and stepped away, though she kept her hand locked tightly in Francesca's.

Quinn's grim face sent a leap of fear through Francesca. "What is it?"

"Tony. He's too messed up to climb down by himself." Gina started moaning again, and Francesca pulled her close.

"Is he . . . is he going to be all right?" Gina asked fearfully.

"I don't know," Quinn said. "I hope so. I called the fire department. They'll take him down with a harness." He gave Francesca a hard look. "Get her out of here. Wait outside for Stellman. I'll stay with the boy."

She searched his face, realized she didn't want to leave him. What if something happened to him while she was gone?

"It's okay," he said quietly, and clearly misinterpreting, added, "You'll be fine."

She opened her mouth to correct the misunderstanding, but he looked over his shoulder, presumably to the injured Tony, then back at her. "Don't want to leave him alone too long," he said, and disappeared.

Arms around each other, she and Gina trudged outside to wait for help. Ten minutes later the sirens started, and soon they were surrounded by police cars, ambulances, and a fire truck. Francesca thought she'd never stop shaking, but knew it must be some kind of adrenaline reaction that would fade eventually. When she could stop hearing the shots, seeing the blood, the faces of the dead and dying.

In between sobs, Gina's story tumbled out. How she and Tony first met at Hadley Park. How she'd been repelled yet oddly fascinated by who he was. How he persuaded her to see him and how she agreed.

"I knew you wouldn't want me to," Gina said, her words halting because she was still crying. "But he's just . . . I don't know, he's just so cute, I couldn't"—she hiccupped—"couldn't say no."

"It's okay," Francesca soothed, but inside she wondered if Gina was also attracted exactly because she knew her sister wouldn't approve.

"We'd go to the mansion and hang out at the p-p-pool." She shuddered. "Remember how we used to do that? Before Daddy . . . "

"Sure I remember." And suddenly it made a kind of sad sense. The Calvinos, the house, the pool, it represented life as they used to know it. No wonder Gina took her chances and grabbed at it.

Gina gulped amid a fresh burst of tears. "I'm sorry, Frannie."

"Ssh. None of this is your fault." She smoothed Gina's matted hair. "So you went over there tonight?"

Gina nodded. "That's why I couldn't tell you."

"Yeah, I kind of figured that out," Francesca said dryly.

"We were in the pool house." Gina blushed ferociously. "We heard a noise. Tony said they were gunshots. He peeked out and saw someone bending over his uncle."

"Who?"

She shook her head. "He didn't know. It was dark and he saw him from the back. Whoever it was, he was all crouched over. But Tony said we had to leave. I didn't even know if the guy was still out there. Tony made us wait a few minutes, then just started running." She was shaking. "I saw him, Frannie. Oh, God, there was blood and st-st-stuff all over. It turned the water in the pool red."

Francesca pulled her sister into her arms. "Don't think about it. Just think that you're safe now."

For a few minutes, they just held each other. Then Francesca asked, "Did you go to Rudy's first?"

Gina gasped; the sound snagged short by a ragged breath. "How . . . how did you know?"

"Quinn tracked you there. And to the park." Francesca hesitated, but she needed to know everything. "Did you . . . you weren't doing drugs, were you?"

Gina shook her head.

"Tony didn't . . . he didn't give you anything?"

"I swear. We were just trying to figure out where to go next."

A whisper of relief ran through Francesca. One less worry to deal with. "And then?"

"Then Uncle Mike called Tony. We didn't even know who he was at first, we hadn't seen him in . . . in forever, but he said how he used to come over and everything, and then I remembered him and Daddy and Uncle Z . . . " Her voice trailed off and she hiccupped.

Francesca stroked her back, soothing her and urging her to continue at the same time. Gina and Tony had been kids when Michael disappeared. They would have had no idea he was supposed to be dead and buried.

"He said . . . he said he would help us, but when we got here, there was n-n-nothing but this . . . this half a building." She started sobbing again. "And he pushed me. And when Tony tried to stop him, he shot Tony."

A medic approached and addressed Francesca. "You need anything?"

She shook her head.

"Okay. Let me take a look at her." He nodded toward Gina, who clung to Francesca and shook her head violently, making the spiny ends of her orange hair dance wildly. Her face was a sooty mess, smudged makeup giving her eyes a bludgeoned look.

Francesca's heart twisted. "It's okay," she soothed. "I'll be right here."

Slowly, she disengaged her sister, whose breath gulped and stuttered as the medic examined her.

"How . . . how's Tony?" Gina asked with a hitch in her voice.

"Last I checked, he's holding his own," the medic said. "With any luck, he'll be fine."

That seemed to comfort Gina a bit, and she gave the medic a watery smile.

Francesca took that moment of distraction to scan the area for Quinn. She didn't see him in the huddles of police inside the fence, but she did see a familiar face. The detective she'd talked to on the phone. Stellman.

She caught his eye, and he tramped through the fence to her, as rumpled and stooped as he'd been earlier, as though the events of the evening had had no effect on him, good or bad. She, on the other hand, was exhausted. She couldn't wait to take Gina home and collapse in bed.

"Miss Bern?"

She nodded.

"Everything all right?"

She indicated the medic with Gina. "We're fine. Just waiting for word we can leave." She hesitated, then continued. "I was wondering about Quinn. I mean . . . Detective Lewis."

Stellman peered at her sharply. "He's doing okay. He's inside going over the scene." He gestured toward the building. "Why?"

She shook her head. "Just . . . no reason." She gave him an embarrassed look. "Well, I'd like to . . . to thank him."

Stellman scrutinized her, evidently battling some inner decision. Finally, he took her by the arm and drew her aside. "Look, Miss Bern—"

"Francesca, please."

"Okay. Francesca. The thing is, Detective Lewis, Quinn, he . . . well, he had a pretty rough time after you dumped him. The thing with your father, it tore him up, I mean really messed with him."

"Did it?" She frowned. From what she'd heard, Quinn had hardly missed a beat.

"Yes, it did," he said firmly. He watched her closely, as though trying to figure her out. "You know, he spoke for your father."

That took her aback. She stared at the older man. "What do you mean?"

"Quinn—Detective Lewis—he spoke for leniency. Did a pretty good job, too, if I remember the way things fell out. The DA went for a lesser charge, didn't she? Check with

Corso," he said, mentioning her father's lawyer. "See if I'm not right."

Her heart thumped. Chuck Corso had never mentioned this to her. Of course, she'd refused to let anyone speak about Quinn in her presence . . .

Stellman looked out toward the half-finished building as though Quinn was there, pleading for her father. "You know, what happened to your father inside . . ." His mashed-in face swung back to her. "It wasn't right. But it wasn't Quinn's fault." He weighed his words carefully. "I've known Quinn since he was a kid, knew his father, the family. He used to be a cocky SOB—pardon my French— but that all changed after, well, after what happened with you. He had a great career going, was a natural as a UC— uh, undercover cop," he explained at her blank look. "But what happened with you and your family, it was too much for him. He went on a three-month drunk, nearly got kicked off the job. As it is, he asked to be transferred out of undercover work—"

That startled her. "He asked? His choice?"

"Oh, yeah, most definitely his choice."

"That's not what he told me."

"No?" Stellman shrugged. "Maybe he didn't want you to know. Didn't want to put that burden on you. Make you feel it was your fault."

Heat suffused her face. If that was true, he'd been kinder than she had.

"Or maybe he was just too proud to say so," Stellman continued. "But he did ask for the transfer. Even went behind a desk for a while. He's only just got his feet on the ground again, and I gotta tell you, Miss Bern—Francesca—I don't know if he can go another round with you."

She saw now where all this had been leading. "Oh." She tossed a wan smile at him. "I get it. Better not ask about him, then. Is that what you're trying to say? Better stay away?"

He spread his hands in a gesture of indecision. "That's up to you and him. But, well, he's punished himself enough, if you know what I mean." Stellman shoved a hand in a pants pocket and jingled some coins. "So . . . " He looked around. "You give anyone a statement?"

"I spoke with several officers. Someone said I could come down to the station tomorrow for the official version."

"Good." He nodded. "That's good." And then he shuffled away.

She watched him go, riveted by what he'd told her. Quinn had shattered, too. His life had changed, just as hers had.

She didn't know what to do with that, would need time to turn it over, examine it, explore the implications.

In the meantime, the medic released Gina, and Detective Stellman arranged for a patrol car to drive them home.

They stumbled through the door, up the stairs, and into Francesca's bed together. Despite their exhaustion, it took them a long time to fall asleep.

The doorbell woke her. Francesca groaned, heard the buzzer again, and sat up. Gina stirred, and Francesca looked down at her. She was curled on her side, clutching a much-worn Raggedy Ann doll. Her crazy hair lay in frayed orange shreds around her still-dirty face. Francesca brushed the hair back, whispered a soothing word, and slipped out of bed.

Sunlight streamed through the windows as she went downstairs to answer the door. She was fully dressed, still wearing the same clothes as the night before, and she checked her watch. It was almost three. They'd slept the whole day.

She yawned, peeked through the peep hole, and saw Quinn on the stoop. He looked showered and shaved and fresher than he had a right to be. And alive. So whole and alive. A nervous flutter of joy leapt in her chest as she opened the door.

"Breakfast?" He held up a Rudy's bag.

She stood aside to let him in. "Thanks," she said.

He paused in the entryway for a quick scan of the place. "So this is where you've been hiding."

She sent him a dry twist of a smile. "Not much compared to Cliff Road."

"At least it's honest."

Their gazes met. "Yes, at least it's that."

He shuffled his feet, glanced away. "So . . . Gina okay?"

She nodded. "She's upstairs sleeping."

"Probably the best thing."

He lifted the bag. "Where can I put this?"

She led him into the kitchen, and he put the bag on the counter, emptying it of three cups of coffee and three cookies: a giant chocolate chip, a linzer cookie with half the sugar rubbed off, and a black and white with a thumbprint in the chocolate half.

"Thought you could use some sustenance." He pushed a cup of coffee and the black and white toward her. "Not to mention a little caffeine and sugar."

For some reason her eyes welled up. She looked from the cookies to his face. It was blank and unreadable.

"Thank you," she said.

"Hey, it's just a cookie." He reached out and caught the tear sliding down her cheek.

She nodded. "I know. But thanks anyway."

He gave her a crooked grin. She remembered that grin. Oh, how she remembered that grin.

"You're welcome," he said simply.

They stared at each other. A flush of heat rose up Francesca's neck. If he noticed, he didn't say.

"So . . . " He cleared his throat. "How's Gina?"

She smiled. "You already asked me that."

"Did I?"

She nodded.

"Damn," he muttered and cleared his throat. "What did you say?"

"She's sleeping."

"Oh, yeah. Right." He took the lid off his coffee, but didn't drink it. "So . . ."

"So . . . " she echoed softly, and for a minute couldn't think of a thing to say except what she couldn't. That she was so glad he was there in her kitchen and they were staring stupidly at each other over cookies from Rudy's. "So," she repeated. "I guess I owe you an apology."

"Yeah? What for?"

"Almost getting you killed."

"Ah." His mouth curled into a tight, wry smile. "What's a little betrayal between friends?"

Her breath caught. How could he joke about it?

Then again, was there any point in crying over it anymore?

"I'm sorry," she said.

"Me, too," he said.

Silence descended between them. The clock on the kitchen wall ticked noisily, and outside someone started a mower.

He broke the stalemate by ripping open a pack of sugar and pouring it into his coffee. "I've been thinking."

"Yeah?"

"Uh-huh."

"About?"

He shrugged and stirred the sugar. "Maybe things between us could be . . . different."

"Different?" She thought about what that might mean. And what it didn't. "You broke my heart, Quinn."

For a second he stopped stirring, as though braced for whatever came next. She gave it to him.

"You broke my heart and wrecked my life." Those tears welled again, and she battled to get them under control. "And then . . . then last night you handed it all back to me. What am I supposed to do with that?"

Slowly, he shook his head, a glimmer of hope in his eyes. "I don't know, Frannie. I wish to God I did. I just know I love you. I want to stop. I do. Life would be a hell of a lot easier if I could. But the truth is . . ." He paused, traced the cardboard rim of the coffee cup, then looked at her. "The truth is I'll probably die loving you."

"You almost did."

His mouth thinned. "That was my job."

"You walked in there knowingly. Without a way to defend yourself. I can't tell you how grateful I am."

"I don't want your gratitude."

She almost asked him what he did want, but she already knew the answer. Crisply, she said, "Sorry, Quinn, you've got it anyway. My gratitude and my forgiveness." And the rest? Why couldn't she say the rest?

Again, his mouth bent into the semblance of a smile. "Well, that's a start. I can't say I haven't hoped for more, but I sure as hell expected less."

He offered to drive her to the Calvinos' to pick up her car, so she left him to shower and change. Gina woke as Francesca was drying her hair. She came into the bathroom sleepy eyed, one side of her hair mashed against her head.

"Where are you going?" She levered herself onto the edge of the vanity and yawned.

"Quinn is here," Francesca said. "I left my car at the Calvinos' and he's going to drive me there."

A flash of fear ran across Gina's face.

"It's okay," Francesca said, thinking Gina wouldn't want to be left alone. "You can come if you like."

Gina shook her head violently. "I don't want to go near that place. Ever."

Francesca put down the dryer. "What if I ask Mrs. Margulies to stay with you? Just until I get back. A half hour." Mrs. Margulies was their next-door neighbor. She was a retired schoolteacher who didn't let Gina get away with much, and Gina wasn't fond of her.

It was a sign of how much she didn't want to be alone that Gina agreed with alacrity. "She can make hot chocolate. She makes good hot chocolate."

"Quinn brought you a linzer cookie."

Her face brightened. "He did?"

Francesca smiled. "He did."

Gina looked at her with wise eyes. "Are you and he . . ." She made a circle in the air as if to indicate oneness.

Francesca thought about it. "I don't know. How would you feel if we were?"

Gina pursed her mouth, taking inventory. "He saved us."

Francesca nodded. "Uh-huh."

"But he also hurt us."

Again, Francesca nodded, the pros and cons stacking up.

"But saving us, Frannie. That was big. That should count for something." She gave Francesca a wide-eyed look. "And he did bring me that cookie. Besides," she said, her mouth turning up in a sly smile, "I saw the way you looked at him last night."

Francesca felt herself blush. "Oh yeah?"

"Yeah. Like *he* was a linzer cookie."

Frannie swatted her sister off the counter and out of the bathroom. "You see way too much for a kid."

Gina hooted as she bounded out. "I'm not a kid. But I am a good observer. That's why I'm going to be a great artist."

When Francesca came down, Quinn was sitting in the living room, where he'd never been before, big and awkward, his hands lolling loosely between his knees. He jumped up when he saw her, and whether it was the shower, the clean clothes, or the sight of him, she didn't know, but the universe lurched again, leaving her reeling.

She stared at him, the echo of the sensation from their first meeting years ago reverberating inside her.

"You look nice," he said into the awkward silence.

She'd thrown on a pair of jeans and an old T-shirt. "Nice" didn't even come close. But she managed to find her voice and say, "Thanks."

On the way out, she stopped in the kitchen where Gina and Mrs. Margulies were arguing over how much sugar to put in the hot chocolate. Gina had tugged on a ratty pair of paint-smeared overalls, but her face was deliciously free of makeup.

"I appreciate you staying," she said to Mrs. Margulies, and to Gina, "Don't drive her nuts."

"She likes it," Gina said. "Why do you think she comes over?"

Mrs. Margulies had a straight back, a large bosom, and a face as hard as iron, but Francesca thought she saw a twinkle in her eyes.

"Go," the older woman said.

"Ready?" Quinn appeared at the doorway.

"Okay." Francesca took a breath, let herself trust that Gina would be all right until she got back, and followed Quinn out.

Behind her, Gina shouted. "Yo, Quinn! Don't forget what I told you."

Francesca gave Quinn a swift look. She could only imagine what that brat had been up to behind her back. "What did she say?"

Quinn opened the front door for her. "Nothing."

"Look, I know my sister. She's not exactly discreet. What did she say?"

He shrugged and led her to his car. "It's between me and her."

Francesca crossed her arms. "I'm not getting in until you tell me."

Quinn looked at her soberly, but the corners of his

mouth twitched. "She promised to break my knees if I hurt you again."

When they got to the Calvino estate, the place looked deserted. A police sawhorse blocked the entrance, no one was milling around, and the cars and ambulances had gone with the night.

Her Saturn was parked where she'd left it, on the side of the road across from the gates. Quinn pulled in behind it and turned off the engine. "What's your schedule?"

"First I have to see if I still have a job. I ran out on Sal last night."

"Can I take you and Gina for dinner? Maybe the Baypointe Inn. It's nice there. Quiet."

She looked at him. In his eyes she saw what neither of them said. This could be a start. A new beginning. Did she want that? She searched her heart and found that she did. But her father used to take her and Gina to the Baypointe Inn for birthdays. If they were going to start over, they'd need new memories. "How about you, me, Gina, and a pizza?"

That slow, sexy grin spread across his face. "Even better. Seven?"

"We'll have to do it earlier if Sal wants me tonight. I'll call you."

He walked her to her car and waited while she opened the door. She started to get in, then turned back. "I . . . I don't have your number."

"Call the station. If I'm not there, they'll know where to find me." He handed her a business card.

She stared down at it, the fact that she didn't even know how to contact him symbolic of how far apart they'd been and how odd that felt now.

She slid inside, and he closed the car door behind her. She rolled down the window. "Talk to you later."

As she drove away she saw him standing beside the driver's door. He raised an arm and waved.

Quinn watched Francesca drive away, a weird warm feeling in his chest. As if the hole that had been there for years was slowly closing up. All at once the sky seemed bluer, the day brighter. He found himself grinning as he started toward his car. He was due back at the station. There were still a few unanswered questions to go over with Stellman, and he wanted to put a dent in the mountain of paperwork waiting for him.

He opened the door, and a voice called out from behind him. "Hands on the roof, Detective!"

He spun around, reaching for his weapon, but a shot rang out before he got there. Something bit into his side.

"Want another one? Grab for your piece again, I'll give it to you."

He'd been hit. Badly? He didn't know. He couldn't look. A wave of nausea washed over him and his heart was beating hard enough to fly. But he forced himself to ignore everything and concentrate on the moment and the familiar voice.

"Hands on the roof where I can see them!"

He obeyed. "This is stupid, Z. A sucker play."

"Who's the sucker here, Detective? And who's holding the gun?"

Footsteps approached from behind.

"Why are you doing this?"

"You killed Michael." Z reached around and took Quinn's gun from his holster.

"Jesus, Z, he would have killed Francesca and Gina."

"That was bullshit. Just a way to get leverage on you. He had no intention of hurting those girls."

"That's not the way it looked last night."

"I don't give a shit how it looked! Turn around. Slowly!"

He followed the command. "Is that why you took out Artie? Because he'd found out you disobeyed him and let Michael live?"

"Artie had a smart mouth. Too smart. I got tired of listening to it."

He was facing Z now. The man's rough face was cold and hard.

"That's why you cut out his tongue. So he couldn't order you to take out your brother again." Quinn shook his head. "What did Michael do, show up out of the blue? He always was a weak, whiney screwup."

"Shut up!"

"It was him shot you at the park, Z. The casing I found matched the shells in his gun. Probably aiming for me, but got you instead. Once a loser, always a loser."

"Shut the fuck up. Move. Keep your hands where I can

see them." He gestured harshly with his Beretta for Quinn to precede him, then followed, poking Quinn in the back with the barrel.

They were almost across the road when a car came careening down the street. Quinn recognized it at once as Francesca's. His breath clogged. What was she doing? If she didn't stop, she was going to—

Z whirled, realized what was about to happen, and raised his gun.

"No!" Quinn slammed into Z's arm, throwing off his aim but also pitching him into the car's oncoming path.

Francesca slammed on the brakes, but too late. Z hit the front end with a stomach-churning thud, flew several yards in the air, and landed with an equally appalling crack.

Francesca leaped out of the car and ran to him. "Oh, my God." She glanced wildly at Quinn and back down at Z. "I saw him in the rearview mirror. I didn't want to—I only wanted to stop him!" She stood frozen and bug-eyed over Z's lifeless body. "Oh, my God. Oh, my God." She kept repeating it over and over.

"It's all right," Quinn mumbled. Now that the immediate danger was over, he felt woozy and unsteady. He managed to get over to Francesca and put an arm around her. "It's all right. Call—" His legs buckled out from under him.

"Quinn!"

Without quite knowing how, he found himself on his knees in the road.

"What's the matter, what's wrong?" Her voice was frantic and her hands, her sweet, soft hands, were all over him. She opened his jacket. "Oh, my God," she moaned. "You're bleeding."

He looked down at his side. The white shirt was covered in sticky red blood. "Shit," he said, and felt like puking all over again.

She called 911, and half walked, half dragged him over to the side of the road, where he collapsed on the ground and leaned against his car to wait for the ambulance. He was cold and the shakes had started.

"You're going into shock," she said anxiously. There were no blankets, so she wrapped her arms around him and used her body heat to keep him warm.

"Never thought I'd have to take a bullet to get you to hold me again," he said, his teeth chattering.

"Don't joke about it."

"Not exactly the new start I was hoping for." God, he felt tired.

She burst into tears.

"Don't, Frannie. Don't. Don't. It's okay. I promise . . . everything's going to be . . ." But he was fading, his eyes felt so heavy.

"Quinn. Quinn! Don't you leave me!"

Not going anywhere, Francesca Bern.

But sleep sounded so good right now . . .

Someone shook him. Violently. A searing pain stabbed into him. "Ouch! Okay, okay, I'll, Christ, I'll stay awake . . . but you have to . . ." The rest was lost in a moan.

"What?"

"Answer a question," he croaked out.

"A question? Are you crazy? Now is not the time for a conversation."

"Last night . . . with—with Zachariah. I told you to leave. Why"—he coughed and it hurt like shit—"didn't you?"

"Lie still, don't talk."

He pushed the words through the pain. "Why, Frannie?"

"Oh, for God's sake."

He closed his eyes, and it did the trick.

"No!" she screamed. "Stay with me!"

He opened them, stared into hers. "You could've left. Run. Why didn't you?"

She avoided his gaze. "You know why."

"I don't." He coughed again. "Ah, Jesus, when is that ambulance getting here?"

"Soon."

He groaned. "I need to know, Frannie. Right now, before I pass out."

"Don't you dare."

"Then answer the damn question," he grunted.

She bit her lip. "I couldn't just leave you there."

"Plenty would. Why not?"

She frowned.

"It hurts to talk. Don't make me ask you again. Why, Frannie?"

"Because I love you! Okay?" She tugged him to her,

resettling him and sending agony up his side. "Happy now? I love you. I don't want to live in a world without you. So lie still and shut up, do you hear me? And stay awake!"

In the distance came the wail of a siren. But all he heard were the words she'd just said.

I love you.

He smiled and drifted off. She loved him.

Everything was going to be just fine.

ENDLESS NIGHT

Carla Cassidy

Chapter 1

She was going to kill her.

Amanda Kincaid narrowed her eyes and smiled at her older sister across the restaurant table. Amanda would pull Cara's bleached blond hairs out one at a time by their darkened roots. It seemed a fitting punishment for Cara setting Amanda up on the blind date from hell.

She cast a surreptitious glance at the man seated next to her. According to Cara and her husband, Harry, Clay Murdock was perfect for her. Harry had met the tall, handsome man at the gym and the two men had struck up a friendship.

"He just moved to town, Amanda, and he's single, gorgeous, and straight," Cara had said.

Certainly the man was easy on the eyes with his dark hair and midnight blue eyes. She'd been aware of other women in the restaurant admiring him.

Dressed in a black shirt that emphasized his wide shoulders and tailored charcoal slacks that molded to lean hips, he had a sexy, utterly masculine aura that drew women.

And he had the personality of a slug.

He'd barely spoken ten words throughout the meal, without ever looking at her after their initial introduction. She'd spent the last two hours with him and had learned that he worked in the construction business and had been in town only three months. He'd offered nothing more personal about himself and hadn't seemed the least bit interested in anything personal about her.

As far as she was concerned, the man was rude and antisocial. She couldn't wait for this date to be over.

She breathed a sigh of relief as Harry asked for their check. Now, all she had to do was endure taking him home and after that she'd never see Clay Murdock again. She hadn't decided if she'd ever speak to her sister and brother-in-law again.

It was bad enough that the date had been so awful, it was insult to injury that she had to drive the man home because he'd had car problems earlier in the day and his car was now in the shop. If it weren't for the fact that he was so clearly reluctant to be out on this date, she might have thought that his car troubles were an attempt to orchestrate some time alone.

The bill was paid, good-byes were said and she found herself alone with him in her car. Fifteen more minutes, she told herself. Fifteen more minutes and he'd be nothing more than a bad memory.

"I hope you don't have to go too far out of your way to drop me at home," he said, breaking the stifling silence that had been the norm for the evening. It was the longest sentence he'd uttered all night.

"It's not a problem," she replied. In truth, it wasn't. His apartment was only a ten-minute drive from her small house. She'd toss him out at the curb, then be on her way.

The Kansas City traffic was light for a Friday night. Even though Clay fell silent once again, it was impossible to ignore his presence.

The scent of him filled the interior of the car, a wonderful blend of spicy cologne and pure male. Despite his silence there was an intensity, a simmering energy about him that sparked in the air and made her stomach twist in an uncomfortable knot.

She couldn't imagine why Cara and Harry thought the man would be perfect for her. There were chocoholics and talkaholics and she was definitely the latter. There was nothing she found more stimulating, more sexy than a spirited conversation.

Clay Murdock appeared capable only of two- or three-word sentences. The only spirited things about him were the two drinks he'd had before dinner.

Isn't that the way it always is, she thought ruefully. In her thirty-one years of life she had discovered that good-looking, well-adjusted men were as unique as two-headed calves.

With a grateful sigh, she pulled up in front of his apartment complex and came to a stop.

"Thanks, Amanda. I had a nice time," he said. It was a lie and she knew it.

"Yeah, so did I," she lied right back. These were the kind of little white lies that were socially acceptable, especially at the end of a very bad date.

He opened the passenger door and stepped out, but leaned down and offered her a smile that didn't quite reach the depths of his thick-lashed eyes. "Again, I apologize for you having to bring me home." He frowned, as if contemplating saying something else. As far as she was concerned there was nothing he could say to put a good spin on a miserable night.

A sharp crack split the silence of the sultry summer night. Almost simultaneously the back passenger window shattered. Amanda screamed; at the same time she saw a man standing across the street, a gun in his hand aimed directly at her car.

Time moved in slow motion. The only thing moving quickly was her heart, which pounded a frantic rhythm. Her gaze locked with the gunman's.

Despite the distance between them she felt the unemotional coldness radiating from his eyes, saw the sheen of his bald head beneath the glow of a nearby streetlamp. What was happening? Her mind worked to make sense of the situation.

He fired again. She saw the spark from the muzzle and instinctively ducked her head and squeezed her eyes tightly shut. The passenger door flung open and she looked to see Clay jump inside.

"Drive!" he commanded.

She stared at him blankly.

He cursed, reached over and threw the gearshift into D, then pressed his hand on her knee, forcing her foot to the gas pedal. The tires squealed in a spin, then gripped and the car shot forward.

Chapter 2

"Turn left," he demanded.

He was practically on top of her as she approached the intersection. The light turned yellow and she braked in automatic response.

"Screw the light. Go! Go!"

She'd never run a red light in her life, but she did now, catching her breath as she managed to slide through right in front of a delivery truck who vented his rage with a blast of his horn.

"Pull over, let me drive."

She'd never been so happy for a suggestion in her life. She slowed, and before the car had come to a complete halt, he half scooted beneath her, unfastened her seat belt and lifted her to the passenger seat.

She'd barely caught her breath before he grabbed the wheel and jammed on the gas, and they lurched forward at warp speed.

Once again she closed her eyes, fear choking in her throat as she heard the roar of a car behind them. She turned her head to see a dark sports car hurtling toward them.

"Buckle up," Clay said.

She gasped and screamed as he shot across two lanes of traffic and made a sharp right turn. She grabbed the seat belt and yanked it across her chest and into the fastener.

Somebody had tried to kill them. Some man she'd never seen before had pointed a gun and fired into her car. Now that person was careening toward them in a vehicle with the apparent intent to finish the job.

The back window exploded. Clay cursed as another scream ripped from her throat. "Get down, get down," he yelled.

She ducked her head, her heart nearly pounding out of her chest as the seat belt half strangled her. Her head slammed into the door as Clay made an abrupt sharp left turn.

Once again she squeezed her eyes closed and tried to make sense of what was happening. She couldn't imagine anyone wanting to kill her. She led a quiet life. She worked in an arts and crafts store, her salary supplemented by an inheritance left to her by her maternal grandmother. She spent Tuesday afternoons reading stories to children in the local library and had good relationships with her neighbors.

This couldn't be about her. It had to be about him.

She raised her head just enough to stare at the man who had been the worst date she'd ever experienced. Where before he'd looked distant but handsome, he now looked deadly and dangerous.

In the illumination from the dash his chiseled features looked stark. Tension knotted his firm jaw and his eyes were narrowed. His hands were white-knuckled as he gripped the steering wheel.

He made a right turn, the car feeling as if it careened around the corner on two wheels. The force of the turn sent Amanda's head banging into his hard thigh. As she pulled away she realized blood seeped through his shirt on his right arm.

"You're hurt," she exclaimed as fear built to a new height inside her.

He grunted, not taking his eyes off the road. Amanda fought back a hysterical giggle. She was being driven down the streets of Kansas City at neck-breaking speed by a man she didn't like who very well might be bleeding to death in the seat next to her.

"You need to get to a doctor."

He cast her a quick, dark glance, then returned his attention straight ahead. "I'm a little busy right now." As if to emphasize his point he screeched around another corner. The momentum forced a scream past Amanda's lips. "And could you stop screaming? You're giving me one hell of a headache."

"Excuse me, but what difference does it make if you have a headache or not? You're either going to bleed to death or we're both going to die in a fiery car crash."

He cast her a quick, sharp glance. "I figured you for an uptight pessimist the moment I first laid eyes on you."

Before she could respond he flew around another corner to the sound of blaring horns and screeching tires. She closed her eyes once again and braced for the impact of another car crashing into hers.

Minutes ticked by and she sensed their speed slowing. She ventured a glance at him and saw that his knuckles were no longer white, although through the tear in his shirt she could see that the wound in his arm still oozed blood.

"I think we've lost him," he said, breaking the tense silence. "What's your address?"

"921 Magenta Avenue." She sat up in the seat, her gaze lingering on him. "Are you going to tell me what's going on?"

He hesitated a beat, then replied, "Hell if I know."

She didn't believe him. She wasn't sure why but she was certain he'd just lied to her. She chewed on her bottom lip and glanced behind them, grateful that there was no sign of the dark sports car that had been following them.

As much as she wanted to get home and get away from him, it was obvious he needed immediate medical attention. "You need to get to a hospital and get your arm looked at, then we need to call the police and report all of this."

"No hospital and no police."

She stared at him once again, wondering if she'd heard him wrong. "Excuse me?"

He flashed her a dark, cold look. "I'm not going to the hospital and we aren't calling the police."

A cold chill washed over her. There was only one reason a person wouldn't go to the appropriate authorities under these circumstances.

Who was this man? What was he hiding? What kind of man had Cara and Harry placed in her path?

She wasn't sure who frightened her more, the man who had shot at them or the man behind the wheel of her car.

Chapter 3

Clay pulled into the driveway at 921 Magenta Avenue. A lamp burned in the window of the neat little ranch house radiating a faint glow into the darkness of the night. He had more important things on his mind than assessing the place where his date for the evening lived.

"I'd like to come in and clean up my arm," he said as he cut the engine and turned to look at her.

It was obvious she wasn't thrilled by the idea. She looked scared. Her green eyes were wide and he saw a pulse beating madly in the hollow of her throat.

She should be scared. If his evaluation of what had just occurred was correct, then not only was he in danger but she was as well.

She appeared frozen, and he didn't have time to sweet-talk or pacify her. His arm was killing him. Despite the burning pain, he thought it was probably just a flesh wound. Still, he needed to get it cleaned up and figure out what his next move was going to be.

"Come on, let's go." He opened his car door, grateful when she did the same.

"You'll clean up your arm and then you'll go?" she asked as she unlocked her front door.

"I promise," he lied.

She led him through a living room that Martha Stewart would have been proud of, one decorated with crafty wall hangings and crocheted doilies and hand-painted furniture.

He wasn't surprised. She looked the type to spend her evenings doing arts and crafts. In the two hours he'd just spent having dinner with her, he'd found her to be quiet and just a little bit boring.

Although she was pretty in a subtle, unassuming way, it had taken him two seconds to recognize she wasn't his type.

The problem was he wasn't sure what kind of woman was his type. He'd spent the last five years of his life with hookers and addicts. Tonight had been his first normal date since the tragedy that had nearly destroyed him.

He followed her into the bathroom. "Do you have a washcloth or something I can use to clean up?" He began unbuttoning his shirt.

She nodded, her gaze wary. "I have a first aid kit." She bent down beneath the sink and withdrew a white box and several washcloths and set them on the edge of the sink.

By that time he had unbuttoned his shirt and winced as he tried to shrug it off his shoulders. "Here, let me help," she said.

Although it was obvious she didn't want to, she stepped close to him and helped him ease the shirt from his body. Despite the searing pain that shot through his shoulder, for the first time he became aware of the scent of her. It was a spicy floral, slightly exotic fragrance and definitely at odds with the bland woman he'd chalked her up to be.

She wet a washcloth and began to clean the blood from around the wound. At least she wasn't the type of woman who fainted at the sight of blood, although he felt a slight trembling in her fingers.

"Are you going to tell me what's going on?" Her long brown hair fell forward to hide her features from his view.

"I don't have a clue." He cursed as she swabbed his wound with something that stung like hell.

"If you don't have a clue, then why not go to a hospital? The police? Some madman shot you and just chased us through the streets of Kansas City for no apparent reason." Her gaze met his, and even though he saw fear there, he also saw a glimmer of challenge.

"It's complicated." He frowned and clenched his jaw as she wiped his arm once again with antiseptic. He needed to think, to plan his next move.

There was no way he could believe that what had just happened to them was a random act of violence. Somebody had sold him out and he needed to get someplace safe and figure out who was responsible and what to do about it.

"You have any money?" he asked as she wrapped a bandage around his arm. "Cash. I need as much cash as you have."

She didn't reply until she'd finished with the bandage; then she stepped back from him and leaned against the sink cabinet. "I don't have much. I don't keep a lot of cash around the house. Less than a hundred dollars."

"You have an ATM card that you can draw more cash off? I'll pay you back."

There was a darkness in his eyes that frightened her. She wished he would put his shirt back on and cover up his impossibly broad chest and the stomach that sported a six-pack of taut muscle without an ounce of fat. She was having enough problems thinking without the sight of his sexy half-nakedness.

He stood and pulled his shirt on, his eyes still radiating a dangerous wildness that made her breath catch in her throat.

She didn't believe anything he said to her. There was no way she was going to hand him what savings she had in the bank.

Was this some sort of crazy scam? Did he know the man who had shot at them? Were they partners? Was this some way to get money from poor hapless females? She was so confused and fear made it impossible for her to sort through her scattered thoughts.

"I don't have any money in the bank to withdraw," she lied. "I work for minimum wage at the arts and craft store. There's never any left over after I pay my bills."

She just wanted him out of her house and out of her life. She wanted this date from hell to be over. As soon as he left she intended to call the police and make a report.

He left the bathroom and she followed him into the living room where he went to the front window and peered outside. Every muscle in his body appeared taut and again a horrifying fear swept through her.

He might be the best-looking man she'd ever gone out with, but he looked like, smelled like, and acted like danger. Amanda had never been one of those women who were drawn to dangerous men. She'd always played it safe.

What was he waiting for? His arm was bandaged. He'd said he'd leave once that was done. Was he waiting for somebody to arrive? A partner, maybe? But that didn't make sense. Why would he take a bullet in the arm to scam a few dollars from her? That just didn't make sense, but nothing else did, either.

He turned back around to face her. "I need your car."

"Fine. Take it." She walked over to her purse that she had flung on the sofa on her way to the bathroom. She pulled out the key ring and removed the two car keys, then grabbed what cash she had and held it out to him.

"I'm afraid things are a little more complicated than that," he replied. The muscles in his jaw clenched tightly.

"What do you mean?" She didn't want to hear what he was about to say. She just wanted him gone.

"You need to pack a bag. You're coming with me."

Chapter 4

"Pack a bag?" She stared at him in horror. She felt as if she'd entered an alternate universe, an alien landscape that scared the hell out of her.

"You have three minutes to gather whatever you think you might need for a day or two, then we're leaving."

She sat on the sofa, her shaking legs unable to hold her up another minute longer. "I'm not going anywhere with you." She'd cooperated with him long enough.

In three long strides he was in front of her. He grabbed her by the arm and hauled her back to her feet. A muscle ticked ominously in his jaw and his eyes were once again narrowed. "You can either get some things that will make you more comfortable while you're away from home or not, but one way or another, you're coming with me."

He loosened his grip on her arm. "Look, you're in danger if you stay here. The man who shot at me, the man who followed us, probably got your license number, and it won't take him any time at all to use that to get your name and address." He dropped his hand from her arm. "If he thinks we're together, if he thinks you mean anything to me, then he'll kill you."

"Then you do know what's going on!" she exclaimed. "Who is that man? Why would he want to kill you, to kill me?"

"We don't have time for that now." Once again he took her arm and steered her down the hallway. "You now have two minutes to get what you need."

He stood at the doorway of her bedroom while she grabbed a small bag from the floor of her closet. Numb.

She'd gone numb with fear. As she grabbed clean under-
wear and a pair of pajamas from her drawer, she eyed the
phone on the nightstand.

If he'd just look the other way for a minute, she'd grab
the phone and dial 911. But, as she finished packing clothes,
he gave her no opportunity to call for help.

Within minutes they were back in her car with him behind the wheel. The numbness that had momentarily
claimed her lifted, and once again icy fear gripped her. Was
he really helping her or had she become his hostage?

He pulled into a bank lot and drove up to the ATM. It
took him only a moment to get a handful of cash; then
they left the bank and drove south.

His gaze alternated between the street ahead and the
rearview mirror, and a dark energy rolled off him. "We're
going to have to lose the car."

"Lose the car? What does that mean?"

"As long as we're in this car, we're sitting ducks."

"Then let me out," she exclaimed with rising hysteria.

"I can't do that. I feel responsible for your safety."

"Please don't. This was just supposed to be a simple,
uncomplicated blind date."

He flashed her a dark look. "And now it's about life
and death."

A wave of helplessness swept through Amanda as she
stared out the passenger window. The first chance she got
she'd run. She'd take her chances against the man with the
gun rather than stay with this virtual stranger who exuded
a terrifying darkness from his pores.

In the meantime, she would not cause him problems and
just prayed that he wasn't taking her someplace to rape
and torture her.

She knew she'd already made her first mistake by getting
back into the car with him. She knew that the worst thing
a victim could do was get in a car with an assailant. She
should have made a stand in the house, but it was too late
to think about that now.

By the time they had driven for twenty minutes, Amanda
was lost. She lived in a northern suburb of Kansas City and
rarely went to the south side of town. The streets they
traveled were unfamiliar to her and she recognized none
of the street names.

He turned into a large car dealership and pulled into the used car lot. He shut off the engine, then turned to look at her. "We go on foot from here."

He opened the car door and got out. Amanda remained seated in the car. She wasn't going anywhere, she decided. If he was going to rape and torture her, then he'd have to do it right here and now.

He stalked around the car to the passenger door and yanked it open. "Come on, let's go. There's a motel about a mile up the road."

"I'm not going anywhere with you. I don't even know you. This date is officially over."

Clay stared at her, surprised at the strength that radiated from her voice. She'd been fairly docile so far. This stubborn thrust of her chin and the mutinous expression on her face made him wonder if she was acting out of character or if perhaps he'd misjudged her when they had shared dinner.

"Look, Amanda, you have no idea what we're up against. You aren't going to be able to fix this with knitting needles or a crochet hook." He looked around, aware of minutes passing, conscious of the dark breath of danger whispering against his neck.

"Just go away. Leave me here. If I think I'm in danger I'll call the cops."

The moment that shot had hit his arm, Clay had entered a zone of self-preservation that didn't allow for stubborn women or delays. They had to get to someplace safe for the night, someplace where he could think what his next move would be.

He jerked his gaze back to her and at the same time grabbed her arm to pull her from the car. She was a small woman but showed surprising strength as she fought his efforts to get her out.

"Dammit, Amanda, I'm not just trying to save my own life, I'm trying to save yours," he said through gritted teeth. He managed to get her out of the car and pulled her up hard against him.

Again he smelled her scent, that heady fragrance that stirred him on a base level. He held her so close against him he felt the press of her soft breasts against his chest and a wave of unexpected lust filled him.

It was an inappropriate response at this time in this situation, and served to remind him how long it had been since he'd been with a woman.

He stepped back from her but didn't release his grip on her shoulders. "I told you I'd explain everything when we get someplace safe."

"I just don't understand why we aren't going to the police," she replied as fear darkened her green eyes.

He drew a deep breath, knowing that what he was about to tell her certainly wouldn't put her at ease. "We can't go to the cops because there's a possibility it was a cop who shot at us."

She stared at him wordlessly. Dear God, what had she gotten herself into? Why would cops be shooting at him unless he was some kind of criminal?

He dropped his hands from her shoulders, his gaze holding hers intently. "I know you have no reason to trust me, but I swear my only concern is for your safety. You've got to trust me, Amanda." He reached up and touched her cheek with his index finger. "For God's sake, please trust me."

He'd been a horrible date, and there had been moments in the past hour when he'd frightened her more than she'd ever been frightened in her life.

But as he held her gaze, she saw something other than wildness in his eyes. She saw a whisper of something that appeared to be torment or grief. She wasn't sure which.

The humid heat of the night wrapped oppressively around her as she continued to hold his gaze. That momentary expression in his eyes coupled with the gentleness of his touch against her face forced her to make an instantaneous decision.

"Okay," she said softly. "I'll trust you until you prove to me I've made a mistake."

She just prayed it wasn't a mistake she'd pay for with her life.

"Good. Then let's go." He reached back into the car and grabbed her overnight bag, then together they took off walking down the street.

They were in an area of the city where she'd definitely never been. It was a blighted area filled with dark, boarded-up buildings. Every other streetlight was broken or flickering erratically. The day's heat radiated up from the sidewalk and the scent of overripe garbage hung in the air.

Clay's strides were long and quick, forcing her to hurry to keep up with him. This was definitely not a neighborhood where she wanted to be alone. Better the devil she knew, she thought.

Of course, she knew nothing about Clay Murdock, and she wondered now just what her sister and brother-in-law had known about the man they'd thought would be perfect for her.

He didn't speak as they walked, but she noticed his gaze seemed to be everywhere, down the darkened alleys and on each car that passed.

Ahead she saw the neon light announcing the Night Owl Motel, and her stomach clenched. What was she doing? She was headed for a motel with a man she didn't know, a man who was probably a criminal. She had no idea if he was trying to save her or use her.

All she knew was that it was too late to turn back now.

Chapter 5

Half an hour later Amanda sat on the edge of the bed and stared at Clay's broad back as he peered out the window of the tiny motel room.

She wrapped her arms and hugged herself, unsure if the chill she felt was from the fact that the air conditioner in the room was too cold or from the situation she found herself in.

Her heart hammered an unsteady beat as she looked around. There was only a double bed, and the thought of lying next to Clay for the night caused her stomach to twist in knots. The nightstands were scarred by cigarette marks, and the one nearest her had the initials "JT" carved into the wood. As dismal as the room appeared, at least it looked clean.

She'd often bemoaned the lack of excitement in her life, but she'd gladly return to her crafts and flower arranging if she got out of this mess alive.

"Did you see the shooter?" He allowed the curtain to fall back into place, then turned to look at her.

She nodded. "Just briefly. It all happened so fast. He had a bald head and cold eyes."

"Would you know him if you saw him again?"

"I think I would."

Clay frowned and moved toward the bed. Her eyes widened and her body tensed. "Don't look so scared," he said. "I told you I'm not going to hurt you." He sat next to her and raked a hand through his thick, dark hair. "I can't do much of anything tonight. I know there's an electronics store not far from here. Tomorrow we'll go there and get

224

a prepaid cell phone, then I can start making calls and see if I can get to the bottom of all this. I can't use the cell phone I've got because the call can be traced."

"Are you going to tell me what's going on?" she asked.

He turned his head and gazed at her, his frown cutting a furrow across his forehead. "I haven't decided yet. I think maybe the best thing to do is get a good night's sleep and then we'll see what the morning brings."

"Do you really think I'm just going to be able to get into bed and get a good night's sleep after everything that's happened?" She stared at him incredulously. "Maybe this is all perfectly normal for your life, but I'm a little out of my comfort zone here."

"Anytime somebody takes a couple shots at me, I'm out of my comfort zone," he replied dryly. "Look, I'm sorry as hell you got into the middle of this, but whether you like it or not, you *are* in the middle of it. Now, why don't you get ready for bed. I don't know what tomorrow is going to bring, and we both better be rested and ready to deal with whatever comes up."

Amanda got up from the bed and grabbed her small overnight bag. It was obvious she wasn't going to get any answers tonight. Now that the adrenaline of the chase was gone, weariness tugged at her, although she was certain sleep wouldn't find her tonight.

Thank goodness she wasn't a silk-and-baby-doll-pajama kind of woman. She pulled her cotton pajamas out of her bag and set them on the sink, trying to decide if she wanted to put them on or try to sleep in her dress and panty hose.

She opted for the pajamas. She'd feel better, less vulnerable, in pajama bottoms. Although she supposed if his intent was to rape her, it would have already happened.

As she washed her face, she stared at her reflection in the mirror. The green eyes—so wide, so filled with fear—looked alien in her slender face. Her safe, uneventful life had been ripped out from under her and for the first time in her life she felt completely powerless and out of control.

It wasn't a pleasant feeling.

She washed her face twice, then brushed her teeth, then stood hesitantly at the door. She was afraid to stay in the bathroom and afraid to leave it.

Despite her apprehension where Clay Murdock was concerned, she couldn't help but remember that moment when he'd pulled her up against him and she'd felt the male solidness of him, smelled the provocative scent of him. At that moment a whisper of desire had slashed through the fear.

Crazy, she chided herself. How could she desire a man she didn't trust, a man who obviously had deadly secrets, a man who hadn't even had the social graces to pretend interest in her over a simple meal?

One thing was certain, she couldn't stay in the bathroom all night. She opened her purse and rummaged around in it. She pulled out a latch-rug hook and clutched it in her hand. It wasn't much of a weapon but she'd feel better with it beneath her pillow within easy reach.

She grabbed her overnight bag and opened the door to see him once again standing at the window, peering out into the night.

He turned at the sound of her and gestured toward the bed where he'd pulled down the bedspread. "You have a preference as to which side you sleep on?"

"This side is fine." She dropped her bag on the floor, then sat on the edge of the bed and slid her hand beneath the pillow and released the latch hook. She had no idea if she had the capacity to use it as a weapon or not and prayed that she wouldn't have to find out.

"Ready for the light to go off?" he asked.

She'd never been afraid of the dark before, but tonight the dark was unknown and fraught with all kinds of imagined dangers. Before she could reply he shut off the light, plunging the room into complete darkness.

She stretched out on the bed, nerves tense as she waited to see if he'd join her there. A flicker of light at the window let her know he was once again looking outside. Did he expect trouble here? She squeezed her eyes shut and wondered if her date with Clay Murdock would ever end?

Clay stared out into the night, not really looking as much as thinking. He'd been functioning on gut instinct, driven only by the need to survive. He frowned as he thought about the predicament they found themselves in. They had no transportation, and he had no real plan.

Even more troubling, he had no weapon and no way to obtain one. He had a gun in a drawer at his apartment, but he'd be a fool to risk going back there.

He supposed if he had enough cash, he could have walked out on the street and within minutes obtained dope, a woman, or a gun. But his ATM card had allowed him to withdraw only five hundred dollars and he had no idea how long he and Amanda might have to live on that money.

Despite the darkness in the room, he felt Amanda's gaze on him and his frown deepened. Everything would be less complicated if she weren't involved. But, if what he suspected was true, then she was in just as much danger as he was. At the moment she was definitely a liability.

They had been seen together, and the people who wanted him dead would think they were a couple. That made her vulnerable. If they thought he cared about her in any way, they wouldn't hesitate to kill her, if for no other reason than to hurt him.

He leaned against the wall and closed his eyes and tried to keep his thoughts focused on what needed to be done, but instead his head filled with a vision of Amanda.

When she'd come out of the bathroom clad in a perfectly respectable pair of green striped pajamas, with her face scrubbed clean of makeup and her hair shining in the lamplight, she'd looked far prettier than his initial assessment had been when they'd shared dinner.

He looked in the direction of the bed where he knew she was still awake. He could tell by the sound of her breathing. So far she'd been fairly cooperative, but he didn't trust her. With a single phone call she could bring death to them. With a cry or a scream she could bring to them the man who had betrayed him, the man who wanted him dead.

He knew next to nothing about Amanda Kincaid. All he really knew was that she was thirty-one years old and was talented when it came to arts and crafts projects.

Initially she'd done a lot of talking at dinner, but he hadn't paid much attention to what she was saying. Harry had coerced him to go on the date. He hadn't wanted to be there, and he had to admit he'd been a jerk.

It seemed ridiculous to apologize now about being a poor dinner companion. Part of the problem was that, after the past five years of his life, he hadn't known how to interact with a normal, well-adjusted female.

Amanda seemed nice enough, but at the moment he

wished he was in this mess with one of the women he'd known in his previous life, women who carried knives and knew how to protect themselves, women who in life had been kicked around and who had learned to kick right back.

If he told Amanda what was going on, he would destroy all that he'd begun to build in the three months since coming to Kansas City.

He liked the city, had wanted to build a life here, but that wouldn't happen if he shared his secrets with her. He'd have to pack up, disappear, and start new in another city, another state.

A bald man with cold eyes. That's what she'd told him about the shooter. He didn't know anybody who was bald, which meant a contract killer had been brought in.

He didn't know how long he stood there trying to figure out who might have betrayed him, but eventually he became aware of the fact that Amanda had fallen asleep.

Her breathing was deep and even. He left the window and moved silently across the floor to the bathroom. He'd take a fast shower, then get some sleep. God knew he needed to be rested and on top of things when morning came.

It took him only minutes to shower; then he pulled his navy boxers back on before leaving the steamy bathroom.

He eased into bed and pulled the blankets up, grateful that he didn't wake her. As he turned onto his side, his hand encountered something hard and pointy beneath the blankets. He pulled it out and ran his fingers over it, recognizing it as a rug hook.

His wife had tried to make a rug a long time ago. He'd found the half-finished product in a box in the closet after her death. An ache filled him as he thought of Jillian, but the ache was no longer as piercing, as devastating as it had once been.

He shoved the grief aside and placed the rug hook on the nightstand. Amanda had obviously intended to use the hook as a weapon against him if necessary. Maybe there was a bit more spunk to the woman than he'd initially thought.

Of course, she had no way of knowing that if he wanted to harm her, if he wanted to take her, nothing in the world, including a rug hook, would stop him.

Chapter 6

She dreamed of warmth.

It infused her, surrounded her, and she reveled in it as the last vestiges of sleep fell away. As consciousness claimed her, her eyes snapped open and her heart seemed to stop beating.

Clay was the heat. She was intimately spooned against him, his arm draped casually across her middle section. Even through the cotton material of her pajamas she could feel the heat of his body.

She tried to tell herself that it was terrible, that he'd taken advantage of her in her sleep, but it was obvious he was asleep, and as much as she hated to admit it, the feel of him curled around her wasn't so terrible at all.

In fact, despite the fact she didn't know him, in spite of the strange situation she found herself in, it felt altogether wonderful. It had been many years since she'd awakened in a man's arms. She'd forgotten how nice it could be.

She didn't move, and as she lay there, she allowed herself to imagine that he wasn't a stranger and they weren't in danger. Instead she fantasized that this was a fitting ending to a wonderful date with a man who was going to be part of her world for the rest of her life.

She allowed herself a momentary flight from reality and imagined that Clay Murdock had fallen madly in love with her, and this was the morning after a night of intense, earth-shattering lovemaking.

His arm tensed around her and she realized he'd awakened. "Sorry," he murmured and rolled away as if appalled to find himself touching her.

He turned on the nightstand lamp. So much for fantasies, she thought. The reality was that she didn't know Clay Murdock, and they were in trouble.

She turned over to see him sitting on the side of the bed. The sight of his naked broad back made her want to reach out and touch it, feel the warmth she knew was contained within.

She wondered if she'd lost her mind. Maybe the intense fear she'd experienced had addled her brains. Hadn't she once read something about a phenomenon where a captive becomes enthralled with the captor? The Stockholm syndrome or something like that?

"You'd better get dressed. We have a lot of things to do today," he said. "Oh, and by the way"—he turned to face her, his expression inscrutable—"I don't know what you intended to do with this, unless you were going to latch hook my chest hair."

He tossed her the hook she'd hidden beneath her pillow the night before.

Her cheeks flamed as she scurried from the bed, grabbed her bag, and hurried into the bathroom. She locked the door and leaned against it.

She'd be a fool to entertain any fantasy where Clay Murdock was concerned. For all she knew he was a dope dealer or a murderer. Just because he hadn't raped or killed her yet didn't mean he was one of the good guys.

She double-checked the lock on the door, then started the water in the shower. She needed a hot shower to clear her head.

The shower didn't help. By the time she'd pulled on the pair of jeans and the blouse she'd shoved into her bag the night before, she was as confused and apprehensive as ever.

She left the bathroom and walked back into the room to the scent of coffee and bacon.

"There's a fast-food place next door," he said and gestured to the foam cup of coffee and a paper sack on the nightstand. "I didn't know if you were a breakfast eater or not."

"I am." She opened the bag to find a breakfast sandwich. She was grateful he was dressed and she didn't have to worry about staring at his bare chest while she drank her coffee and ate the sandwich.

As she began to eat, he pulled open the curtains to allow the morning sun to stream into the room. For some reason the sight of the sun after the long, dark, frightening night reassured her. "So, when can I go home?"

The gaze he shot her was less than reassuring. "I can't answer that. When this is all resolved." He stepped away from the window and checked his wristwatch. "As soon as the electronics store opens, we'll walk down there and get a prepaid cell phone. With that I can contact some people and see if I can get to the bottom of all this."

"When this gets resolved . . . when you get to the bottom of this—I'm not going anywhere with you until you tell me what 'this' is." Sometime in the course of the past few seconds she'd made up her mind.

She sat on the edge of the bed and stared at him. "Last night you told me to trust you, and despite all my instincts to the contrary, I did. Now I think it's time you trust me and tell me just what in the hell is going on here." She was pleased that her voice sounded stronger than she felt.

He picked up his foam cup of coffee and took a swallow, his gaze never leaving hers. She saw the muscle that ticked in his jaw and tensed with wary expectation.

With slow, deliberate motion he set the cup back on the nightstand, then walked around the bed and sat next to her. Every nerve in her body screamed as she saw the utter blackness of his eyes, a soulless look that terrified her more than anything that had happened.

"Five years ago I was a Chicago cop. The department came to me and asked if I was willing to go undercover to work at bringing down a drug lord who had gained a lot of power on the south side of the city. They explained to me that I would be deep under, without backup, without friends. I agreed."

"Why?" She felt herself begin to relax somewhat. Finally she was going to get some answers. "Why would anyone choose to do a job like that? I've read accounts of undercover police, how they have to give up all contact with their families and friends and live in a world where one false move could mean their death. Why did you want to go undercover?"

He stared at the wall opposite them, and once again she sensed a darkness falling over him. It wasn't a darkness that frightened her. It was one she sensed was bred in pain, in grief.

"At the time I was in a bad place in my life," he continued. "I chose to do it because I thought I had nothing to lose."

"What about your family?"

"I didn't have any. My parents had died two years before and my . . . there was nobody left."

My wife? Was that what he'd been about to say? Had his wife left him or had she died? Certainly the grief that etched his features for a moment spoke of deep tragedy.

He stood suddenly and paced the narrow area at the foot of the bed. "Anyway, for the next five years I worked to get close to Ben Correl. He worked what appeared to be a legitimate import/export business, but we knew he was dirty."

He stopped pacing and stared at her again, his eyes still dark, haunted. "For almost five years I ate, drank, and slept with the dregs of humanity. By the time the assignment ended, I felt as if I'd been walking in the shadows for too long."

"So how did you get from the police force in Chicago to working construction in Kansas City?" Although there was a ring of truth to his story, she wasn't sure if she believed him.

He rejoined her on the bed and raked a hand through his thick hair. "I testified at the trial, and Ben got a life sentence. The last thing he said before they took him away was that I'd never live to see thirty-five. My thirty-fifth birthday is next month."

"That still doesn't explain what you're doing here in Kansas City," she replied. He sighed and frowned as if deciding if he intended to tell her the whole story. "I'm not moving from this bed until you tell me everything," she said and meant it.

She'd allowed herself to be pulled into his drama. She'd left her house, given him her car and what little cash she had, and now, unless he offered her a viable reason for what had happened, she was through. One way or another she'd get to the phone and dial 911 or she'd scream so loud and so long somebody would come to see what the ruckus was about.

She looked at him steadily with her chin raised in a show of defiance. He held her gaze for a long moment; then one corner of his lips curved upward. "I believe you mean it."

"Damn right I do," she exclaimed. Although he hadn't offered her a full smile, the hint of one shining momentarily in his eyes and relaxing the tension in his face increased his attractiveness. She reminded herself that Ted Bundy had also been an attractive man.

Once again he stared at the wall opposite her, and all traces of levity disappeared from his features. "I tried to go back to the force after the trial, but nobody wanted to partner with me and my heart wasn't in it anymore. I'd become a liability to the force. After talking to my chief, I decided to enter the witness protection program. I got a new identity, a new city, and a new job to start life over again."

"And you think this man, this Ben, has hired somebody to kill you?" She didn't wait for his reply as her mind worked to wrap around everything he'd told her. "But how would he know where you were, that you're here in Kansas City?"

He turned to look at her, his blue gaze once again hard and dangerous looking. "The only way Ben Correl could know where I am, could know the name I now have, is if he's working with somebody on the inside, somebody in law enforcement."

"That's why you didn't want me to call the police."

He nodded. "I have no idea who might have sold me out, and until I know, it isn't safe to talk to anyone."

"But I thought when you entered the witness protection program, nobody knew where you were."

"There are only two people who know my new identity— Jeffrey Smith, a local FBI agent, and Larry Mitchell, my contact within the program. If somebody sold me out, it's probably one of those two men."

"But why would you think I'm in danger? I don't know any of these people."

"Ben Correl is one of the most amoral, evil men I've ever known. If he gets word that I'm with a woman, he'll think nothing of making sure the woman is on the hit list as well. He'd do anything to hurt me, including killing the people who are close to me." He checked his watch and stood. "And now it's time to take a walk up to the electronics store."

She remained seated for a moment, trying to decide if she believed his story. She did. If he was going to rape her or kill her, he'd had ample opportunity already. He'd done nothing so far to harm her.

Despite her intention to stay awake the entire night, she'd fallen asleep. In sleep she had been utterly vulnerable, and all he'd done was cuddle with her. Despite a million reasons not to, she believed him—and what was more, she thought she trusted him.

"If you're in the witness protection program, then Clay Murdock isn't your real name, is it?"

He frowned. "It's not the name I was born with."

"So what is your real name?"

His frown deepened. "I think I've given you enough information for the moment. Now, let's get to that store so we can get this over with."

She got up from the bed and together they left the chilly motel room and stepped out into the hot humid morning air. "What's your plan?" she asked as they began to walk down the sidewalk.

"I'm still trying to come up with one."

"That's not real reassuring," she said dryly.

"I don't want to give you a false sense of security. If everything I believe is true, then the danger to both of us is very real. Somebody will be watching our homes, checking our bank accounts and monitoring calls."

"But nobody can trace a prepaid phone, right?" she asked.

"Right."

For several minutes they walked without talking. The neighborhood looked less threatening in the light of day than it had the night before. Still, it was an area where she wouldn't have felt comfortable alone.

Usually on Saturdays she worked at the arts and crafts shop, but she'd taken the weekend off. Nobody would be looking for her because she missed work.

She'd always believed that if you were in trouble you went to the police. It felt strange to recognize that a call to law enforcement might bring death.

She cast Clay a surreptitious glance. She had a feeling he hadn't told her the whole story, but he'd told her enough for her to know that by the circumstance of chance they were partners in danger. Until he resolved his situation, she had to depend on him to keep her safe.

She imagined by now her sister would have called, and when she didn't get Amanda at home, she'd assume that perhaps a love connection had been made and Amanda had spent the night with Clay. Cara was a hopeless romantic. She'd never imagine the truth of the situation.

"Why arts and crafts?" he asked as they skirted around a pile of trash. "You didn't mention last night what got you interested in that kind of work."

"Last night you didn't seem interested in much of anything I said," she retorted. "In fact, you were pretty rude."

"I wasn't that bad."

"On a scale from one to ten, ten being the best date I've ever been on, last night was a minus two."

He winced, but one corner of his lip turned up in a half smile. "That bad?"

"That bad," she replied.

They walked again in silence, the electronics store visible in the next block. "I'm sorry that I was a bad date," he finally said. "I spent too much of the last couple of years living, working, and interacting with the worst kind of people. I guess I have forgotten how to socialize with normal people."

She smiled at him. "What makes you think I'm normal?"

He laughed, the sound a wonderful burst of deep male mirth. She liked the sound of his laugh, just as she'd liked waking up that morning with his arms around her. Crazy. She was definitely going crazy from the stress of the situation.

"You never answered my question."

She looked at him curiously. "What question?"

"Why arts and crafts?"

"I've got an MBA, and I worked in the corporate world for five years and hated every minute of it. I've always loved handmade things and floral arranging. Last year my grandmother passed away and left me a little inheritance. I decided life was too short not to do what you loved, so

I took the job at the craft store. I know it sounds cheesy, but I like creating beautiful things that make people feel good."

"Nothing cheesy about that," he replied. He sighed. "For the past two months I've been working as a Sheetrocker on new homes. I liked doing it for the same reason. I come in with nothing but framework done, and when I leave there are rooms where people will eventually live. I'll miss doing it when this is all over."

"Why would you have to stop?"

They paused just outside the door of the electronics store. The laughter that had momentarily lit his eyes and softened his chiseled features disappeared. "If my cover here has been blown, then I'll probably have to reenter the program. That means a new state, a new name, and a new profession." It was obvious the thought didn't please him.

"Come on, let's get what I need so I can get us both out of this mess." With these words he opened the door to the store and they went inside.

Chapter 7

It took Clay only minutes to get the phone he needed. The first step to solving their dilemma was to contact the suspects he thought might be responsible. He wanted to talk to them, preferably face-to-face so he could see their body language, stare into their eyes.

Years undercover had given him an edge when it came to reading people. His intuitiveness had kept him alive in situations when the potential for death had been a heartbeat away.

As they left the store, his thoughts went from the difficult task before him to the woman walking beside him. He'd been shocked to find her in his arms that morning, her warm slender body spooned against his and her hair fragrant with a clean, slightly fruity scent.

For just a moment he'd remembered what it had been like to live a normal life, to wake up in the morning and look forward to living with a woman he loved. He'd remembered mortgage payments and morning passion and evenings at the movies.

The remembering had hurt, but not as much as it had in the past, and in that quiet moment with Amanda's body pressed so close against his own, he'd recognized that sometime over the past five years he had begun to heal.

He'd thought Amanda Kincaid plain, but that was before he'd noticed the spark of life in her eyes, the shine of the sun in her hair. He'd thought she was boring, but he no longer trusted his judgement where she was concerned.

Of course it didn't much matter what he thought of her.

When this was all over, he'd move on to a new life in a new town.

The thought depressed him. He hated the idea of once again starting over.

"What was her name?"

He looked at Amanda in surprise. "Excuse me?"

"I was just curious about the woman in your past."

"What makes you think there was any particular woman in my past?" he countered.

She shrugged. "Just a feeling."

They walked for a moment in silence. "Jillian," he finally answered. It had been almost five years since he'd said her name aloud. "Her name was Jillian. We'd been married eight months when she was killed coming home from the grocery store by a drunk driver."

"Oh, Clay. I'm so sorry."

It was his turn to shrug. "It was a long time ago. It was two months after her death that I decided to go undercover." He'd been so angry, so filled with rage and grief that he hadn't cared how dangerous the assignment, had harbored a death wish that now half shamed him.

"What about you?" he asked.

"What about me?"

"What about the men in your life?"

She smiled and he wondered if she had any idea what a pretty smile she possessed. "There haven't been a lot of men in my life." Her smile faltered and fell away. "Only one that got serious enough to talk marriage, but before we could take the plunge I found out he was dating somebody else while he was dating me. That was three years ago."

"And so now you hate all men, and only date when your sister and brother-in-law blackmail you into going."

She laughed. "Not exactly. I don't hate all men, only liars. But I've realized I don't have to have a man in my life to be whole. I'd love to share my life with somebody special, but I'm not desperate to grab on to just anyone."

They reached the motel room. He unlocked the door and they went inside. Clay's thoughts shifted from pleasant conversation to the matter at hand.

He sat in the chair at the desk and opened the bag that contained the phone. As he unboxed the instrument,

Amanda made the bed, then sat on the edge and watched him.

"What are you going to do?" she asked.

He rubbed his fingers across his forehead, where the beginning of a headache was making itself known. Dammit, he needed a plan. "I need a place to meet with these men, a place where there will be people, a place where a man wouldn't attempt to get off a shot at me." He plugged in the phone to begin charging.

She frowned thoughtfully. "What about a mall, like maybe the Oak Grove Mall? You could arrange to meet them by the fountain on the lower level. I could be on the upper level watching to see if the shooter shows up."

"You aren't going to be anywhere but here in this room," he replied.

"Don't be stupid," she replied. "You don't know what the shooter looks like. I do."

"And it's possible the shooter knows what you look like." He shoved back from the desk and stood. As far as he was concerned this point was nonnegotiable. He wouldn't risk her life to save his own.

"I've been thinking about that." She stood as well. "I don't see how he could have seen my face. The interior of the car was dark when he shot. I'm betting he couldn't pick me out of a lineup."

"It's still out of the question. The best thing you can do for yourself is to stay here and let me take care of it."

"That's not going to happen." Her chin shot up a notch in an expression of stubbornness he now recognized.

Clay's headache pounded with a vengeance. He didn't have time for this. It was bad enough she was in trouble by mere association with him. He wasn't about to make it worse for her by putting her in more harm's way. "Amanda, you need to be reasonable."

"I think I've been very reasonable. I've been driven through the streets by a man I barely know chased by a man trying to kill us. I ditched my car and don't know if I'll ever see it again and slept in a motel room that probably rents by the hour. I'd say I've been exceptionally reasonable."

Her eyes flashed with a touch of annoyance and she reached out and jabbed a finger into his chest. "And there's no way you're going to leave me here while you ride off like the Lone Ranger."

He grabbed her hand with his and pulled her up against him. Jillian had been a stubborn woman, too, and he'd butted heads with her more than once. But they'd argued about the color for the living room paint and evening plans, about what to have for breakfast and where in the house to store his gun.

This was different. This wasn't about wall color or a choice of food. "This is life or death," he said, and tried not to notice how well she fit against him, how full her lips were as she stared up at him.

"I know. My life, my death, my choice," she replied. "Whether you like it or not, we're in this together, and you aren't going anywhere without me."

He wasn't sure why, but more than anything at that moment he wanted to kiss her. Maybe it was all the talk about life and death, or maybe it was because she looked so charmingly earnest as she told him they were in this mess together. Whatever the reason, he didn't question it. He indulged it by crashing his lips down to hers.

He had no right to kiss her. He'd known her less than twenty-four hours and he half expected her to respond by shoving him away and slapping his face.

What he didn't expect was the white-hot fire that shot through him as she wound her arms around his neck and opened her mouth to welcome his kiss.

A primal need swept through him as he tasted the honeyed heat of her mouth, felt her small breasts thrust against him. The desire that stabbed through him, the need to possess her was madness and he knew it.

He wound his fingers in her soft, silky hair as his tongue danced with hers. The scent of her surrounded him and he found it intoxicating, found her intoxicating.

He reluctantly ended the kiss, but she tightened her arms around him. Her eyes shimmered with heat as she gazed up at him. "Don't stop," she said, her voice a mere whisper.

Blood flowed thick and hot through his veins as he held her gaze. "Amanda, if I don't stop now, I can't promise that I'll stop later," he warned. It was the truth—that single kiss had enflamed him as none other he could remember in a very long time.

"Maybe I won't want you to stop." Her husky voice was breathless. "Clay, I've played it safe my entire life. I'm not looking for promises and I won't have regrets. Just this moment here and now."

He was her walk on the wild side, and at the moment she felt like a tranquil port in the storm of his life. No promises and no regrets. A man would be a fool not to take advantage of that kind of deal.

Clay was certainly no fool.

Chapter 8

Amanda wasn't sure at what point she'd lost her mind, but as Clay's mouth possessed hers once again she knew she had and she didn't care. He might have been a horrid date, but the man certainly knew how to kiss.

Someplace in the back of her mind she knew this craziness was prompted by the fact that for the first time in her life she was staring at her own mortality. But her desire to be with Clay was driven by more than that.

It was as simple as how warm and safe she felt in his arms and as complicated as the emotion he'd wrought in her when he'd talked about his wife's death.

His mouth was hot as it left hers and trailed kisses down the length of her neck. She pulled his shirt from his pants and ran her hands up beneath it, caressing the warm flesh of his back.

He cupped her buttocks and pulled her more intimately against him. He was aroused, and the knowledge that she was responsible for his physical state sent a wildness through her.

Together they tumbled to the bed, arms and legs tangled as they tugged and pulled on each other's clothing. Thought was impossible as Clay's hands and mouth seemed to be everywhere and she was swallowed by the sweet sensations his caresses evoked.

His thumb grazed her nipple, followed by his greedy mouth, and an electrical current sizzled in every nerve in her body. His other hand slipped down the flat of her stomach to find her wet heat.

There was no hesitation in his touch, no awkward fondling

or tentative fumbling. He knew exactly what he was doing, and she cried out and moved her hips to meet his touch.

If she had to choose one lover before she died, she would have chosen Clay. He was both commanding and tender, demanding and giving. Within minutes of foreplay she was gasping with need for him to take her completely.

He entered her in one smooth thrust. She moaned with sheer pleasure and wrapped her legs around his back, bringing him deeper into her.

His heartbeat crashed in rhythm with her own as he gazed at her. "This is crazy." His voice was deep and husky.

"Crazy wonderful," she replied.

"Yeah, crazy wonderful," he repeated, then kissed her as he stroked into her.

Faster and faster they moved together in the rhythm of passion. Higher and higher she climbed until she spun out of control and her climax shuddered through her, leaving her shaking and weak. Almost instantaneously he stiffened against her and groaned as he found his own release.

She expected him to immediately roll away and get up, but he surprised her by pulling her into his embrace and remaining beside her.

As their heartbeats slowed and their breathing became more regular, a sudden burst of embarrassment swept over her. What had she been thinking? She'd never done anything like this before in her life.

"You said no regrets," he said softly.

She looked at him in surprise. "What makes you think I have regrets?"

"All your muscles stiffened just now."

"It's not regret, it's a bit of embarrassment." She felt her cheeks warm. "I want you to know that I don't usually fall into bed with a man on the first date."

He smiled and looked breathtakingly handsome with his hair tousled and his features relaxed. "This hasn't exactly been a normal first date. Besides, I didn't take you for a fast woman."

"No, you obviously took me for somebody who didn't warrant your attention."

He looked chagrined. "I'm sorry about that. I agreed to the date because I like Harry, but I didn't really want to be there."

"And I agreed to go because I love my sister and she's a hopeless romantic."

He leaned up on one elbow and gazed down at her. "And what about you? Are you a hopeless romantic?"

She shook her head. "Not as much as she is, but I guess there's a bit of a romantic inside me." She knew these moments in the warmth of the bed, the conversation about anything and everything, were nothing more than a respite from the danger and uncertainty that lay ahead.

They remained there for over thirty minutes, talking about favorite pizza, movies they'd seen, politics and life experiences. As they got to know each other a little better, she realized they'd done everything backward. They'd shared their passion before they'd shared much of anything else.

When he glanced at his watch, she knew the respite was over and a cold chill swept over her as she thought of the immediate future.

If she believed everything he'd told her, then she had no life to go back to until he found out who had betrayed him. By the mere circumstance of being seen with him, she'd gotten her name on some sort of hit list.

What if his plan didn't work? What if he didn't find out who was responsible for the attempted murder last night? How could she return to her home, her work, knowing that it was possible somebody might try to kill her?

"Your muscles have all tightened again," he said.

She sat up. "I was just wondering what happens if you don't find out who's behind all this?"

He sat up as well and his eyes were once again dark and dangerous-looking. "Trust me, Amanda. I will find out who's responsible. If not today, then tomorrow."

"And what about me? What happens to me in the meantime?"

He smiled once again, only this time the gesture didn't reach the darkness in his eyes. "Until I fix this, we remain together. I won't let you get hurt. Until this is over, our first date continues."

She wasn't sure if this reassured her or not. She watched as he swung his legs over the side of the bed and stood. Wearing only the bandage on his arm, he padded into the bathroom and a moment later she heard the shower water run.

Amanda lay back once again, her thoughts as jumbled as decorative rocks in the bottom of a vase. She'd just made love to a man she hardly knew and now would risk her life to help save his and reclaim her own.

The most difficult thing she'd faced in the past year was working with grapevines to make holiday wreaths. Nothing in her past experience had prepared her for the man she was with and the situation she was in.

The witness protection program. The only thing she knew about it was what she'd seen in movies, and she doubted if half of that was accurate.

She liked Clay. She liked him a lot. Little good it did her. He'd told her that once this was over he'd probably go back into the program, start a new life with a new name in another city and state.

She did know that an important part of the program was that the people who entered it were never supposed to contact anyone from their past. She would never know what kind of a life he built elsewhere, if he would eventually find a happiness that would erase the shadows in his eyes.

Just her luck to find a man she liked, a man she'd like to get to know better, and within hours or days he'd disappear like a mirage in the desert.

He came back into the room clad only in a towel, and she watched while he dressed. "While you shower, I'll make my phone calls and set things up," he said as he sat on the edge of the bed to put on his socks.

"You know, I'd feel better if I knew your real name."

He slid his feet into his shoes and stood. A frown creased his brow and he held her gaze for a long moment. "It's better that you don't know. It's safer for me and safer for you. Now, you'd better get showered and dressed." He walked to the window and stared outside.

She got out of bed and went into the bathroom, uneasiness weighing heavily on her shoulders. It bothered her that he didn't want to tell her his real name.

As she started the water for a fast shower, she prayed she hadn't put her trust in the wrong person.

Chapter 9

It was a bad plan. Clay and Amanda stood on the upper level of the Oak Grove Mall, half hidden by a decorative planter containing six-foot-tall plant fronds. Below them on the bottom level he could see the fountain where in thirty minutes he was to meet with Larry Mitchell, his contact within the program. An hour after that he would meet with Jeffrey Smith.

He'd told both men about the shooting the night before, but had been unable to detect anything in their response that would let him know if either man was responsible.

"What's wrong?" Amanda asked.

He looked at her, surprised that after less than twenty-four hours of knowing him she seemed attuned to his thoughts, his moods. "Setting up a meet here wasn't such a good idea." He returned his gaze to the fountain area, where a group of teenagers were hanging out and several elderly couples sat on the nearby benches.

She followed his gaze, then looked back at him. "I thought you wanted a place where there were people."

"I thought it might be safer that way, but I can't take a chance on one of those kids or anyone else getting hurt." He pulled the cell phone from his pocket. "I've got to abort this whole thing, figure something else out."

"Wait." She stopped him with a hand on his arm before he could dial. "Maybe we can still make this work." A delicate furrow cut across her brow as she frowned thoughtfully. "There's a loading dock just outside of those doors. You could meet there and nobody else would be around." Her frown deepened. "What worries me about this whole setup is that once you go down by that fountain you're a sitting duck. Either man had enough time to let the shooter know where you'd be at what time."

"That's why you're here, to see if you spot the shooter," he replied.

Her eyes were dark as she held his gaze. "What if I screw up? What if he's wearing a cap and I don't recognize him? Or I just miss him?" She shook her head. "No, this isn't going to work. I have a better idea."

"What?" He eyed her curiously. For a woman he'd initially thought boring, she was certainly rising to this occasion with a surprisingly clear mind and courage.

"You point out each man as they arrive. I go down and get close enough to tell them to meet you on the loading dock in two minutes. That way if the shooter is in place he won't have a target to hit."

"Except you." He shook his head. "I don't want you putting yourself in danger."

She gripped his arm. "Clay, you've spent the last twenty-four hours trying to convince me that I am in danger. Nobody is going to take a shot at me if they think you're anywhere around. That would tip their hand. Think about it, Clay. If we do it my way, the shooter won't have an opportunity to position himself on the dock."

As much as he hated to admit it, her plan made sense. "I still don't like the idea of you getting anywhere close to either man."

"But they don't know me. They'll have no idea I have anything to do with you until I'm next to them giving them the message."

"They might try to detain you in some way," he protested.

She opened her purse and pulled out her rug hook. "Let them try. They touch me, and I'll jab them and scream to high heaven." She looked over the ledge to the level below. "Those people aren't going to allow somebody to manhandle a poor helpless female."

He frowned. "You don't have to do this, you know," he said softly.

"I know. But it's the best way to keep us both safe."

Emotion rose up inside him. It had been a very long time since anyone had cared about his safety. As much as he hated to admit it, her plan was good. He just prayed nothing went wrong.

"All right," he agreed reluctantly. "We'll do it your way."

She nodded, with that familiar determined thrust to her chin. She humbled him, this woman he hardly knew, this woman who was willing to put herself in danger's path to minimize the danger to him. He watched as she scanned the people on the upper level and the lower level. He knew she was looking for the bald man who had started all this.

"Amanda."

She turned to look at him.

"If we ever had a chance to go out on a date again, I'd be a ten."

She smiled, and he saw a flash of wistfulness in her eyes. "Just my luck, the first man who has interested me in years will within the next couple of days be swallowed back into the witness protection program and disappear forever."

Amanda redirected her attention to the people around them. An unexpected ache resounded in her heart. How was it possible she would miss a man she'd only known for a day? How was it possible that in such a brief time Clay Murdock had managed to touch her heart like no other man had done before?

She couldn't dwell on that now. Neither of them would have a future of any kind if things went horribly wrong in the next couple of hours.

As minutes ticked off, nerves coiled taut and painful in the pit of her stomach. Her gaze shot left and right in an effort to spot potential death in the form of a burly bald man with cold, dead eyes. But so far there had been no sign of him.

"There he is," Clay said, his voice radiating taut energy. "That's Larry on the right side of the fountain."

He was a tall, blond man wearing jeans and a T-shirt. He looked like dozens of other men she'd seen walking the mall in the past hour. He stood perfectly still, not far from the benches where people sat chatting and laughing.

Amanda's heart felt as if it stopped beating as she realized the time had come. "Two minutes and you'll be at the loading dock on the north side of the mall," she said to herself as much as to Clay.

He grabbed her arm, his fingers biting into her skin.

"Amanda, are you sure you want to do this?" His eyes bore into hers. "I can go down there and you can stay safe up here."

She shook her head. "No, we do it the way we planned. You just watch yourself on the dock, and I'll meet you back here in fifteen minutes."

She didn't give him another opportunity to talk her out of it, but rather pulled away from him and headed for the nearby escalator that would take her to the fountain area. Her legs trembled, and as she rode down she fumbled in her purse for the rug hook.

Gripping it in her hand didn't make her feel much better. She was more frightened than she'd ever been in her life.

She consciously kept her gaze from the upper level where she knew Clay stood. She didn't want to give away his location to anyone who might be watching her.

She tried to look like any other woman shopping on a late Saturday afternoon. She walked leisurely toward the fountain even though every nerve in her body screamed with tension.

He looked bigger up close. Larry Mitchell easily stood six feet tall, and she'd guess that under different circumstances his features would be pleasant. At the moment they radiated a grimness that was daunting. As she drew closer, she noted that his eyes were cold and that cold clutched at her soul.

Was this the man who wanted Clay dead? Was this the man who had sold him out for a drug-dealing thug? She wondered what a man's life was worth these days?

Anger mingled with her fear and surged inside her. It was obvious Larry Mitchell didn't recognize her, had no interest in her. As she walked closer his gaze touched on her, then slid away, and some of her nervous tension ebbed.

"Mr. Mitchell?" she said when she was close enough. "If you want to talk to Clay, you have two minutes to get to the loading dock on the north side of the mall."

They had been afraid that she might be grabbed or detained, but Larry Mitchell did neither. He turned and raced for the escalator that would take him to the loading dock.

Amanda looked up at where Clay had stood, only to find him gone. The agreement was that she would return to the area by the planter to wait for him to conclude his meeting.

She returned to the escalator and clung to the railing, aware that her vision had blurred with tears. The tears were a release of the tension that had built to overwhelming proportions.

Beneath the shadows of the plant fronds she waited for Clay to return, prayed that he would return. If Larry Mitchell was the one who wanted him dead, then Clay could be shot on that loading dock.

Her heart nearly stuttered to a stop at the thought. It was one thing to tell him good-bye as he started a new life someplace else, it was quite another to lose him to death.

In the brief time she'd known him, she'd come to care about him, and she hoped when this was all over he'd find happiness in whatever life he lived.

As the minutes ticked by and Clay didn't return, tears burned once again. What was taking so long? It had been a stupid plan after all. He'd gone without any kind of a weapon, without any kind of backup to meet a man who might want him dead. He was either the bravest man she'd ever met or the most foolish.

Just when she was about to surrender to despair she saw him approaching from down the corridor of the mall. She ran toward him and when he got close enough, threw herself into his arms as sobs choked in her throat.

"Hey, hey. It's all right. I'm all right." He held her tight and she swallowed her tears, appalled by her emotional outburst.

"I was so afraid for you." She stepped back from him and hurriedly wiped her tears.

He led her back by the planter and cupped her face in his hands. "Are you okay?" His fingers were warm and his gaze bore into hers intently.

"I'm fine. Did you find out anything?"

He dropped his hands to his sides and sighed. "No. Mitchell said all the right things. He's going to begin an investigation, try to get to the bottom of this, and he offered me a safe house to stay in until we find out who leaked my identity."

He pulled a hand through his hair in a gesture she recognized as sheer frustration. "I thought I'd know if he lied by looking at his face, staring him in the eyes. Either he told me the truth or he's a damned good liar. I just don't know which to believe."

"You still have to meet with Jeffrey Smith. Maybe after you talk with him you'll have a better idea of who is a liar and who isn't."

He looked at his watch. "Are you up to doing it all over again?"

"Absolutely," she replied and swallowed against a new burst of apprehension. "Hopefully Jeffrey Smith will go as smoothly as Larry Mitchell did."

"We'll know in about thirty minutes." He threw an arm around her shoulder and they both looked down at the fountain area below.

As they waited, Amanda continued to watch the other people, looking for the shooter who might appear as just another shopper. At the same time, she and Clay talked.

There was an intimacy to their conversation, as if they'd known each other forever. She supposed facing danger created a strange, rather comforting intimacy between people.

She saw Jeffrey Smith before Clay did. Clad in a dark suit with a white shirt, he looked like what she'd imagined an FBI agent would look like.

"Is that him?" she asked. A muscle ticked in Clay's jaw as he nodded. "Then let's get this over with."

She started to walk toward the escalator but paused as Clay softly called her name. She turned back to him. "Adam," he said. She frowned in confusion. "Adam Blackburn, that was the name of the man I used to be."

"I think I like Clay better," she replied, then turned toward the escalator. As she rode down her heart swelled, momentarily banishing any trace of fear.

Any lingering doubt she'd had about him and what was going on vanished. The fact that he'd told her his real name meant he'd handed her his complete trust.

It was a gift from a man she suspected didn't trust easily. Now she'd do what she could to help him stay alive.

Chapter 10

It was just after seven when Amanda and Clay sat in the rear of a taxi that would take them back to the Night Owl Motel.

Clay's mood was as dark as he could ever remember. His talk with Jeffrey Smith had been an echo of his talk with Larry Mitchell. Jeffrey had also said all the right things, made all the right promises, but there had been something in the depths of the FBI agent's eyes that Clay hadn't quite trusted.

"Are you all right?" Amanda asked.

"Yeah. I guess." He reached out and took her hand. Her dainty, slender fingers entwined with his. "I just don't feel as if we accomplished a thing today. I'm still not sure who is responsible."

"Neither of them gave you any hint that they might be guilty?"

He frowned thoughtfully. "There was something about Jeffrey that seemed kind of off." He replayed the conversation in his mind. "I know what it was," he said with sudden clarity.

"What?"

He turned to look at her, her features painted golden in the whisper of dusk seeping in through the car windows. How had he ever imagined her plain-looking? She was beautiful.

"I just realized that at least three times during my conversation with Jeffrey he asked where I was staying."

"And Larry didn't?" she asked.

"Larry told me to stay in touch, but didn't ask me specifically where I had holed up."

"Which makes you wonder why Jeffrey wanted to know specifically where you were staying."

"Exactly," he replied.

"So, you have another plan?"

"I'm working on it." He squeezed her hand as a burst of renewed desire for her warmed him. He tamped it down, knowing this was no time to indulge himself.

One thing was certain, while he would never, ever wish any harm to Amanda, he was glad she was by his side and saddened that when this was finished he'd probably never see her again.

They arrived at the motel and once again entered the room that had been home since the night before. Amanda turned on the bedside lamp against the encroaching darkness, then sat on the edge of the bed as Clay threw himself in the chair at the desk.

They'd grabbed a sandwich before leaving the mall but Clay was hungry for a plan that would put an end to this surreal experience.

Clay's gut instinct told him that Jeffrey Smith was involved, that the man had pressed too hard for his location. He rubbed a hand down the lower portion of his jaw as a plan formulated in his head.

He stood and gestured for her to get up from the bed. "I've got a plan," he said as he ripped down the bedspread.

She eyed him curiously. "What kind of a plan?"

"Call the motel office and ask if we can get a couple of extra pillows." He was grateful she didn't ask any questions but instead moved to the phone and made the call.

"Somebody will bring us a couple in just a few minutes," she said as she hung up.

"Good. And now I need all your spare clothes and your overnight bag."

Again she asked no questions and got him what he'd requested. "What's the plan?" she finally asked as he pulled her clothes out of the overnight bag.

"Jeffrey wanted to know where I was going to be for the night. I'm going to tell him," he said.

"And we won't be here," she said.

Before he could reply a knock fell on the door. She
started to answer it, but he stopped her with a hand on her
arm. Instead of going directly to the door, he went to the
window, moved the curtain aside, and peered out.

"Okay, you can answer it," he said.

It was a young woman with two pillows. Amanda took
the pillows, thanked the woman, then closed and locked
the door once again.

"What do you think about spending the night in the
parking lot of this place?" he asked and took the pillows
from her.

"I think if it keeps us alive, then it's a wonderful place
to spend the night."

He grinned at her. "Of all the women in the world I
could have gotten stuck with, I'm glad it's somebody as
agreeable as you."

"I seem to remember you telling me you'd pegged me
as a pessimist from the moment you laid eyes on me."

"Guess that just proves you can't judge a book by its
cover." He began to arrange the pillows and her clothing
to look like two bodies lying in the bed. When he was
finished and had once again pulled up the bedspread, he
stepped back to view his handiwork. "What do you think?"

"I look a little skinny and you look a little short." She
disappeared into the bathroom and returned with several
of the thin motel towels. She rolled them up and added
them to the bottom of his fake body. "That's better. I don't
mind being skinny, but if you're going to fool somebody
you have to have the additional length."

"They only have to fool somebody for a split second."
He turned on the television, then turned off the bedside
lamp. With only the glow from the television in the room
the bodies in the bed looked more realistic. "What do
you think?"

"If I were a hit man, they'd fool me," she replied.

He looked at his watch. It was just after eight. Too early
to make the call that he hoped would bring a hit man out
of his hole. They needed the darkness of night to set things
in motion.

"Is it possible neither Larry nor Jeffrey are guilty?"
she asked.

"Yeah, it's possible. If they aren't guilty, then they'll

eventually find out who is." He reached out and grabbed her hand and led her to the foot of the bed where they both sat.

"One way or another, I promise you'll have your life back," he said. "You'll go back to creating beautiful things that make people happy. You'll eventually meet a terrific guy and sew your own wedding gown and crochet blankets for the babies you'll have."

"I'm not concerned about getting back to my life, I'm concerned about making sure you stay alive."

He released her hand and instead touched the soft downy skin of her cheek. "Don't you worry about that. I'm a survivor, Amanda, and no punk drug dealer or corrupt official is going to be the death of me. I'll go back into the program and start over and you'll go back to your wonderful life and be happy."

He stood, surprised by the emotion that pressed tightly in his chest as he thought of telling her good-bye. "We need to get outside and see if we can find a place to hide."

If this plan didn't work, then he was out of ideas and he'd have to let Larry and Jeffrey investigate, which would take time.

Spending more time with Amanda seemed nearly as dangerous as facing a hit man. Spending more time with her would only make it more difficult to tell her good-bye.

If this plan didn't work, then he'd request that she be taken into protective custody and placed in a safe house until they found the guilty party. He would remain on the streets depending on himself and his own skills for survival.

One way or another, it was in both his interest and Amanda's that they say good-bye to each other as soon as possible.

Chapter 11

A Dumpster on the edge of the parking lot provided them adequate cover. It was just after ten when they took their positions behind the rank trash container.

Night had fallen, hiding them in deep shadows that made it impossible for Amanda to read Clay's features. But she didn't have to see his face in order to feel his tension.

She knew what he hoped would happen. He hoped that while they hid out here the gunman would come to the motel, break down their door, and shoot the bodies they had created in the bed. If that happened, then he would know that Jeffrey Smith was an agent gone bad.

There had been a moment in the room when she'd stared at the forms in the bed and imagined bullets riddling the bed. It had been a horrifying mental picture.

"Showtime," he said, his voice a soft whisper in the otherwise silent night. She saw the light of his phone as he flipped it open to make the call. Her stomach twisted as she realized that faint glow might bring death closer.

She was aware that things could go horridly wrong. If the gunman came, he might spy them hiding here. He might burst into the room and know instantly it was a ruse. He might go hunting for them, and she and Clay had no real defense, no weapons to use against the threat.

"Jeffrey, it's me," Clay said into the phone. "I found a place for the night and figured I'd give you the phone number here so you can reach me if anything breaks."

She listened as Clay gave Jeffrey the motel room phone number. "Yeah, it's the Night Owl Motel. I'll be here until morning. Yeah, that's right. Okay." He clicked off.

The taste of fear filled her mouth and she scooted closer to Clay. The bait had been cast; now they would see if they caught a killer whale.

"Amanda, here." He handed her the phone. "The minute anything goes down, you dial 911 and tell them to get a unit here."

She gripped the phone tightly. "What will you be doing?"

"Whatever I can to bring down a killer." His voice held the hard edge of a man who was intimately acquainted with danger.

"And take this." He grabbed her free hand and gave her what felt like a wad of money. "There's enough there for cab fare. If anything happens here, you run. You run as fast and as far as you can. No matter what you see or hear, you get the hell away from here. Take a cab and get someplace safe. If Jeffrey shows up tonight, then get away from here and call Larry Mitchell. He'll tell you what to do. If anything bad happens, you forget about all this, you forget about me. Promise me, Amanda. Promise me you'll do that."

"Okay. I promise." She would do as he asked, but there was no way she could ever forget the past forty-eight hours. There was no way she'd ever be able to forget her walk on the wild side with a man who might have stolen her heart.

He put an arm around her shoulder and she leaned her head against his broad, strong chest. "It's going to be a long night," he murmured.

And it was.

The minutes ticked by at an excruciating pace. With her head against his chest she could feel the slow, steady beat of his heart in direct contrast to the fast fluttering of her own.

She hoped Jeffrey Smith wasn't guilty and the night would pass uneventfully. She hoped the worst that would happen was that they would both be sore in the morning from having spent the night crouched on the hard concrete.

"Did you and Jillian want children?" she asked in a whisper.

"We'd talked about it and eventually we wanted a couple, but we weren't in any hurry. We were young and still enjoying the novelty of being newlyweds."

"You must miss her very much."

His chest rose and fell with a sigh. "Initially I think I wanted to die. I couldn't imagine living without her. But, you know, it is true what they say about time healing wounds. I'll always love Jillian, I'll cherish the memories I have of her, but I know now there is life after Jillian."

"So where do you think you'll eventually end up? On a horse ranch in Montana, or maybe working an oil rig in Texas?" She consciously worked to keep her tone light.

"Who knows? Maybe I'll be a short-order cook in some truck stop in South Carolina or a garbageman in Oregon."

"No matter where you go or what you do, I want you to know one thing," she said.

"What's that?"

"This was the best first date I've ever had in my life."

His laugh was a low rumble in his chest. "That's just because I'm your one and only walk on the wild side," he replied.

"No, it's much more than that," she protested. She wanted to tell him that she liked the way his smile began at one corner and slowly swept across his lips. She wanted to say that she admired the choice he'd once made to work undercover to bring a bad guy to justice. She liked the fact that when he'd eaten his sandwich he'd torn off the crust and that his arms around her felt so completely right.

Instead she drew in the scent of him and memorized how his arms enfolded her and made her feel safe despite the situation they were in.

She must have fallen asleep, because the next thing she knew Clay said her name with an urgency that instantly brought with it full consciousness. He pushed her from his arms and she became aware that a car had entered the parking lot.

It crept in slowly and extinguished its headlights before parking. It was a dark sports car, just like the one that had chased them through the streets the night before. The engine shut off, and in the ensuing silence Amanda heard her fear screaming through her.

Moments passed, agonizing moments when nothing happened. Nobody exited the car. The moonlight cascading down from a plump, nearly full moon gave the parking lot a ghostly glow. The night held the quiet, deserted feel of an abandoned town. She knew it had to be after midnight.

The driver's door finally opened, and Amanda stifled a gasp as the moonlight shone off a bald head.

"It's him," she whispered as terror ripped through her.

"Remember your promise," Clay whispered from beside her, and then he was gone, leaving the cover of the Dumpster and moving behind a nearby car.

She watched as the bald man walked toward their motel room door. He paused just outside the door and looked left, then right. Her heart was in her throat as she felt his gaze move in the direction of the Dumpster.

Even though she knew there was no way he could see her peeking around the corner of the structure, despite the fact she couldn't make out any features on his face, she felt the coldness of his eyes through the darkness.

She glanced back to where Clay had hidden, and panic shot through her as she realized he was no longer there. Where had he gone? Surely he wasn't really going to attempt to take down the bald man. The killer had a gun. Clay had nothing but his bare hands. He didn't have the ready cash to buy a gun on the street, nor did he have a source for such a purchase. He'd considered returning to his apartment to retrieve his gun, but had been afraid the apartment was being watched.

She leaned back against the Dumpster, opened the phone, and quickly dialed 911. "Night Owl Motel, please come quickly. There's a man with a gun," she whispered, then shut the phone and once again peered around the corner of the Dumpster.

The killer grabbed the doorknob and did something. He was either picking the lock or using a credit card or something comparable to spring the lock. Even though this was what they had hoped would happen, had been expecting to happen, the reality of it sent icy chills down her spine.

The bald man stepped back from the door, once again looked to his left, then to his right, then opened the door. She saw the flash of the gun, heard the *psst* of the bullets that riddled the bed, and imagined she felt the searing pain of those bullets tearing into her.

She cried out and stood just as Clay appeared behind the

gunman. "Run!" He shouted the single word as he leapt onto the big man's back.

Amanda froze as the two men tumbled into the room and out of her sight. Her first instinct was to run into the motel room and help Clay, but the sound of approaching sirens filled the night and she remembered the promise she'd given to Clay.

With fear crashing through her, she left the cover of the Dumpster and ran. She ran as she'd never run before, without looking back, without conscious thought.

When she'd gone about four blocks, she stopped to catch her breath. Leaning with her back against the front of an abandoned building, she drew deep gulps of the humid night air.

The sound of sirens had stopped. Had the police arrived in time to help Clay? Was he still alive or had the bald man managed to shoot him and escape?

She didn't realize she was crying until she opened the phone to call information for the number to a cab company. The numbers on the keypad swam and a sob choked from the depths of her.

She should have stayed. She should have done something to help him. She should have called the police sooner. Recriminations flooded her, along with an overwhelming sense of grief.

It was over. It was time to go home and forget any of this had ever happened. As if she could forget. She asked the operator to connect her to a local cab company and requested a pickup.

As she waited for the cab to arrive, her thoughts, her heart, her very soul filled with Clay. Had he survived this night? She would probably never know. She had a feeling that there would be no news coverage about what had occurred at the Night Owl Motel.

The cab arrived, and she slid into the backseat and gave the driver her address. She saw on the clock on the dashboard that it was just after three a.m. Weariness sat like a rock on her shoulders. She knew it wasn't just an exhaustion from lack of sleep, but also from the emotional stress of the night.

Numbness swept over her, and she leaned her head back

against the seat as the cab carried her closer and closer to home.

She should have felt relief when the driver pulled into her driveway and the sight of her safe little house greeted her, but she didn't.

She'd never known that a mere forty-eight hours could change a life, but hers had been changed. She'd never known that a man she'd known for forty-eight hours could touch her heart so deeply, so profoundly. But Clay had.

And she knew with miserable certainty that she would never see him again.

Chapter 12

Amanda awakened to brilliant sunshine streaming through her bedroom window. She knew it had to be early afternoon because she hadn't fallen into bed until sometime after eight that morning.

When she'd gotten home, it had taken her forever to unwind. She'd made a cup of coffee and had drunk it while staring at a local channel on the television. She'd channel surfed for hours, looking for any kind of news story pertaining to the Night Owl Motel. There was none.

She'd played and replayed the events of her time with Clay in her head, from the moment she'd first laid eyes on him to the last time she'd seen him.

She got out of bed and headed for the bathroom. Minutes later, standing beneath a hot steamy shower, she remembered every smile, every touch they had shared. His lovemaking had been beyond breathtaking and had stirred her like none other that she had ever experienced.

When she'd found out what the situation was with him, that he wasn't some dope dealer or criminal, she'd felt one hundred percent safe with him. There had never been any doubt in her mind that he wouldn't take care of her.

Forget him, a little voice whispered inside her head as she dried off. You'll never see him again. He's gone. Either he died in that motel room last night or he was whisked away back into protective custody. Either way he was gone forever, and all she had left were memories of what might have been.

As she left her bedroom, dressed in a pair of shorts and a sleeveless blouse, the phone rang. She walked into the kitchen, where the caller ID showed that it was her sister. She didn't feel like talking.

"Amanda, are you there?" Cara's voice filled the kitchen as she left a message on the answering machine. "I called you all day yesterday and you never returned any of my calls. I suppose you're mad about the date the other night. How was I supposed to know a man who looked as yummy as Clay would turn out to be such a dud? Anyway, call me. Harry's secretary has a brother who I think might be just right for you."

Amanda sighed as her sister's message ended. The last thing she wanted anytime soon was to entertain the idea of another blind date.

Maybe the best panacea for now was work. Although she didn't have to return to the store until the next day, she had plenty of things she could work on here at home.

She pulled a large plastic tub from the garage into the kitchen and took off the lid. Inside was ribbon of all colors and designs. Even though it was only August, she decided to start making fall-colored bows to decorate wreaths and arrangements.

Where would he be in the fall? Would he be walking through lush autumn leaves in Boston? On a sunny beach in Florida? It would be so much easier for her if she knew he was okay, if she knew for sure that he'd gotten out of that motel.

It was some comfort that if he was alive, she knew he'd eventually live a wonderful life. The depth of emotion he'd displayed for his lost wife proved that he was capable of loving, and people who loved once rarely went through life without loving again.

One thing had become clear in her mind since coming home. For the past two years she'd thought about going out on her own, opening her own shop. She'd put every dime she could in a savings account for that eventuality. But the risk of the venture had kept her from following through.

Risk was going undercover for five years and putting your life on the line. Risk was knowing some creep with connections had vowed you'd not live to your next birthday.

Her walk on the wild side with Clay had given her the

courage to reach for her dream of owning her own shop. Tomorrow after work she would begin scouting locations.

She'd just made her third bright, beautiful bow when a knock fell on her front door. She frowned and got up from the table. The last thing she wanted was a visitor. She was in the middle of her own personal pity party.

She opened the door and gasped. Clay grinned at her, that wonderful, sexy smile that instantly brought tears to her eyes.

"You're okay!" she exclaimed as he stepped into her living room.

"Not only am I okay, but I come bearing gifts. I brought you a rental car." He handed her a set of keys. "Unfortunately, your car is going to be tied up with the police for a few days."

Her car. She'd forgotten all about her car. "That's not important," she replied and tossed the keys on the coffee table. "What's important is that you're alive."

She wanted to throw her arms around his neck, kiss those gorgeous sexy lips of his, but the circumstances that had forced them together no longer existed. While she was clear on her feelings for him, she had no idea what he felt about her.

"I didn't think I'd ever see you again," she said. "I thought you'd be setting up work as a rodeo clown in Texas or a miner in Alaska."

"I've spent the last couple of hours down at FBI headquarters talking to Jeffrey Smith and considering my options."

"Is he in custody?"

Clay walked over to the sofa and sat, then motioned for her to sit beside him. "He's in custody and singing like a canary. It seems Jeffrey was in the middle of a financial crisis and about to lose his house when he contacted my old friend, Ben Correl. Ben offered Jeffrey two hundred grand to see that I disappeared permanently from the face of the earth."

"So Jeffrey hired the hit man."

"Exactly. According to Jeffrey, only he and the hit man knew my identity and now both of them are going to be sharing a cell for a very long time."

"And what about you? Are you going back into the program?"

He leaned forward, bringing with him the scent of clean male and spicy cologne. "I've been thinking about my options all morning. According to what Jeffrey told us, Ben Correl doesn't know my real name. It was in Jeffrey's best interest not to share that information with him."

"Why?" she asked curiously.

"If Jeffrey told Ben my name, then nothing would have prevented Ben from hiring out the job to somebody else. My identity was Jeffrey's assurance that Ben had to deal with him and him only. Mitchell offered me a new identity, but I've decided I like my life here." His midnight blue eyes warmed her. "How are you doing?"

"Better now that I know you're all right," she confessed. "What happened when you went into the motel room? I was so frightened for you."

He shot her a charmingly crooked smile. "I've got to admit, my heart was beating a little fast, too. I managed to jump on the back of the shooter and he dropped the gun. We grappled around, but before either of us could get possession, the cops arrived and we were both arrested and taken downtown."

"So it's really over."

He reached out a hand and toyed with the strands of her hair. "Yeah, it's really over." He dropped his hand and stood. "You've got your car back. You've got your life back." He headed for the front door and she got up and hurried after him.

She'd thought it had been difficult to come home this morning and not know what had happened to him, but it was not half as difficult as telling him good-bye now.

She would always be grateful that he'd come here to let her know he was all right and that the bad guys were behind bars. But she hadn't realized how seeing him again, talking to him again would warm her heart and make her long for something more.

He stopped at the door, reached out for her, and drew her against his hard, muscled chest. "I don't usually leave my dates without a good-night kiss."

Then he kissed her, and in the fire of his kiss she realized that what they had begun to build might have found its birth in danger and circumstance, but it hadn't ended when the danger had passed.

He ended the kiss and smiled down at her. "It wasn't too bad, our first date, was it?"

She laughed. "I can honestly say it was the most exciting first date I've ever been on."

The smile left his eyes and a dark intensity filled them. "What do you say we try it again? Go out on another date?"

She laughed again, tremulously, happily, and threw her arms around his neck. "I'd love to. If our first date was any indication of the good time you can show a girl, then I can't wait to see what you do to top it."

The darkness in his eyes lifted and his features relaxed. "I was thinking maybe we'd do something totally wild and out of the ordinary, like a nice quiet meal at my favorite Italian restaurant, then a night of sweet lovemaking," he said and tightened his arms around her.

"How about we skip the nice meal and start the second date right now," she said breathlessly.

He slammed the front door and turned the lock, then scooped her up in his arms. "I knew the moment I laid eyes on you that you were my kind of woman."

She smiled. "That's just what I was thinking—I knew we were meant to be together," she said, laughing with him.

It was the end of an impossibly long first date, but the beginning of something wonderful.